D0251346

ALSO BY CARO KING

Seven Sorcerers

SHADOW
SPELL

BY CARO KING

ALADDIN
New York   London   Toronto   Sydney   New Delhi

ALADDIN

An imprint of Simon & Schuster Children's Publishing Division
1230 Avenue of the Americas, New York, NY 10020
First Aladdin hardcover edition May 2012
Copyright © 2010 by Caro King
Originally published in Great Britain in 2010 by Quercus
Published by arrangement with Quercus Books
All rights reserved, including the right of reproduction in whole or in part in any form.
ALADDIN is a trademark of Simon & Schuster, Inc., and related logo is a registered trademark of Simon & Schuster, Inc.
For information about special discounts for bulk purchases, please contact Simon & Schuster Special Sales at 1-866-506-1949 or business@simonandschuster.com.
The Simon & Schuster Speakers Bureau can bring authors to your live event. For more information or to book an event contact the Simon & Schuster Speakers Bureau at 1-866-248-3049 or visit our website at www.simonspeakers.com.
Designed by Lisa Vega
The text of this book was set in ITC Esprit.
Manufactured in the United States of America 0312 FFG
2 4 6 8 10 9 7 5 3 1
Library of Congress Cataloging-in-Publication Data
King, Caro.
Shadow spell / Caro King.
p. cm.
Sequel to: Seven sorcerers.
Summary: Nin Redstone and her friends make their way to the strange mansion of Simeon Dark, the most powerful sorcerer in the land of Drift and the only one who can stop the evil Strood and save the Drift from dying.
ISBN 978-1-4424-2045-8 (hc)
[1. Brothers and sisters—Fiction. 2. Missing children—Fiction.
3. Adventure and adventurers—Fiction. 4. Fantasy.] I. Title.
PZ7.K5743Sh 2012
[Fic]—dc23
2012004010
ISBN 978-1-4423-3908-8 (pbk)
ISBN 978-1-4424-2046-5 (eBook)

SHADOW
SPELL

PART
1

THE NATURE
OF SPELLS

1

THE BELL RINGER

Perched on the very edge of a ragged cliff, the Terrible House of Strood towered against the summer sky in a mass of dark stone walls and pointed roofs. Far below, waves crashed over the rocks at the foot of the cliff, surging into every crevice and filling the air with spray that hung like salty mist.

The roof of the Terrible House, with its jumble of chimney pots and towers, was familiar territory to Bogeyman Skerridge since his unauthorized entry into the building a couple of days ago, shortly after he had gone rogue and left Mr. Strood's service forever.

And now he was back again, scanning the rooftops with his sharp red eyes until he spotted the creature he had come to find—the bell ringer, whose job it was to keep watch for the exact moment when the edge of the sun slipped below the horizon and then to ring the Evebell.

Skerridge grinned. It wasn't a nice grin. In a recent fit of remorse he had promised himself never to harm another living Quick, but this creature wasn't exactly living and was only slightly Quick so it didn't count.

And, anyway, he was only going to torture it a little.

The creature was not at its post in the weathered stone bell tower that rose high above the rooftops. Sundown was still an hour away, so instead it was perched on an outcrop of roof enjoying the view out to sea. Treading as quietly as only a bogeyman could, Skerridge headed that way. When he was right behind the unsuspecting bell ringer he leaned close and said, "'Ullo."

The creature hooted through its beak and did a twisting leap that brought it around to face Skerridge, who grinned, taking care to show a lot of jagged teeth.

"Halloo," said the bell ringer, quickly working out that there was no harm in being polite. He had been sitting with his knobbly back to the beach, looking out over the waves as they dashed themselves on the rocks below and trying to forget about the handful of Quick cluttering up the seashore away in the distance behind him. The sudden arrival of a horrible, hairy, bony figure in tattered trousers and a fancy waistcoat wasn't an improvement on his day.

Skerridge settled down on the roof next to the gargoyle. "I'm Bogeyman Skerridge," he said cheerfully. "Wha's yore name then?"

"Jibbit," said Jibbit nervously. Being the only gargoyle in the Terrible House, he had the roof all to himself apart from the pigeons. He wasn't used to people, Quick, Grimm, or Fabulous, and found them untidy and difficult. This one had a definite air of untidy and positively radiated difficult. With extras.

"Bet it's nice an' quiet up 'ere."

"Yes."

"Lotsa time to listen to all the goin's on, eh? Bet it's

been an excitin' afternoon, what wiv all the escapin' and everyfin'! Ninevah Redstone breakin' outa the 'Ouse like that, givin' Mr. Strood the runaround jus' when 'e fort 'e'd won. Not t' mention rescuin' 'er bruvver an' gettin' 'er mem'ry pearl back."

"Y-yes."

"So, what I wanna know is what 'appened next? Fink you can tell me that?"

Jibbit swapped nervously from foot to foot and hunched his stubby wings. He had a bad feeling about what he was going to do, but his duty was clear.

"If you're Bogeyman Skerridge, then yoo've gone rogue," he said trying not to hoot too much. "And if yoo've gone rogue then I mustn't say anything . . ."

Skerridge shot out a hand and grabbed the bell ringer so fast that Jibbit barely saw it happen. One second he was sitting on the roof, next he was dangling upside down over nothing.

"Fort ya might say that. Now, if ya wan' my advice, I fink ya should tell me everyfin' ya know, 'cos if ya don' then I'll drop ya."

Jibbit glared at the bogeyman from underneath his own feet.

"I know," went on Skerridge cheerfully. "Yer finkin' that no self-respectin' gargoyle is gonna be scared o' heights. And if ya gets broke ya can be stuck back t'gevver again, right?"

"Yes," snapped Jibbit.

"But isn't there somefin' yer fergettin'?" Skerridge leaned over to bring his head closer to the dangling gargoyle. "Look. Down," he whispered.

Jibbit glared for a second longer then turned his gaze downward. It had a long way to go. The wall plunged away from him. Jibbit followed it with his eyes until he saw where it led. The ground—in this case rather rocky and involving a lot of breaking waves, but still the ground. Jibbit hooted in panic.

"Didn' fink o' that did ya?" Skerridge chuckled. "By my understandin', gargoyles don' like places what aren' 'igh, right? An' ya don' get much more not 'igh than the ground! So, 'ave we gotta deal?"

Jibbit squeaked pitifully.

Skerridge grinned. "Right oh." He pulled his arm back and dropped Jibbit on the tiles, wrong side up.

"Thanks." Jibbit scuffled onto his paws.

"Fink nuffin' of it. Off ya go, then."

Staring thoughtfully into space while he got his scattered nerves together, Jibbit settled back on the tiles, making sure he had a firm grip.

"That chimney pot at the back there," he said at last, "is the one to the furnace in Mr. Strood's laboratory. I . . . um . . . happened to be sitting next to it just as Ninevah Redstone got away, so I climbed down the flue tooo see what all the racket was about. The furnace has got a glass door, so I could see right into the laboratory. Mr. Strood wasn't pleased." Jibbit warmed to his story. "In fact, he was so angry he tripped down a hole . . ."

"Eh?"

"A hole. In the ground. Left by the new Fabulous when he came up through the floor to rescue Ninevah Redstone. Yoo know, the mudman?"

"Yeah, Jik, I know 'im. Go on."

"Mr. Strood was already coming apart on account of the faerie poison getting over him, and his leg broke off and he went down the hole, see?"

"I'm gettin' the picture," said Skerridge grimly.

"And then the earth fell in on top of him and he

4

was buried, deep in the heart of the house, far below the foundations."

"So tha's what they've been doin' then," the bogey-man murmured, "diggin' 'im up. I wondered why they weren' pourin' outta the door looking fer us."

"The servants, the guards, everybody had to dig. It was taking a long time, so the Housekeeper sent for the bogeymen. There's no daylight in the House, so three of them came to dig even though it wasn't night." Jibbit looked at Skerridge thoughtfully. "They can do super-speed, yoo know."

"Course I know, I am one! Still, superspeed diggin' ain't like superspeed runnin'. My guess is it'd still take 'em all afternoon." Skerridge blew out his cheeks, feel-ing oddly anxious. "Carn' 'ave been fun, bein' stuck down there, buried alive in the earf fer 'ours. Bet 'e'll be in a good mood after that!"

Jibbit considered. "I wouldn't call it good," he said carefully.

"They've found 'im then?"

"Yes. He must have been digging upward too, because suddenly the Housekeeper said . . ."

"STOP!" Strood's housekeeper, Mrs. Dunvice, held up a hand. Everyone stopped.

"There," she said after a moment, "can you hear that?"

Down in the earth, somewhere below the bottom of the deep well that used to be the laboratory floor, something stirred. It did it with a lot of cursing and unpleasant squashing sounds, but it definitely stirred. The cursing was garbled, as if it came from a mouth that was half missing and choked with dirt into the bar-gain. Most of the cursing involved unpleasant things happening to somebody called Ninevah Redstone.

Secretary Scribbins gulped. "It's him," he whispered hoarsely.

A murmur ran around the gathered workers. Some of them edged away. Even the bogeymen.

"Right," said Mrs. Dunvice decisively. "Everyone out, except for the bogeymen and guards Stanley and Floyd. NOW!"

Bodies tumbled toward the complicated scaffolding running up the sides of the well. The servants got there first, scampering up and out as quickly as they could. The goblin-Grimm guards followed.

When the others had gone, the werewolf-Grimm Housekeeper pointed at the three bogeymen who had been doing the tunneling.

"Dig some more, but do it carefully, okay?"

One of the BMs, the one wearing a pair of sacking trousers and a bow tie, blew out a slow breath. None of them fancied having to dig out a furious Mr. Strood. But then, on the other hand, they would be HELPING him, so maybe he wouldn't want to give them the sack. The BM straightened his bow tie and stepped forward, crouching down just about where the muttered curses were coming from. The others joined him.

Now they could hear scraping, scuffling noises, like a giant mole digging its way up toward the light. One of the BMs snarled and jumped back as a hand shot out of the earth. It was a slender hand half covered in scars that made it look like a bad patchwork glove. The other half was still mostly skinned.

"We found 'im!" yelled the one with the bow tie, unnecessarily.

The hand felt around and its owner hissed.

"Ged be oud, you worthlesh bunch of idiotsh!"

Mrs. Dunvice leaned forward and held out a hand, then realized that Mr. Strood couldn't see it as his head was still below the surface. So she grabbed his wrist instead and pulled. The earth heaved like a small volcano as his head rose slowly from the ground, followed by the rest of him. Or, at least, what was left of the rest of him.

Mrs. Dunvice cleared her throat. "Welcome back, sir. We found your ear. You must have lost it on the way down."

Scribbins bobbed forward, holding out the ear wrapped in a napkin. Someone had cleaned the mud out of it.

"Don'd bother," hissed Strood, "I'b growd a dew one."

"And the arm, sir? And what about . . ."

"The leg? Yesh, yesh, id'sh growd back. Sho has by jaw. Almosht."

At last, Arafin Strood stood before them, wobbling badly and holding on to the rung of a nearby ladder for balance. Mrs. Dunvice thanked her lucky stars that she had sent all the others away. They could do without all the screaming and throwing up. Scribbins was bad enough.

Several hours had passed since the accident in the laboratory, in which a shattered bottle of faerie venom had showered Mr. Strood with flesh-dissolving poison. Even so, the venom was still at work eating him away and Strood was less than whole. His clothing had suffered too, and he was left with only half a ragged pair of trousers and a badly crumpled shirt collar. Most of his ribs were exposed, giving an interesting view of the workings of a heart and lungs for anyone who liked biology. His lower jaw was trying hard to grow back in spite

7

of the persistent venom, and one hand had just about managed to re-form completely. Because it was new, it was free of the scars that covered the remaining parts of Strood like an insane road map. One leg was mostly bone. One eye socket was busily refilling itself. The other was filled with a horribly gleaming eye. It was a good thing he was immortal, or he'd have been well past dead by now.

Mrs. Dunvice licked her lips nervously. Behind her, Scribbins whimpered, a pathetic sound that made the werewolf in Mrs. Dunvice want to bite him. The BMs gazed on, silent and wary.

Mr. Strood slowly raised his head. His eye was a pool of darkness in his horribly mangled face.

"Guard Shtanley and Guard Floyd," he said in a voice like cracked ice, "brig be one of by ped digersh and a human Quick. Any Quick will do. Then ged the bordal dishtillation bachine ready. There'sh work to be done."

"Yesh . . . I mean yes, sir!" Stanley turned smartly and hurried toward the scaffolding, half falling over himself in his eagerness to get away. Floyd followed hard on his heels.

Mr. Stood switched his attention to Scribbins. "A bath. Clothesh. Coffee. Five binutes or you're doast."

Scribbins gave a strangled squawk and ran for it. Finally, Strood turned to the BMs and Mrs. Dunvice.

"Only three?"

"They were the only ones we could find, sir."

Strood considered for a moment. Then he leaned forward and smiled a smile that made even the werewolf part of her nervous.

"Id will do for now, we can always ged bore later. The girl may think she'sh shafe for the moment," he said, his voice strengthening as his jaw finally achieved wholeness, "but nightfall ish on its way." His chilling one-eyed stare swiveled to the bogeymen, who bunched up together nervously. "So one of you is to bring me Ninevah Redshtone, EVEN IF THERE ARE WIT-NESSES, understand?"

The BMs swapped a look. Snatching kids in front of witnesses was against the bogeyman code, but then again . . .

"DO YOU UNDERSTAND?" Strood's eye gleamed feverishly. "I need bogeymen who can be adaptable . . ." He didn't need to finish the sentence. They knew what he meant. Adapt or be fired.

"Yessir!" One of them even saluted. "I'll do it, sir!"

Strood's eye fixed on him, the gleam incandescent. "Remember, I want her alive. I've got plans for Ninevah Redstone and they don't involve an easy end."

He switched back to the other BMs. "And as for you two, well . . ."

There was a long pause while some old emotion struggled to show on Strood's ravaged face. Mrs. Dunvice shuddered. She could feel something coming and it was making her blood tingle.

"I've let their pathetic leftovers linger on all these years," Strood hissed at last, "but I know they'll try to help her. So now the time has come to deal with the last remains of the Seven Sorcerers. These are your orders . . ."

Jibbit stopped. "That's when I left."

Skerridge groaned. "Gimme a break! Couldn' yer 'ang on five more minutes!"

"There was a pigeon," said Jibbit coldly, "and I was hungry."

"Sheesh! Which bogeymen were they? D'ya know that?"

"They were just bogeymen. How should I know?"

"What were they wearin'?" said Skerridge patiently. "Ya can always tell a BM by what 'e's wearin', even when 'e's in anovver shape."

Jibbit huffed. "Erm. Torn red trousers and a rope belt. Ordinary trousers like yoo and a bow tie. And . . . and . . . a pair of blue dungarees with paint on."

"Bogeymen Rope, Pigwit, and Bale, then. Fanks."

"No problem." Jibbit glanced anxiously over Skerridge's shoulder. Skerridge turned to look. Out across the sea the sun was drowning in a pool of light, sinking lower and lower toward the blue rim of the horizon. The bell ringer began to fidget.

"I got tooo ring the bell in a moment," he said, hooting nervously. "It's my job and I got tooo dooo it. Every sundown I ring the Evebell so people know that the day is turning into night."

Although Skerridge chose to be different, as a general rule bad things didn't like the light and that included bogeymen. So, even though the BMs would not leave the House straightaway, he knew that Mr. Strood's instructions would be put into action the moment the sun dipped below the horizon. Which gave him little more than a few minutes to act.

Sending a glance back over the top of the House to where Ninevah Redstone was still sitting on the beach far below, unaware of what was about to happen to her, Skerridge did some fast thinking. He couldn't superspeed over the roof because superspeed generated a lot of heat and he would simply turn the tiles into blobs of molten lead, which would fall into the attic and do some fairly serious damage to the servants who lived there.

10

But the bogeyman that Mr. Strood had sent to get Nin would be able to superspeed all right.

On the plus side, the girl wouldn't be alone. Taggit was still there, along with Jonas, of course. Toby didn't count because he was too small to do anything anyway. And although it was taking a while because he'd been so badly damaged, hopefully the mudman would be done baking soon.

While the bogeyman worked things out, Jibbit was inching toward the bell tower. Just as the edge of the sun touched the dark curve of the horizon, he made a break for it, skittering away over the tiles. Skerridge jumped, landing just in front of the fleeing gargoyle, who darted left to go around him.

"No ya don't," said Skerridge. He picked the bell ringer up and held him by his legs, upside down and thrashing wildly.

"I got tooo! I got tooo! IT'S MY JOB!" hooted Jibbit.

"Not today it ain't," said Skerridge. "See, I need to send a message and I'm bettin' that the goblin or the boy will be bright enough, even if the kid don' work it out."

As the sun began to slip below the edge of the world, the darkening sky was filled with the bell ringer's howl of anguish.

2

NIGHT FALLS

Jonas sat up and turned to stare back at the cliff, where he could just make out the rooftops of the Terrible House, black and jagged against the liquid glow of the evening sky. Taggit, dozing by the fire, opened one eye and frowned. "Uh-oh!" said Nin, sensing danger.

She got to her feet, pulling on her grubby pink rucksack as she did so, then glanced at the fire still burning around Jik. They had been feeding it all afternoon and the core of the flames, where the mudman was baking, glowed red-hot.

"You thinkin' what I'm thinkin'?" said Taggit, glancing at Jonas. The nine-foot-tall Fabulous goblin's face creased into an expression that was probably worry, but that looked more like a Halloween mask having a bad day.

"Come on, Toby," called Nin, hurrying over to her little brother, who had fallen asleep in the middle of the sandcastle he had been building. He mumbled sleepily as she pulled him to his feet and dusted him off, talking to him reassuringly.

"Yep. It's sundown. We should have heard the Evebell

by now," said Jonas. "There's something's going on."

Taggit called over to Nin, his voice urgent. "Get to the sanctuary. I'll bring yer brother."

Nin hurried Toby over toward Taggit, then got going, heading inland toward the stone ladder cut into the cliff face that led to up to Strood's garden and the Lockheart Sanctuary. Behind her, she could hear Toby laughing excitedly as Taggit picked him up and began to run.

The light was fading fast. Night was falling, and with the night came the Dread Fabulous, the bad things that didn't like the light. Bogeymen for example. Super-fast, superstrong, fire-breathing bogeymen that could run up walls as easily as Nin could walk across a living room floor.

She hauled herself up the cliff face as fast as she could, her heart hammering like it wanted to get out. Her breath was harsh in her throat and her hair kept flopping in her eyes. She could hear Jonas right behind her, and below him came Taggit with Toby hanging on around his neck. Toby had worked out that this wasn't about fun and had stopped laughing. "You're nearly there!" Jonas called up. "Follow the path, but turn in through the arch of stones."

By now Nin could barely see one hand in front of the other. Tumbling off the top of the ladder, gasping for breath, and with her legs like jelly from the climb, she hurried on up the path. Ahead of her swept Mr. Strood's garden, rising steeply through many levels of tall trees and shaggy lawns dotted with follies and grottos until it reached the dark walls and bricked-in windows of the Terrible House.

The Lockheart Sanctuary was perched on the land-side edge of the cliff. It was so heavily wreathed in ivy and overhung by trees that it was barely visible even without the magical spells that protected it from view, spells cast by the long-dead sorcerer who built the sanctuary many decades ago. Following the path that wound on through the crazy growth of wild roses and vivid peonies, Nin searched desperately for the entrance. And then, off to one side, she saw a low arch of huge, mossy slabs, nearly invisible in the twilight. Stumbling through it, she fell into a small cave dimly lit by a golden lamp that burned on the wall, next to a door set in the rock. "We're here!" she called back to the others, as she ran toward the door and hammered on it.

There was a crackle of heat and the hiss of something moving very fast overhead and coming to a halt right behind her. "Gotcha!" snarled a voice in her ear as Nin felt herself seized and lifted from the ground. Her world spun and she got a glimpse of paint-stained dungarees and long, hairy, bony arms.

Everything happened dizzyingly fast. Hanging upside down in the bogeyman's grip, Nin screamed and reached out, seeing the sanctuary door slip away as he hauled her roughly back across the ceiling of the cave. She fought hard, trying to break free, but Bogeyman Bale's arm was wrapped firmly around her hips. All she could do was scream helplessly, until she felt something fasten onto her forearm and saw Jonas appear right below her.

"I've got you!" he yelled, holding on with grim determination.

Bogeyman Bale jerked to a startled halt as Nin slithered in his grip, dragged downward by Jonas. For a split second she was hanging in midair looking back between her own boots to the front of the cave.

The bogeyman roared with fury and lurched back

into movement, dragging Nin and Jonas several steps across the ground toward the stone arch. And Taggit.

Seizing Jonas around the waist, Taggit pulled back in the opposite direction, barely breaking his stride as he dragged them all toward the sanctuary, Bogeyman Bale snarling and yelping desperately as they went. Nin screamed again, this time with pain as well as fear. The bogeyman's grip had slipped to her legs, but he was still holding on hard, and she had Jonas and Taggit hauling on her arm. She could feel the strain in her joints and back and had a terrifying vision of herself flying apart in their grip, her spine snapped and her arms ripped free.

Ahead of them, the door to the sanctuary opened, spilling light into the cave. A woman stood in the entrance taking in the fight with astonishment.

"Elinor!" yelled Jonas as he struggled, seeing the Lockheart Sister who had cared for him after his escape from the Storm Hounds.

Elinor pulled the door wide and then spotted a terrified Toby hovering in the background. She held out her arms and he ran toward her, darting around the struggling knot of figures in his path and into the safety of the Lockheart Sanctuary.

Hauled along by the combined strength of Taggit and Jonas, Bale howled with fury, raking down chunks of rock as he scrabbled to hold on. His hands slid down Nin's legs and she gasped, feeling the clawed fingers dig through her jeans, tearing the cloth and her skin beneath.

Nin was half in and half out of the sanctuary door when the tip of the bogeyman's claw crossed the threshold and something happened. The cave shook and there was a moment of white light so brilliant, Nin could see nothing else. The light went out and was replaced by a

grinding sound loud enough to drown out all the screaming and shouting.

Bogeyman Bale gave one last haul on Nin, his claws
raking deep, then let go. Holding Toby, Elinor sprang
back as Taggit and Jonas collapsed just inside the door.
Suddenly released, Nin flew over their heads, whirling
through the air into the sanctuary. The last thing she
saw before she smashed against the wall was the bogeyman drop to the ground and turn to run as the rocky
ceiling and floor of the cave began to move, rumbling
together with a sound like thunder.

Then the door swung shut. The walls shook and
Jonas, trying to get back on his feet, fell to the ground
again.

"What's happening?" cried Jonas.

Around them, the cool stone of the corridor rippled
into a deep gold wood. There was a smell of fresh air and
a sound like wind. In front of them the blackened oak
door bleached gold and started to grow taller. "Sanctuary's movin'," yelled Taggit over the noise.

"Nin!" wailed Toby from behind them.

They turned to look.

Elinor was kneeling beside Nin, leaning over her
as she lay horribly still. She was crumpled on the floor
where she had fallen, the walls rippling around her. And
there was blood.

"Here now." The sister's blue clad shape leaned over
Nin, supporting her head, holding something to her
lips.

"Will she be all right?" asked Jonas. He looked ash
gray in the candlelight.

Nin spluttered, half waking as she took a sip of the
bitter-tasting liquid. It had a smell like iron and blood.

"Drink a little more." Elinor tipped the cup again, persuading. "She split her skull, her leg is torn, and she's lost a lot of blood," she said, answering Jonas. "All she needs to heal is time, but we don't have time. Strood is already at work."

Jonas sent a glance out through the half-open door into the narrow hallway of twisted wood and interlaced branches—so different to the cool stone that he remembered. He could sense a feeling of growing unease in the air. It made him wonder exactly what Strood was up to that could even disturb the safety of the Lockheart Sanctuary.

But there were more immediate things to worry about. "It's just . . . I always thought taking crowsmorte in a dissolved form was dangerous?" he asked.

"True," said Elinor, "but we need Nin to get well quickly and so it is a risk we must take."

Nin half opened her eyes and murmured. She could hear their voices, but the words meant little. She was unspeakably tired; every single particle in her body ached and she was so, so cold. She took a last sip and lay back, hearing a gentle humming that seemed to come from a long way away. She wondered if it was outside, or maybe just in her head. "But," Elinor went on, settling Nin on her pillow, "I made this potion with my own hands and as carefully as I could."

Nin sighed and murmured. The heaviness in her limbs was already growing less, and soft clouds were gathering around her, cushioning her against the pain. Lights glimmered in the corners of her eyes and the humming drew closer. "Now let her rest," said Elinor softly. "The crowsmorte will do its best work when she's asleep."

Nin drifted, the world around her moving away

faster and faster. And as Elinor's voice receded, so the humming grew until it was not just a tuneful sound but real singing, low and soft and so warm it made her spirits rise. The glimmers were there too, dim like candles, dancing in a pattern of soothing light and shade. "That's right, sleep the pain away," said Jonas, although his voice was deeper and more musical than it should be.

So she did.

3

THE TIGER AND THE HUMAN QUICK

J ik awoke to the sound of the waves crashing onto the beach. The tide was in, but far enough away not to be a problem. He lay for a moment, watching the sky. The electric feel of gathering magic crackled in the air, and out over the sea, flames licked the horizon. He thought that he must have been cooking for a long time if morning was on its way. A very long time. He wondered if it was because he was a Fabulous now, and Fabulous took longer to mend than mere Land Magic.

Dawn ignited and billowing flames raced overhead, filling the sky with a fierce light. It was a red so deep it was the color of rubies. "Weird, if yer arsk me," said a voice. "Not yer normal Drift mornin', eh?"

Skerridge was crouched on a rock, looking down at Jik. He was still in Natural Bogeyman shape, just in case anything turned up that called for a burst of super-speed or a good dousing in firebreath. Superspeed and firebreath didn't work in anything other than Natural Bogeyman.

"Yik!"

"Gold's yer norm. Or a nice 'ot orange, but not *that*. Looks kinda doomy. Fink it means anyfin'?"

Jik sat up, scattering ashes. It was the second dawn he had seen that red, the first being just a couple of days before, and he definitely thought it meant something. He just didn't know what, though he was pretty sure it wouldn't be nice. It made him think strange thoughts about cataclysms and The End of the World.

Skerridge squinted down at him. "Looks t' me like yer've grown! Yer'll be up t' Ninevah's middle, I reckon."

Hopping to his feet, Jik shook off the dusty remains of the fire. The ground certainly seemed a little further away than it used to be. Overhead the glow died, the flames burning out into a clear morning. He looked up and down the beach.

"Wik Nik gik?"

"Oh, the Redstone kid's in trouble, wouldn' ya know it! Or at least she was. Now she's safely cozied up wiv the sisters. That racket I 'eard last night while ya was still cookin' was the sanctuary closin' its door and movin' somewhere less tricky."

"Kik dik thik?"

"Course it can do that!" Skerridge sniggered. "Reckon tha's one sorry bogeyman what fort 'e could catch Ninevah Redstone, eh?" His snigger turned to a frown. "Wonder what the ovver BMs are up to? Accordin' t' the bell ringer, Strood's plannin' t' finish off the Seven." He shuddered. "I know they ain't sorcerers anymore, jus' the remains of sorcerers, but the Seven are . . . well . . . they're the last breff of Celidon, see. An' if 'e wipes out every last trace of the old world, then it really 'as gone ferever."

Jik had never known the Land back when it was called Celidon and had been the home of many different Fabulous, from cruel faeries to graceful elves and powerful sorcerers. He had been born far too late, long after the plague had come from nowhere and killed most of the Fabulous, wiping some species out of existence altogether. Now the Land was lived in mainly by Quick and was called the Drift. And it was still dying, still being devoured slowly by the plague that was turning its wild woods and green valleys back into misty Raw—the base magic it had all been created from back at the dawn of time. Soon it would all be gone. Every last bit. Like a fantastic sandcastle washed away by the sea.

But Jik knew even more than that. He had crossed the Heart of Celidon, the oldest patch of Raw in the Drift, and knew that the plague was not just killing the Drift by sending it back to its original state. If that had been all, then there would have been hope that one day the Raw might give birth to a new Land and a new kind of Fabulous. But Jik knew that such a thing would never happen. He had seen that at the heart of the Heart was *nothing*. Not even Raw. The plague was killing magic itself, and once the Land had gone, *nothing* was all there would be. Forever.

Jik sent a glance back at the dark shape of the House towering over the beach. A stiff breeze had got up and the sea horses were throwing themselves against the rocks in a frenzy of foam.

Skerridge huffed thoughtfully. "Not t' mention the consequences," he went on. "Somefin' as big as killin' off the last breff of Celidon is bound to 'ave 'orrible consequences."

Jik stared at him anxiously. "Fing is, what're we gonna do about it, eh? I 'spect yer finkin' o' trackin' down Nin. Bet yer can sense 'er whereabouts already, eh?"

"Yik!"

"Fort so. But she's wiv the sisters, right? So she's

safe fer the moment, which leaves yew an' me free t' do somefin' useful." Skerridge bared his jagged jumble of teeth in a grin. "See, I've been turnin' fings over while ya was cookin', an' I gotta plan. It ain't much, but it'll get up Strood's nose a lot, which by my reckonin' is worf it. Wanna come along?"

Jik knew in his mud that Skerridge was right and Nin was safe from Strood, for now at least. And it would be good to help slow down the darkness gathering around the last remains of Celidon. So he nodded.

"By the way, d'yer know yer glintin'? Mus' be somefin' t' do wiv all that salt an' sand mixed in wiv yer earf. S'gone all quartzy."

The mudman checked himself over, turning his arms this way and that, and then holding them up to the sun. Skerridge was right. Set in the mix of red and dark earth that made up his body were tiny glints of crystal, most of them concentrated in his hands and feet, though there was a general scattering everywhere else.

"Good fing too," said Skerridge approvingly. "It'll make yer nice an' tough. Come on then." He jumped off the rock and started lolloping up the beach in a flurry of sand.

"Wik?" asked Jik, falling in next to the bogeyman.

"We're off ter the Widdern, tha's where. We're gonna be a nice surprise fer someone!" Skerridge chuckled. "Then after we get back, we can go an' find Nin. Strood ain't daft an' 'e's bound to 'ave a backup plan. He frowned. "Fing is, I carn' 'elp wonderin'—what did 'e want wiv the tiger an' the 'uman Quick?"

Jibbit watched the red dawn burn itself out and wondered dismally what to do next. He was huddled in the crook between two chimney pots, struggling to face the fact that the Evebell had gone unrung for the first time since Strood had taken over the House, nearly a hundred years ago. It had not been the ex–bell ringer's fault—after all, what hope did a small stone have against a large Fabulous—but Mr. Strood was not the sort to accept excuses, and Jibbit knew that he was doomed. He would be ground to dust or reduced to molten lava. Or even—he shuddered—subjected to one of Mr. Strood's horrible experiments. Jibbit was the result of an experiment in the first place when Strood had brought him to life with the leftover magic in a sorcerer's wand, and then infected him with a trace of Quick to give him thought. But that didn't mean that he couldn't become part of another one. Arafin Strood was not above recycling.

The gargoyle moaned quietly and wrung his three-toed, stony paws. The useless wings on his back hunched pathetically against the early morning wind that blew in from the sea. He had had a nice life up on the roof of the House, tucked out of the way of the more horrible aspects of working for Mr. Strood, but now it was all over.

A sound echoed over the roof. It came from the back of the House, far away from the bell tower and down a roof or two from where Jibbit was crouching. The Suna-torium. He listened for a moment, then crept slowly closer.

Mr. Strood's Sunatorium was a woodland walk at the back of the Terrible House. It was encased in living crystal that grew out from the House's walls to join with the cliff and surround the wood, leaving the occasional hole for extra long branches to poke through. The sounds Jibbit could hear were coming from one of those holes.

Jibbit perched on the very edge of the roof and

peered through the crystal top of the Sunatorium. He didn't dare step onto it for fear of falling through, or—if the crystal didn't break beneath him—of sliding off it to his doom on the rocks at the foot of the cliff.

Below him were Mr. Strood, Secretary Scribbins, a tiger, and a ragged-looking man. Both the tiger and the man were in cages. The Mortal Distillation Machine was there too, dragged in from the ruined laboratory along with the cages. A whole range of bottles and strange-looking implements had been laid out on a trestle table to the left of the machine. There was also an armchair, set facing the machine, with a small side table on which sat a steaming cup of coffee and an uneaten slice of toast.

"What do you mean, he hasn't come back?"

Mr. Strood had had a bath and had changed his rags for one of his usual black silk suits. Fortunately, along with his jaw, his right arm and his leg had finally grown back. The missing eye had managed to heal too, but had done it around a small lump of quartz that must have got lodged in the socket during all the crawling through the earth. It gave the eye a splintered gleam that reflected the early morning sun. Altogether it was not a pretty sight. "J-just th-that, Mr. Strood sir. B-bogeyman B-Bale hasn't come back," stuttered Scribbins.

There was only one conclusion to be drawn from this and Strood drew it. He let out a slow hiss.

"She got away AGAIN," he said in a voice so full of sharp edges it made the watching Jibbit feel sick with fright.

Scribbins held his breath. Mr. Strood was normally a controlled sort of person, even when he was in a temper, but it was becoming very clear after the incident in the laboratory that Ninevah Redstone was the one thing that could make him go absolutely no-holds-barred nova.

Strood switched his gaze to the tiger and the Quick, and his eyes brightened. Scribbins let out his breath slowly and his heart started beating again, though in a disturbingly fluttery way.

"I thought she might," Strood said, "that's why I have a backup plan. Always have a backup plan, Scribbins." He laughed. It was almost friendly. "Y-y-yes, sir." Scribbins bobbed nervously a couple of times. "Truth is, I rather look forward to the challenge. Since I dealt with Gan Mafig, my old master, and took over his House, things have been a little quiet around here. Now I have a real test of power. Time to show the Drift just what I can do, eh?"

Scribbins had begun to shake so badly he could hardly hold his notebook. It was experiment time, he just knew it. "Put the man into the distillation machine," said Strood, "and move the tiger's cage closer."

"B-b-but . . ."

Strood rolled his eyes. "All right, get one of the guards to do it. Really, Scribbins, pull yourself together or I'll send you down to the Engine and get Mrs. Dunvice to take notes instead."

The watching Jibbit shuddered. He had heard about the Engine, where men, women, and children ran all day in the great wheels that spun electricity to power the Terrible House. Stories about Hathor, the giant-Grimm guard who kept them all running until they fell to the ground and died, were often repeated among Strood's servants. Below him, Guard Floyd appeared and shoved the tiger's cage into position. Then he grappled the screaming man into the Mortal Distillation Machine and shut the door on him. Strood got busy with the needles and tubes, linking the human and the tiger, so that the distilled essence of the first would flow directly into the second. "Now, I expect you to take detailed notes,

Scribbins. This is only part one of my plan. The end
result will be a first, you understand. Nothing like this
will have been seen before. By the time I have finished, I
will have made legend."

Scribbins wiped a clammy hand on his jacket and
tried to get a grip on his pencil. With a flourish, Strood
released a clamp, allowing a cloudy pink potion to flow
down the tube and drip into the victim's veins. The
potion was a key part of the distillation process and
drove the victim insane, locking him into his worst
nightmare, magnified a thousand times. His spirit would
be completely crushed by the sheer weight of terror, and
its squeezed-out essence could then be either collected
into a beaker for Mr. Strood to use later, or fed straight
into the body of victim number two. In this case, the
tiger.

Jibbit couldn't tear himself away. He crouched there,
shivering, while the horrible experiment went on. He
had never personally witnessed distillation, but he had
heard the screams echoing up from the chimney pots,
even when he was up on his perch at the bell tower.
Now, watching the poor man reduced by degrees to a
leftover husk, he saw the real horror of it.

The tiger's fate was little better. When Mr. Strood
had made Jibbit he had used only a small drop of distilled human to infect the gargoyle, just enough to give
him some intelligence. But the tiger was getting an entire
body's worth. Judging by all the roaring, it wasn't a nice
experience.

Strood hummed contentedly as he watched the ago-
nizing transformation take place, the pure essence of
human forcing its way in to mingle with that of the tiger.

In the corner of the room, Scribbins was trying hard
not to throw up. Especially since he might be sick over

his notes, which were going to be hard enough to read as it was, what with all the trembling.

Suddenly the room fell silent. Strood stopped humming. In the distillation machine a wispy husk hung from the restraints like crumpled-up tissue paper. In the cage, the transformation was complete.

Something uncurled from the floor. It was gold and black, and its amber eyes glowed with savagery. Six-inch-long claws scraped on the tiles as it pushed itself up to rise gracefully to its full height. It couldn't speak much, its mouth was too full of teeth, but it made a low purring sound.

"Perfect," said Strood quietly.

Scribbins sighed with relief.

"Now, clean out that mess in the Distillation Machine and put the tiger-man in there. It's time for phase two. And while *he's* distilling, fetch me some crowsmorte and a bucket of blood." Strood smiled. "On second thoughts, make that a barrel."

4

A PLACE OF SAFETY

ello, Ninevah Redstone."

Nin had been dreaming about being on a mountain in the dark, with the wind howling around her. Now she gasped as fiery light bathed her. She could feel something too, a tingle in the air that meant dawn was happening. She opened her eyes, though she knew that she wasn't really opening her eyes. In reality she was still asleep, but in her mind she was just . . . seeing what was there.

She was in a bed and a woman was sitting beside her. The woman's shape was clear and so bright it must have been made of the dawn fire. She was slender and her close-cropped hair was silver-white. Her long robe was of the same ruby color as the sunrise.

The woman smiled. It was such a gentle smile that a little warmth began to creep back into Nin's icy limbs. "Hello, Ninevah," she said again. Her voice could have broken hearts.

The woman was only an image made of light, an echo of something that had once been real, but Nin understood completely that a vision so vivid and clear could only be the remains of one of the Seven Sorcerers. "You have to be Enid Lockheart!" Nin stirred, trying to sit up, but her limbs felt like lead so she lay quietly, her eyes fixed on the woman's face. She knew she was right, this was the once-sorceress who had created the Sanctuary. "Indeed I am." Enid smiled. "Now, we have little time, Ninevah, for it is only in the moment between oblivion and consciousness that I can be seen, and you are waking up. I will hang on to the moment for as long as I can. There are things I have to tell you and you must listen carefully."

The sound of the wind seemed distant now, a gentle murmur. Nodding, Nin sighed inwardly. She had a feeling she knew what this visit was all about.

She had been longing to go home and had done everything she needed to do to achieve that, but in her heart she knew it wasn't over yet. While rescuing Toby and finding both of their memory pearls—the spell that would restore the memory of their existence in their world, the world of the Widdern—she had made an enemy of Arafin Strood. And if last night's attack by bogeyman was anything to go by, he was not about to let her walk off happily into the sunset.

"Tell me," Enid went on, "when you met Nemus Sturdy, did he explain about the Seven Sorcerers? About how we tried to cheat the plague by becoming something else? Good, then you'll know about how I poured all my magic into a spell to make a place of safety, where Quick may come to be healed and find comfort."

"Yes, you made the sanctuary." Nin paused as a chill ran though her. "I just realized what I did!" she gasped. "I led the bogeyman straight to you! He'll tell Strood where you are and then . . ."

Enid laughed and for just a moment Nin caught a

glimpse of steel in her eyes. "No Dread Fabulous will ever cross my threshold." She leaned forward and Nin felt golden eyes on her face and smelled wild flowers. "You have to understand the nature of spells," Enid went on. "Listen to me, Ninevah, because this is important. Spells are not just words that you say and that have an end result and then they are over. They are much more than that. Think of them as a living thing, a creation of the sorcerer who casts them. They evolve and sometimes you could almost believe they are intelligent. Sometimes, with a powerful spell, even their creator doesn't know how it will achieve what he has set it off to do. Look at Simeon."

"Simeon Dark? The last sorcerer. The only one of you who might still be alive and still a sorcerer?"

"Simeon cast a spell that hid him so completely, it is as if he has vanished from the Land. And even those closest to him do not know what the spell did to achieve that." Enid smiled warmly. "It's possible that even Simeon Dark doesn't know what happened to Simeon Dark!"

Nin frowned, trying to understand. "So, like, the sorcerer assigns his spell a . . . a task and starts it off. And it will do what it's told, but how it does it is up to the spell?"

"Right. That is why the bogeyman who came after you was no threat to me. I cast a spell to make a safe refuge for the Quick, and that spell is still alive, fed by the desire of millions of Quick."

"Safe," said Nin, thoughtfully. "So when the sanctuary was found by the BM, someone who threatened its safety . . ."

"My sanctuary moved. Every last patient, sister, bottle, and bandage." Enid laughed with delight and Nin joined in, feeling suddenly happy. "It moved because if it hadn't, it wouldn't be safe anymore, and it has to be safe because that's what I made it to be."

"Neat! So Strood will never find you?"

"No, but there is one way that Strood can kill the spell and so kill me. He's trying it right now. You'll see what I mean when you wake."

"I'm sorry."

"Don't be. It's not your fault that he is what he is. If it's down to anybody, then it's down to us, the Seven, for what we did to him." Enid smiled her warm smile again. "He's left us alone for many years, no doubt taking pride in the knowledge that he is the most powerful person in the Drift, while we are shadows of the sorcerers we used to be. But now he has decided to have his revenge, both on us and on you. He's killing us all and there will be consequences."

Now Enid's eyes were full of ice and Nin shivered. The sound of the wind seemed close again. "What should I do?"

"I think that fate . . ."—Enid hesitated—". . . or something, anyway, has chosen you to stop Strood. And I think the Seven, the Land, and all who live on it will stand or fall along with you. You have to survive, and to do that you'll need help, the most powerful help you can get."

"Simeon Dark," said Nin, understanding at once. "I have to find the last, living sorcerer. Because he's the only one who might be able to help us stop Strood."

"Right." Enid laughed. "But it's not going to be easy." She leaned close, her smooth brow crumpled with thought. "There are many stories about Dark and what happened to him. I'm sure you'll come across them in your travels. But we were his friends and knew him best and I can tell you that he always loved disguises." She

31

laughed softly, remembering good times. "Sometimes he'd turn up to his own parties looking like a complete stranger—a different kind of Fabulous, a Grimm perhaps, or even a Quick."

"So he could be disguised as anyone or anything?"

"That's right. And you see, around the time of the Final Gathering, Simeon fell in love. He never said who it was, but I think she was a Quick. So I've often wondered if, at the end, the spell disguised him as a Quick so that he could be with her."

"But she'd be dead by now, wouldn't she?" The sound of the wind was louder, getting in the way.

"Oh yes, but he may have kept the disguise even after her death. There may have been children, and if so, then they would have been Grimm and may still be alive. Besides, Simeon loved company, so he'd be in a place where there are people, I'm sure."

Nin thought about it. "Okay, so that's one possibility. But where do I start to look?"

"In Dark's Mansion," said Enid promptly. She looked almost transparent now, her form thinning, blending with the fiery glow of dawn. "There's a story that when Simeon emptied his house, storing away everything he owned for the day when he might return, he left one great treasure behind. If I know Simeon it's not a treasure so much as a clue, a hint of some kind."

Enid Lockheart leaned close, her golden eyes fixed on Nin's, and even though the once-sorceress was only a vision, Nin felt breath on her cheek, warm and full of something so vital it made her gasp. "We need you, Nin. More depends on your success than you could possibly understand. And time is running out. All night, while you were lying here so badly injured, while your friends waited and watched, Strood has been getting things done."

Nin shivered as Enid's words blurred in her head. "You're fading!" she cried urgently, "where is Dark's Mansion?"

"Here," said Enid. "Simeon built it high enough to touch the heavens, and what you are hearing is the ceaseless wind that blows about its peak."

"Here . . . !"

"My spell knows, you see," Enid went on, "that to keep the sanctuary safe, Strood has to be stopped before he finally ends us all." Now, the once-sorceress was nothing more than a formless shape of light. "So when the sanctuary had to move, the spell chose to bring it to Dark's Mansion. It brought us here because of you, Ninevah. My spell knows that you are its only hope and it is helping you so that you can help it, so that it can go on keeping me safe, you see?"

Enid smiled, though by now Nin could hardly see the curve of her lips anymore. "Good luck, Ninevah, though I'm told you already have it! You must succeed, for all our sakes."

"Whatever happens, I'm glad I saw you," said Nin, as her inner eyes closed and her real ones began to flicker open. "You are so lovely."

"We all were," Enid's voice was a whisper now, her shape a glimmer of ruby in the after-dawn light. "But, remember, sometimes beauty hides a rotten heart."

And then her light went out and Nin opened bleary eyes on the morning.

The world had changed. Nin had never been to the sanctuary before this, but Jonas had told her about it and she had seen into its cool stone corridors. Now the walls were twisted wood, baked by time and sunlight to a deep gold. Unevenly spaced windows looked out onto a clear sky of delicate turquoise. But the thing she saw straightaway as she walked its halls in the early morning light was that the sanctuary was shrinking. The once airy corridors and many rooms were changing, and this time not by design. Enid was right. Mr. Strood had been Getting Things Done.

"It started that night, after the BM nearly got you," Jonas told her, while she dressed and ate a hurried breakfast. "At midnight the sanctuary was full of rooms and doors and long hallways. By dawn it was two-thirds the size."

"But how?"

"We don't know for sure, but we think Strood has sent his BMs to kill the Quick who were once patients here, who left to go back home to the Widdern, having got back their health or their sanity. The ones who kept the spell alive by telling the story to others."

"So, all over the Widdern, people are dying?" Nin looked up at him, horrified. She was feeling overwhelmed by the task ahead of her, and if she had had any glimmering of hope that Strood might change his mind and give up, it died right then. "It's awful. *He's* awful."

"That's why we're going to do something about it, right?"

Nin sent a glance at the two stuffed rucksacks propped against the wall. They were getting ready to leave.

"Taggit's gone on ahead," said Jonas. "He's going to see if he can find Skerridge and Jik, then we'll all meet up at Hilfian. Taggit thinks that with Strood on the warpath, Hilfian is the place everyone will go. Good place to gather and make a stand, see? We might find help there. Plus, the Savage Forest is not far beyond Hilfian, so if we want, we can go on and speak to Nemus. He might be able to tell us more."

Nin's appetite had gone, but she forced down her last mouthful and smiled up at Elinor as she came to take away the plate and cup. The sister smiled back, her golden eyes lovely but still nothing more than a pale reflection of Enid's.

Sorcerer-Grimm, thought Nin, and wondered who her Fabulous father or mother had been.

"I'll take Toby back to the Widdern," Elinor said. "So you need not worry."

"Toby?"

"I think we'd better send him home, don't you?" Jonas smiled. "The kid's been through enough already."

"I'll deliver him right to his door," promised Elinor, "and he can take his memory pearl and be safe with his mother by lunchtime. She'll be shocked at first, but if I know Quick minds, she'll blame forgetting him on the trauma of his disappearance."

Nin nodded. She wanted so much to go home with Toby that her eyes stung with unshed tears. Jonas must have seen the look on her face, because he put an arm around her and squeezed, though he said nothing.

"All right," said Nin, sniffing hard, "but I want to say good-bye."

When they were all packed and ready to go, Elinor woke Toby and brought him along to the doorway that led out into Dark's Mansion. By now the Lockheart Sanctuary was beginning to stir and other sisters, going about their morning business of waking up their patients, turned their heads to look at Nin. The shrinking seemed to have stopped for now—presumably because the BMs who were doing the damage were hiding from the daylight—but there was a feeling of tension in the air, of anxious waiting.

While Jonas stood by, Nin watched Toby hurrying

up to her, his blond hair flopping over his face, his wide eyes so blue they were nearly purple. He gazed at her worriedly, but to Nin's relief there were no tears. "I can help, if you like," he offered. He was wearing a pair of slightly too big pajamas and was holding Monkey, the toy that had come all the way across the Drift with Nin to rescue him from the Terrible House of Strood. Nin shook her head.

"It's okay, Toby. But I've got another job for you, a really important one." Nin bobbed down so that she could talk to him eye-to-eye. "Look after Mum, right, because she won't remember me at all. But when she does, she won't know why she's forgotten in the first place so she'll be all upset. And when that happens, when she cries out my name or something, then it means I'm right outside the door. Do you understand?"

Toby nodded.

"And then you can open the door for Mum and I'll be there waiting, see?"

She didn't think about the ending where they didn't make it, Strood won, and she never came home, just in case it showed on her face. She gave him a hug and a kiss, and then turned back to the door. "Ready?" asked Jonas.

Nin paused, settling her rucksack more comfortably on her back. It was her old pink one, the one with the horrible fairy embroidered on it. Packed inside she had the rest of the beeswax candle that brought peace of mind, the bottle of bee venom painkiller, and some food. Slung around her waist was a leather flask of fresh water. She still had her old boots and jacket, and Elinor had found her a pair of someone's jeans and a shocking pink T-shirt, to replace the things that had gotten ripped and bloodstained. The sister had even come up with a new black coat for Jonas, his having been ruined when they used it to wrap up Jik for their undersea escape. Jonas still had his old red scarf wound around his neck.

"Ready," she said as firmly as she could.

Jonas pushed open the door to Dark's Mansion and they stepped through into a howling wind that smelled of ice and early morning.

5

GETTING THINGS DONE

I t was early morning in the Widdern on an ordinary main street in an ordinary town. People rushed in and out of shops, keen to get things done before the day wore too far on. Occasionally one or two of them paused in front of Sandy's Electrical Store to stare at the images flicking across the TV screens, images of homes and cars, each one burned to a horrible wreck during the previous night by some cause unknown. Each one containing the charred remains of bodies that had been the center of the blaze. The morning newspapers were calling it "Britain's Blowtorch Butchery."

Next to the TV store was The Little Garden Shop, and here people who didn't want to know any more horrible facts about the rash of fire tragedies sweeping the country were pausing to comment on the garden statues arranged along the front. "Very modern," said one old but elegant woman with a floaty scarf. "Rough-hewn of natural materials, but with an almost occult feel about it."

"Give me a gnome any day," muttered her husband.

Something snuffled near Skerridge's elbow and he squinted down at a small dog attached to a leash, which was attached to the woman with the scarf, who was studying Jik intently. "So organic, a wonderful representation of the Earth Incarnate," Floating Scarf went on.

"Blimmin' creepy, if you ask me."

Jik glared.

Skerridge chuckled. He was sitting on the pavement next to Jik and right underneath Floating Scarf's nose. But Skerridge was a bogeyman in the Widdern, and, to a grown-up Quick, he was invisible. They could hear him though, and Blimming Creepy backed off looking nervous.

"Ya betta watchit. One of 'em'll buy ya if yer not careful," Skerridge whispered.

Blimming Creepy went pale and grabbed Floating Scarf's arm. "Did you hear that?"

"What? For goodness' sake, Bernie, it's just a statue."

"It's glaring at me and I HEARD SOMETHING SPEAK."

Skerridge chuckled again. Floating Scarf blinked. The dog snuffled some more and made a nervous yipping sound. Skerridge hissed like an angry kettle. A small child being wheeled past in a stroller burst into a fit of spontaneous screaming.

Floating Scarf squeezed Blimming Creepy's arm. "On second thought, dear, you're right. Definitely creepy."

The dog whined. Skerridge leaned over and snapped twice. An empty leash dangled against Floating Scarf's legs, but she was already on the move, hurrying Blimming Creepy in the direction of home and not even noticing that her pet had gone. Skerridge munched thoughtfully as he watched her cross the road, clutching her husband tightly, the empty leash flapping along behind her. The inattentiveness of the Quick never ceased to amaze him.

He chuckled. Jik looked at him sternly. "Ik!"

"I was 'ungry! S'all right fer some of us what don' 'ave a stomach, but we're gonna be 'angin' around 'ere ferever, so I gotta take some nourishment while it's about."

It was a good thing that BMs knew the name and address of every living Quick—at least, the ones that hadn't already been stolen—as it meant that Jik and Skerridge were able to go straight to the home address of Hilary Jones. Hilary was the last surviving descendant of the once-sorceress Senta Melana. After she had cut off her own left hand and earthed herself, Senta poured all of her magic back into the Land and went to live in the Widdern and have babies. They knew that she was the *last* surviving descendant because they had reached the homes of the other descendants far too late to save them. Strood's BMs had been getting things done all right. "There's two fings 'appenin' in the Widdern, see," explained Skerridge heavily. "On the one 'and, 'e's killin' off Senta's descendants so as to end 'er line altogevver; and on the ovver 'e's killin' off a bunch o' Quick what I strongly suspec' 'ave 'ad doin's wiv Enid Lock'eart."

Jik ikked quietly. It sounded right. It sounded just like Strood. The thought made him feel anxious, not just for the poor suffering Quick, but for some other, deeper reason that he couldn't quite put his finger on. One thing was sure though, he knew in his mud that what Skerridge had said on the beach was right. There would be consequences.

Unfortunately, they had turned up at Hilary's flat— two floors up on the elegant block opposite the garden store—a bit too late to stop her from going out that morning. "'Spect she's been called out ter identify the remains." Skerridge sighed. "Poor fing. That ain't gonna be fun! But she'll be 'ome soon 'cos I 'spect she's gotta bit o' cryin' t' do—well, a lot actually—and then we'll stand 'ere an' watch over 'er till somefin 'appens. Which it's bound t' do, though prob'ly not till nightfall. BMs don' go out in the day."

"Yik dik."

"Yeah, but I made a choice, see. Ovver BMs jus' wouldn'."

Jik didn't look convinced and Skerridge could see his point. If Skerridge could make a choice, surely so could the others. Not that they would; somehow Skerridge was sure of that.

Skerridge burped loudly, fished around in his teeth and then spat out a small silver disc with the name "Tuffin" printed on it in curly letters. Jik sent him a look and then turned his gaze to the flickering TV screens next door. The many images were now showing an interview with a senior police official who looked pale but calm and who was answering a battery of questions from the press.

He sighed. Skerridge was right. Nothing more was likely to happen here until nightfall.

"Well," said Skerridge cheerfully, scratching his ribs under his fancy waistcoat, "time fer me t' be movin' on."

Jik glared.

"Le's face it, yer perfectly suited t' standin' in one spot impersonatin' a statue an' watchin' over fings. An' I'm perfectly suited t' superspeedin' back ter the Drift t' look around an' see wha's goin' on."

Jik glared some more.

"Tha's the spirit. Keep that up an' no one'll buy ya!"

The air fizzed. Jik glared at the empty space where a bogeyman used to be, then he switched his gaze back to the block of apartments across the road, heaved a sigh, and stood guard.

✳ ✳ ✳

41

In the Sunatorium, Mr. Strood was getting even more things done.

Below Jibbit, who was still watching through the Sunatorium's crystal roof, a large barrel of blood had been added to the bizarre collection of things in the wood. It stood to one side and was already covered in crowsmorte grown from the single bloom Strood had thrown into it a short while earlier. Guard Stanley, who was topping off the blood with a couple of bucket loads, had a job finding a gap to pour through. And as soon as the fresh blood tipped into the barrel, the whole thicket of blooms quivered and rippled, as if they were one great body sucking up the gore. And growing. Unfurling new blooms and putting out more shoots. Spreading.

Jibbit shuddered. He didn't have any blood, but even so, he knew what it meant to a Quick to lose it all. He wondered how many humans and animals would be bled dry to feed this growing crop and where Strood would get them all from.

"That will do for the present," said Strood cheerfully.

He was settled in his armchair, one silk-clad leg crossed tidily over the other, his quartz eye glittering with satisfaction. He went back to studying the bottle on the table beside him. It was full of a golden liquid, shot through with dark ripples. Essence of Tiger-Man.

In the machine the remains of the original tiger-man bore no resemblance at all to the exotic creature of this morning. Its vitality and spirit had been distilled out of it and all that was left was a dried-out yellow skin with a few pale stripes. Scribbins was gingerly gathering it up to put in a sack, handling it carefully in case it crumbled into dust and got all over the place.

As he studied the essence, Strood hummed thoughtfully. It was the sort of hum that meant he was ready to move on to the next stage of an interesting experiment. Hearing it, Scribbins paused in his work and shivered.

Strood got to his feet. He picked up the bottle carefully, carried it from the small table to the workbench, and set it down again next to a beaker of blood.

"A bloom, Scribbins."

Scribbins laid down the sack and went to pick a crowsmorte flower. He didn't have to go far. By now the plant was spreading across the Sunatorium floor. He took the bloom over to Strood who had opened the bottle and drawn off a syringe full of golden liquid. "Now, Scribbins, pay attention. I want this recorded in full."

With a trembling hand, Scribbins reached for the notebook. Far over their heads, Jibbit leaned a little further forward, listening.

"According to the story of the Seven Sorcerers— although as we all know there is always a large gap between story and truth—this plant was developed by Morgan Crow using the best of his magic and was meant to grow a new body for him. Crow's plan is said to have failed, because the plant ate him instead. Whatever the truth of that tale, the fact remains that he left behind a plant that has a taste for flesh and blood and is saturated with creative magical power. Now, it may be nothing more than a side effect, but crowsmorte is known to have amazing healing properties and to me that indicates a deep regenerative force, which, I suspect, has never been fully tested. You understand, I hope?"

Scribbins gulped. "The m-magic in the crowsmorte bloom g-grows people back?"

"Well done, Scribbins." Strood leaned over the flower lying on the table and injected it with one tiny drop from the syringe. Next he laid down the still-full syringe, dropped the flower onto the ground, and tipped the beaker of blood over it. Then he stood back to watch.

The crowsmorte bloom quivered. It began to expand, its stem fattening and its petals growing broader and paler. The color leaked out of it, purple turning to red and then to gold. Only streaks of darkness remained. Shoots split from the stem and thickened in their turn, coiling in on themselves, doubling back and twisting, some parts growing larger, some longer until the whole mass had a horrible innards kind of look.

"More blood," snapped Strood.

Guard Stanley threw on more blood.

And now it went faster. The newly pale petals turned back on themselves, wrapping their soft velvet around the innards like skin. Four more shoots detached from the bulk, shoots that grew in an oddly jointed way, and the petal skin covered those too. The whole thing started to throb as if a pulse had begun to beat somewhere inside. Both ends lengthened. The bottom end grew longer and thinner in a tail that began to twitch. The top put out a short stem that soon stopped growing, then thickened and rounded, the front part hollowing and curving and splitting. Thorns grew in the split, but they looked horribly white and sharp to the watching Jibbit.

And then eyes opened in the hollows, the mouth yawned widely, and the new tiger-man uncurled and rose to its feet in one sinuous movement.

This tiger-man was smaller than the original, though not by much. The pattern carried in the single drop of tiger-man essence had shaped it, but it was still grown from crowsmorte, and the plant's coloring showed through. The creature was softly golden, but the stripes across its velvet skin were dark purple. A scarlet flash ran down its spine from the top of its head to the tip of its tail. Its purple eyes somehow managed to glow red.

Guard Stanley shuddered. Scribbins nearly dropped his pencil. Strood beamed.

"So, Scribbins, how many blooms do you think we have here?" He waved an arm over the coated woodland. "And how many drops do you think a bottle that size can hold?"

"Y-you're going t-to make more?"

"Oh, lots more, Scribbins. We are going to war with Ninevah Redstone and anyone who dares to aid her."

The tiger-man opened a mouth fringed with needle teeth.

"Morrrr blood?" it asked.

"Plenty," said Strood quietly. "Do what I ask and you can have all the blood you want."

The door opened and Dunvice came in. "Ahh, perfect timing." Strood beamed. "Now, while Scribbins gets on with making more tiger-men, you and I can start recruiting officers."

6

DARK'S MANSION

Nin turned to send one last look back into the Lockheart Sanctuary. Through the doorway she could see Toby, waving. She waved back and smiled. Then the door closed, shutting them out of the Sanctuary's warmth and safety. They were alone in Dark's Mansion, standing in a stairwell laced with narrow windows through which the wind howled, clean and clear and sharp as glass.

Leaning to look out of the window next to her, Nin could see nothing but sky above, around, and below. Far beneath them, clouds swirled in a gray mass. She couldn't quite make out what they were being today, they looked like a tangle of wispy hair twisting and waving in the wind. One thing was sure though, Enid had been right when she said that Dark had built his home tall enough to touch the sky. And the sanctuary had set itself right at the very top.

Jonas had set off down the spiral stairs. Nin glanced back at the sanctuary door for the last time. It had blended into the wood of the walls, only the thinnest crack betraying its presence. She wished they could go back in, but they had a job to do. Two jobs. Find Dark. Stop Strood. Sighing, she hurried after Jonas.

So," she said, catching up to him, "tell me, just *how* do sick people manage to climb all the way up here to reach the sanctuary?"

"For the sick and desperate there are many ways into the sanctuary. We're neither, so we have to use the real door, the one that opens exactly where the sanctuary is and not where the desires of Quick need it to be." Jonas laughed. "Just be glad Enid's spell brought us here!"

"It's only trying to help itself," muttered Nin. "Anyway, where's the Mansion in relation to Hilfian? I mean, when we've found the clue, whatever it is, we're going on to Hilfian, right? To meet up with the others and find out what's going on before we go and see Nemus?"

"Right. Let's hope the Drift folk are gathering there like Taggit thinks; we could do with some help against Strood. But the problem for us is that Hilfian is a long way from here. Dark's Mansion is right down in the southwestern part of the Drift. Hilfian is a lot further up and way over east, near the Giant's Wood, remember that? But we'll find a way somehow. And if Taggit manages to find Skerridge, then he might be able to carry us there at sub-superspeed."

"And how is Taggit going to get to Skerridge? If Skerridge and Jik are still on the beach then Taggit's got to go . . ."—she thought about it—"even further east and north, out beyond Hilfian and the Forest and even the Heart. And then get back again to meet us."

Jonas laughed. "I dunno, but the Fabulous have their ways."

They hurried on, winding down the narrow stairwell. The walls on either side of them were rough wood, touched here and there with twigs, moss, and the occasional plant. They had to pay attention as they went, because the steps were uneven in height and depth, each tread different to the last, each surface dipped or raised underfoot as if they had formed naturally instead of being made.

After a while Nin stopped again to look out. Now, gazing first down, then craning her head up and back, she could see that Dark's Mansion was half Gothic castle and half mountain. Its summit was a vast tree growing out from the uppermost part of the Mansion to tower against the sky, with the sanctuary perched at the top like an oversized bird's nest caught in a net of branches. She and Jonas were traveling down inside the tree's hollowed-out trunk and were only about halfway, even after all that walking.

"So what's the deal with this place? It's pretty amazing."

"Sorcerers can't leave the Land," said Jonas, "but as long as they've got a direct line of contact, they're okay. Story goes, Dark formed the Mansion straight from the rock of the Land. So he could be high above everything but still be in touch with the ground, see?"

"So we really are inside a giant tree! Cool!"

"He liked to push the rules a bit, did Simeon Dark."

As they went farther down, the wood walls darkened, becoming blackened and losing their mossy look. "Dawn," said Jonas shortly. "The dawn fires must burn through it about here."

Nin was about to say how much she would love to see that, then bit back the comment. Since Jonas had nearly lost his soul to the Storm and become one of the Gabriel Hounds, she was always wary of mentioning the dawn. She had been there with him, as part of the Storm, and had felt the raw power of the dawn fires as they burned across the Drift sky. She still felt a stab of loss whenever she remembered it, and she knew that what Jonas felt must be a hundred times worse, even though he had conquered the Hound inside him. So she said nothing and just kept on following him down the twisting stairway.

The lower they went, the wider the trunk of the giant tree became. The hollowed-out part widened with it until the stairs seemed miles away from the walls, spiraling down through empty air like a wooden corkscrew. Fortunately for Nin, a thick coil of stringy stalk dotted with large ivy leaves followed the turns of the stairway—sometimes on the right, sometimes on the left—so she had something to hang on to. She didn't think she would have been able to move an inch otherwise. The sense of standing there with nothing but a thin wood step between her and vast amounts of empty air made her head spin and her insides turn to jelly.

Cool silver-gray light came in through the ragged windows, which had grown with the tower and were now as big as doors. Bigger. There was no glass in them and the cold air blew through, moist with unshed rain. Thin gray clouds drifted in too, coiling their way through the tower, in one huge window and out the other.

As they traveled downward, drawing closer to the clouds, Nin began to make out their shape. They were imitating mermaids, with long locks of misty hair floating around them. A few more twists of the stair and their feet were disappearing into the clouds that rose about them like thick fog, swallowing them up. She hung on extra tight and moved closer to Jonas.

At last they stepped off the bottom stair onto a stone floor, polished until it looked like deep, dark water. Looking up, Nin could see the stairway twisting above her up the hollow funnel of the trunk tower, until it disappeared into the drifting clouds. Silver light fell through the mermaids' wispy hair, rippling over the floor like water. "It's beautiful!" Nin sighed. "Kind of spooky, but beautiful."

Here, the walls around them were made from the twisted roots of the giant tree, and there was one large window level with the floor. Nin went to look out.

Far below, the Drift was veiled from sight by another, lower layer of wispy mermaid cloud from which Dark's Mansion rose in a tower of greens and grays, its rugged mud-and-stone outer walls wreathed in ivy and moss. Directly beneath her, Nin could see a sweep of green lawn jutting out, just above the clouds. "There's, like, a garden down there. A garden in the sky!" she called over her shoulder to Jonas. "It must be a sort of huge balcony!"

A stream ran across the lawn. The silver strip of water trickled to the edge of the garden, then out through a hole in the surrounding wall to tumble into nothingness and vanish into the clouds.

Behind her, Jonas sighed. He was studying something in the corner of the room. "So," he said, "where do we start? What do you think this clue looks like?"

Nin shrugged. "It'll be magic and I'm betting we'll know it when . . ." She turned and saw Jonas staring. Her gaze followed his. "What's that?"

"Skeleton. Thought you'd've worked that out!"

"Yes," said Nin with exaggerated patience. "But what's it doing here? *Other than being dead,*" she added sharply.

Jonas gave her a steady look. "This is a sorcerer's home, Nin. It may not be the Terrible House, but that doesn't mean it's SAFE."

Nin glared at his back as he started walking toward

an arch on the other side of the room. A horrible thought crossed her mind. What if Simeon Dark was . . . *not friendly?* Worse, what if he was EVIL? She had been seeing him as a hero, a champion who would use his powers to save them. But just because he was the only sorcerer left alive, and their one hope to stop Strood, didn't mean he had to be on their side. With a sigh, she put it out of her head and followed Jonas. The Mansion looked big. Best not to get lost!

On the other side of the arch was a staircase down to a smaller room, which in turn led to a maze of other rooms, all connected by arches and stairways. They walked on through Dark's mountain home, with Jonas in the lead and Nin staring around her as they went. Here the walls and floors were mainly rock, sometimes polished until they shone like glass and sometimes rough and sporting patches of moss or tiny flowers that sparkled like stars. In places the rock was seamed with agate or crystal and there were pillars like stalactites. It wasn't like being in a cave, though, for every room was full of light that poured in through windows of every shape possible. Many of them were filled with stained glass that spilled their color across the floor in swirls of blue and green, touched with vivid scarlet.

It would have been nice, but for two bad things. The first Nin noticed straight away. There were voices.

They began as a background murmur, but quickly grew to a constant chattering and laughing—almost as if they were getting used to the intruders' presence and growing bolder. After a while, Nin began to feel like they were the only living people at a very large party of unseen ghosts.

"It's spooking me," she grumbled. "I wish we could find the clue and get out of here."

"There's just so much of it," sighed Jonas, meaning the Mansion.

He looked worried and Nin knew why. It brought her straight to bad thing number two. The bone count was growing, from leftover bits of skull and oddly scattered bones, to whole and fairly new-looking skeletons. She frowned at the one they were just passing. It was still sporting tufts of hair and looked unnervingly familiar. As if she had seen it before.

Bad thing number three was just about to arrive.

Jonas stopped dead in his tracks. "We've seen that before," he said sharply. He threw up his arms. "Oh hell! I've been getting the feeling we're going round in circles and that just proves it!"

There was a moment of silence as the voices around them fell suddenly quiet. It gave Nin the creepy feeling that they were listening.

"We can't be," she said firmly. "We've been going *down* every stairway we've found. To cover the same ground, we'd have to go *up* at least sometimes, right?"

"This is a sorcerer's house, Nin. What's the betting normal rules don't apply?"

"So . . . like . . . doors might not lead where you think they lead?" Nin's heart sank as she caught on. "There might be some that take you all the way from the top to the bottom in a step. And some that take you from the bottom to the top again."

"The whole place is a 3-D maze," groaned Jonas. "At this rate, we'll never find our way out, let alone track down the wretched clue. We could starve to death in here!"

They stared at the skeleton in desperate silence. The voices got going again and Nin was sure there was more than the usual amount of sniggering.

"It's the story about him leaving treasure behind, I suppose," she said thoughtfully. "That's why so many people have come here."

"And died, you mean? Yep, sounds about right. What worries me is the skeletons that aren't whole, the ones that look like something tore them up."

"Oh, thanks for that thought!" Instant images crowded into Nin's head, things with big teeth, things with claws, powerful things that could be waiting round the very next corner. Fear settled in, making a cold nest somewhere around her middle. She had a nasty feeling it was going to stay for a while. Suddenly, the bad things were stacking up.

Jonas laughed grimly and shifted his pack to settle it more comfortably. "Come on, kid. Better give it another go. Maybe now that we know what we're up against, we'll stand a better chance."

They set off again, with Jonas marking the rooms and archways carefully as they went, using a piece of chalk dug out from the bottom of his pack. It soon became clear that things were pretty hopeless. There were so many rooms that Nin thought it would take months to look in them all.

On top of that, not only did the arches not lead where they ought to, but sometimes they were one way only, making it impossible for them to retrace their steps. They would go through an arch and find themselves in a familiar room, then turn back to find the single entrance they had come in by replaced by three different arches, all of which led to unknown rooms.

Jonas was concentrating hard, trying to work out if there was a system. In each room he would go over to the windows to look out and get his bearings as to where they were in the Mansion. Nin could see that it didn't help much. There didn't seem to be any logic in the way it was laid out at all.

And now, as well as worrying about being lost, Nin kept expecting some horrible THING to leap out at them and rip them limb from limb. It would be just like a sorcerer, she thought, to set a horrible guardian to watch over his home.

Gloomily, she followed Jonas through yet another arch.

7

ECHOES

To distract herself from her fears, Nin began to listen more carefully to the voices. She wondered if they were echoes of all the things that had been said and done here, the parties that Simeon Dark had held, the gatherings of his friends and fellow sorcerers. Perhaps she was listening to their dinner-party conversations. When one discussion ended, another always began straightaway, usually with different voices and about an entirely different subject. If she listened carefully, she could pick out individual people. *"Really, Simeon,"* said a voice that she thought belonged to Nemus Sturdy, the oldest and most powerful of the Seven Sorcerers, *"I don't think it's quite appropriate for you to pretend to be one of the Dread. Werewolves are so . . . unpleasant."*

Nin smiled to herself, remembering what Enid had told her about Dark. It sounded like the sorcerer was getting a talking to for his habit of turning up to his own dinner parties in disguise. It would be fun though, she thought, if you could be anybody, an actual person or a made-up one. With magic, the disguise would be as real as the real thing.

There was no response from Dark, but Nin was sure she heard a stifled yawn.

"Simeon!" snapped Nemus. *"This is serious, you know."*

Nin laughed. Without realizing it, the more interested she became, the more she fell behind Jonas. There was silence for a moment and then a different conversation started up, so she tuned in to listen. Soon she began to see the owner of each voice in her mind's eye.

"So what does it mean, exactly?" asked a new voice that just had to belong to Senta Melana. It was a soft, slightly husky voice, not as beautiful as Enid's but lovely enough to make the listener shiver. Senta had been the most beautiful of all the Seven Sorcerers. To escape the plague she had poured all of her magic back into the Land and gone to spend the last years of her life in the Widdern.

She's over there, thought Nin as she slowed right down, standing by a window, bathed in blue and golden light. And then it was more than just seeing Senta in her head. The sorceress was there in front of her, clear and sharp, though faintly transparent. Her beauty took Nin's breath away and she stopped to stare. There was something familiar about her, but although Nin had met Hilary Jones once before, she didn't quite make the connection.

"How should I know, my dear," said another voice, this one with a masculine beauty that easily matched Senta's. It was a lazy voice too, one that didn't care. Or at least, one that pretended not to. Nin turned her head and saw Azork. For a moment she felt a chill run through her; but this was not the tombfolk King he would become, this was the old Azork, the way he had been before he had cast a spell to make himself into a Dread Fabulous.

"It's just one of Morgan's foolish sayings." Azork moved over to stand opposite Senta, his silver eyes bright in his dark face as he watched her. His look made Nin feel strange, like she was spying on something private.

Senta laughed and the sound of it made Nin smile. It made Azork smile too, a gentle smile.

He's in love! Nin thought, amazed.

"Don't confuse foolishness with stupidity, Azork. Morgan isn't an idiot, whatever you may think of him. He just gets carried away sometimes." Senta moved, her long hair falling about her like golden silk, her dress a shimmer of pearly white.

Azork scowled. He obviously didn't like Morgan Crow much.

"Even so," put in another voice, *"I don't think the prediction has to mean anything specific. It's just an image, an impression snatched from a future time."*

Nin spun around, excitement gripping her. She saw a man she didn't know. His hair was pale gold, his eyes were a curious mix of gold and silver, and his slim shape was clad in a white shirt with black trousers and a scarlet waistcoat that hung open. He looked like a man who was at home.

"Surely, visions of the future can't be exact," Simeon Dark went on, taking a bite out of an apple, *"not when they are about EVERYONE'S future. It's all very well telling some little girl to beware the tall, dark stranger, but when Morgan makes a prophecy it's about the Land and that means something that will affect everyone alive, something that may be decades away. So all he can give is an outline, a snatched view, see?"*

"Hmmm." Azork sneered.

Senta gave a dreamy sigh that made Azork's scowl even darker.

"He makes such lovely prophecies though, doesn't he," she said. "A tide of golden darkness will rise in the east and sweep the Land, carrying death to the heart of one and dread to the souls of many."

"We could all make pretty sayings," muttered Azork irritably. "And we'd have just as much chance of them coming true at some time in the future as Crow." He struck a pose, one arm outstretched and his head thrown back. The light from the window turned his eyes to a glowing yellow-white, but didn't seem to touch the purple velvet of his robe. He hesitated.

"Go on," said Senta, looking amused.

"When there is life again in the Heart, so shall the lost be found and the ruined made whole."

"Is that the clue?" asked Nin eagerly. "Y'know, the lost being . . ." She stopped, her head spinning slightly. She was standing in an empty room talking to a window.

A very empty room.

"Jonas!" she called, hurrying through the nearest archway. On the other side was another empty room, so she turned around to go back. In front of her were two arches and through neither of them was a room lit with blue and yellow light.

Her stomach did a slow roll and a chill spread down her back in prickles.

"Jonas!" Although she shouted, her voice sounded horribly reedy and thin, floating on the empty air. Even the ghosts had gone quiet. "JOOONAAAS!" she yelled.

There was no reply.

She was alone.

8

PRESS-GANGED

It was early afternoon and while Ninevah Redstone wandered Dark's Mansion looking for Jonas, far over the other side of the Drift, Jibbit had taken refuge on the lower-left roof of the Terrible House. He was huddled against an outcrop of chimneys, trying to look like wall. He had been there all day.

He tensed. Out of the corner of his eye he saw movement, a gray shape slinking toward him over the sloping roof. Yellow eyes glowed as the shape passed through the shadow cast by a block of chimneys. Giving up on the disguise, Jibbit ran, scampering over the tiles on all fours and hooting with fright. The gray shape came after him, also on all fours, managing the steep rooftops almost as easily as the gargoyle. Soon any advantage Jibbit gained from his agility was lost because the gray shape was just as fast, and also much longer, so it could cover the tiles more quickly. It was gaining on him, its yellow eyes shining with the chase.

Jibbit screamed as a thin hand shot out and grabbed his foot. "Got you," said Mrs. Dunvice. "Come along, Mr. Strood wants a word."

Jibbit struggled and thrashed, gouging marks in the tiles and hooting like crazy. The half-werewolf House-keeper dragged him easily toward her, bundled him into her apron, tied the strings, and picked the whole bundle up in her teeth. Then she set off, still on all fours, heading for the roof door. "It wasn't my fault!" wailed Jibbit, still struggling. "It was the bogeyman! He made me! I never missed an Evebell till now. It's not FAIR!"

"Shtop making shuch a fush," snapped Mrs. Dunvice through a mouthful of apron. "You're caushing me bother. If you break my teesh, you're gravel, got that?"

The door onto the roof of the Terrible House was in one of the lesser attics toward the back. Once inside, she stood upright and smoothed her skirts and hair, then swapped Jibbit to one hand and started downstairs.

Jibbit screamed, "NOT DOWN!!!!"

"Oh for Galig's sake," muttered the Housekeeper. She hoisted the gargoyle up so that they were face-to-face and her yellow, werewolf-Grimm eyes glared straight into his gray, stony ones. A lifetime passed.

"SHUT," she said, very quietly, "UP."

The gargoyle gave a tiny nod and they went on in silence.

In the Sunatorium, the scene was like something out of a bizarre dream. Even allowing for Mr. Strood's arm-chair, the Mortal Distillation Machine, and so on, the Sunatorium was unrecognizable, and the thing that had really made the transformation was the crowsmorte.

It was everywhere. The path through the woodland walk had gone and so had the shrubs and ferns. Now crowsmorte covered the ground in a dense carpet of purple flowers touched with scarlet. Wiry stems twined and twisted up the trunks of the trees like ivy, coating them in a thick growth of soft blooms and vivid leaves.

They were laced around the table legs, draped over and inside the Distillation Machine, and even growing up the back of Strood's chair.

Here, a long way east and north of Dark's Mansion, there was no rain. Sunlight poured in through the crystal windows, throwing some nice dark shadows under the canopies of crowsmorte. Shadows that could hide things. Like a bogeyman for instance.

"So," Strood said, leaning back in his chair and taking a few more sips of his afternoon cup of tea, "tell me, why is it quivering like that?"

"It's downphobic," explained Mrs. Dunvice, "and we're on the ground. But I stopped it screaming. It also thinks you want to punish it for missing the Evebell."

The watching Skerridge felt an inner twinge that might have been guilt but was probably just indigestion. "Shoulda spat the collar out too," he mumbled to a particularly large bloom pressing against his nose, or at least, where his nose would have been had he not been in Dark-Space-Underneath-the-Crowsmorte form. He had been there since midmorning, just as Strood had finished growing his first tiger-man.

"Missing the Evebell?" Mr. Strood was saying with a frown. "Did it? Oh well." He went back to looking thoughtfully at Jibbit. He leaned forward. His quartz eye glittered eerily. "So, erm, Giblet, can you fly with those wings?"

Jibbit quivered. He opened his mouth and dribbled on the crowsmorte.

"Well, it is made of stone, I suppose." Strood sighed. "So, Dunvice, do you think it will be of any use?"

"Absolutely none, sir, while it's in that state."

Strood thought for a moment. Then he beamed. He fixed Jibbit with his glittering eye. "So, you don't like down, eh? And I bet you think you can't get any more down than the ground, eh? But you can. So if you don't stop shaking and start talking, I'll BURY YOU!"

Jibbit's eyes went wide. For a moment he froze. Suddenly, he had a new worst nightmare.

"I c-can climb," he croaked suddenly, in between panic-stricken hoots. "And I c-can s-sit totally s-still . . ."

Strood didn't look impressed.

"And I can go for days and days . . . *forever* without food or drink, though the odd pigeon is nice tooo chew. And I don't need tooo breathe. . . ."

Strood sighed and raised a dismissive hand. "Cross the bell ringer off the list and send him to the gardener for the rockery, then bring in whoever's next," he said, waving a hand at the large Grimm guard hovering by the door.

"AND I CAN KILL PEOPLE WITH MY FREEZING RAINWATER SPIT, AND SPLIT THEIR HEADS BY FALLING ON THEM. . . ."

Strood's hand stopped midwave. "Now, that's more like it. What do you think, Dunvice, shall I let the gargoyle join my army, or shall we bury him anyway?"

Dunvice smiled, her yellow eyes fixed on the agonized stone. "I think he might be useful, sir," she said.

While Mr. Strood was occupied interviewing other candidates for his army, Jibbit had managed to climb on top of the Distillation Machine and the relief of being UP again was so deep, it made his spine tingle. He drew a shuddering breath.

Around the Sunatorium a few chosen servants were harvesting the rest of the crop. When they had a basket full of the best, largest blooms, they carried it over to the far corner of the Sunatorium where the trembling

Scribbins was injecting each flower with a tiny drop of the essence created from the original tiger-man.

A purple bloom dangled over Jibbit's eyes. He tore it off his head and bit it angrily. It tasted foul. "Wanna lift?" muttered a voice in his ear.

Jibbit stifled a hoot. There was no need to look round because he knew who it was.

"Yooo!"

"Can it, will ya. I'm doin' yer a favor. Wanna lift?"

Jibbit nodded speechlessly, then wished he hadn't as the air around his ears grew hot and everything got so blurry he thought his eyes were going to implode.

Skerridge came to a halt halfway up the main stairs where he had a good view of the central hallway and the rooms off it. They were on a nice high stair, so Jibbit leaned over to peer through the banisters.

If the scene inside the Sunatorium had been strange, the one in the House was insane.

The Terrible House of Strood, once so quiet and orderly, was now bedlam. Strood was growing crowsmorte, and crowsmorte, like any other plant, needed sunlight. The once bricked-up windows had been smashed open to the world and it looked as if someone had done it in a hurry with a sledgehammer, and without worrying about bringing down large parts of wall.

On top of that, there was crowsmorte everywhere, or at least everywhere that wasn't covered in freshly grown tiger-men. The stuff was growing up the walls and out of the smashed-in windows; it was wound around banisters and cupboards and even hanging off the wall lamps. Skerridge suspected it covered the floor too, but since it was being used as a comfortable bed by the tiger-men, he couldn't quite tell. Their golden, velvet bodies, striped with bands of purple and fringed with ivory claws and needle teeth, curled and coiled over every inch of ground. Eyes gleamed here and there, slits of eerie purple that somehow managed to glow red.

Terrified servants scurried around and over all the obstacles, their faces white with fear, laden down with plates of meat and bowls of blood for the tiger-men to eat and drink. Skerridge knew that the servants were part mouse and so the tiger-men (which were, when you got right down to it, great big CATS) must be giving them the horrors. Still, they were Strood's servants and so they had no choice but to do their job.

Everything was a terrible mess, too: the floor (what you could see of it) was covered in blood, mud, fur, and worse. There were horrible stains on the wallpaper, not to mention claw marks, and the furniture was beginning to look frayed and battered. There were smells all over the place, some of them very nasty and some of them the usual ones having to do with cooking and fresh air. On top of all that, the racket was dreadful. Everyone shouted orders or replies, the tiger-men yowled or snarled, doors banged, feet scurried or plodded, and when the tiger-men got bored with waiting their turn for dinner, there were the screams of those servants near enough to provide them with a timely snack. Fortunately, the crows-morte was there to clean every last scrap off the bones or things could have been very unpleasant indeed.

Just below Skerridge and Jibbit, Guard Floyd walked past, looking gloomy. On impulse, Skerridge left his perch on the stairs and fell into step behind the goblin-Grimm. Feeling the bogeyman start to move, fortunately at normal speed, Jibbit did a sideways flip and scrabbled onto Skerridge's back. Judging by the direction Guard Floyd was going, he was heading out of the House. Jibbit was finding the cacophony of sound, sight, and smell almost unbearable after the lonely quiet of the rooftops, and although Mrs. Dunvice had forbidden him to go back to the roof, she hadn't said anything about outside.

"Ullo," said Skerridge cheerfully, as soon as they had stepped through a gap in the broken walls, "whatcha doin'?"

Floyd came to a sudden halt, realized who it was, and got walking again without even looking around.

"Well, well, if it ain't Bogeyman Skerridge," he muttered to the empty air in front of him. "Yew've gotta cheek!" He stomped on down the overgrown path.

"Come on, mate, I only arsked. Carn' a feller arsk?"

"We're musterin' an army, tha's what," snapped Floyd. It was a polite snap. After all, Skerridge might be a traitor, but he was still Fabulous. "An' now Mr. Strood's recruitin' . . ."

"Press gangin' more like," snorted Skerridge.

Floyd glared at him, his brow creased. He was partly puzzled by the fact that Skerridge had a gargoyle on his head, and partly by some nameless worries that had been nagging at him all day and had suddenly got a lot worse, though he wasn't sure why.

"I'm off ter ask Lord Grayghast if e'll kindly pop up an' 'ave a chat wiv Mr. Strood," said Floyd at last. "Yew ain't gonna tell me we'll be doin' any browbeatin' there!"

Skerridge's heart sank at the name of one of the most powerful Fabulous left in the Drift. Lord Grayghast wasn't a lord. There weren't any nobles left in the Drift these days, but Grayghast thought his name sounded good with "lord" in front of it, and since nobody was prepared to argue with a Fabulous werewolf, that was what he was called. And he was going to join Strood's army, Skerridge would bet on it. There was killing involved and werewolves always felt at home where there was killing.

They crossed the remains of a once-smooth lawn and walked through a tangle of dark trees. Jibbit could see the Large Folly looming ahead and made ready to jump. He could hang about out here where it was quiet until somebody came looking for him.

"Look," Floyd went on with exaggerated patience. "We work fer Strood, an' that means we follow 'is orders, see? We don' worry about consequences. If some dumb kid 'as t' go an' get up Mr. Strood's nose, then it's 'er look out, ain' it? If Mr. Strood wants t' pull the Drift apart bit by bit an 'ave 'is cruel revenge on ev'ry livin' fing, then that's jus' 'ow it is. If we don' do it, someone else will an' we'll jus' end up on the side what suffers an' 'orrible fate or gets eaten or whatever. See? Common sense. Believe me, yer picked the losin' side."

The guard stopped in his tracks, thinking over what he had just said. Seeing Floyd's face crease up with the effort of working it out, Skerridge gave him a nudge in the right direction.

"Yer right. It's only common sense," he said cheerfully, patting Floyd on the shoulder as he spoke. "On the balance o' probabilities, the Redstone kid's gonna croak along wiv all 'er friends, the remains of the Seven, an' an awful lot o' innocent Quick. So, wanna know why I'm on the ovver side?" Skerridge leaned close. "Yore the ones tha's gonna live . . ."—he paused just long enough to give a bit of dramatic effect—"*wiv the consequences.*"

Then he was gone, leaving a trail of smoldering undergrowth behind him.

Floyd watched him go. The BM's words hung about in his head, taking up a lot of room and looking very ominous. Consequences. Floyd didn't know what the consequences of killing the entire population of the Drift would be, but he had a nasty feeling he wouldn't like them. He wrestled with his thoughts for a while and then sighed. He couldn't work out the twists and turns of it all, but one thing he was sure of. His current future, the one where he stayed working for Mr. Strood, was full of an awful lot of screaming. Besides, regardless of the consequences, he thought the Redstone kid was okay and somehow it just didn't seem fair.

"Enuff is enuff," he said firmly.

Then he dropped his spear, turned his face to the southwest, and started to run.

From the top of the Large Folly, safely out of the way for the time being, Jibbit watched him go.

9

A CLUE

Nin got slowly to her feet. She had been sitting down with her head in her hands wondering what on earth to do next. "I should have just stayed where I was and let *him* find *me,*" she said out loud. They could have been just missing each other for ages and the voices weren't helping. Every time she thought she heard him she wasn't sure because all the chatter got in the way.

"And you can be quiet," she snapped, feeling both irritable and near tears.

Something hissed behind her, a slow hiss. Spiteful.

"*Ava, do you have to?*" sighed a female voice that Nin recognized as Enid.

"Enid!" called Nin on impulse. "Help me, I've lost Jonas."

There was a long silence and then more whispering, but no answer. The ghosts weren't playing—if they could even hear her in the first place.

One of the voices began singing something, a daft little rhyme about "*when bogeymen come to play.*" It wasn't nice. It made the BMs sound even more horrible than they were. Especially the bit about rending things limb from limb and "holding the darkness," whatever that meant.

Nin got moving again. She had to find Jonas. Had to. Or her bones would join those scattered throughout the Mansion. Trying not to let panic take over, she went through the nearest arch into the next room and then the one after that. And the one after that. Then down some stairs. She called out, then stopped to listen and wished she hadn't.

The song about the bogeymen was still going, or maybe the singer was singing it over and over again. The goriness of *". . . and then they pulled the bones apart and stripped the flesh right off them, and digging free the beating heart they squeezed till it burst open . . ."* clashed so horribly with the tinkly nursery rhyme tune that Nin began to feel sick. She plugged her ears with her fingers, trying to block it out. The singer raised his voice. There was a hard edge to it.

Perhaps it's Vispilio again, she thought, although if she was honest it sounded more like Dark. She didn't like to think he could be so horrible. *Perhaps he's just teasing me,* she thought, *trying to scare me. I wish he'd stop.*

Spinning around, she wondered which way to pick next. *"And held the dark around their forms, so hidden they could claim, the poor and hapless children, that they wanted for their game. . . ."* The voice rose steadily to a boom.

"STOP IT!" yelled Nin. "They aren't THAT nasty!"

"What do you know of the Dread Fabulous, little girl?" The voice chuckled. *"What do you REALLY KNOW about bogeymen . . . ?"*

Silence fell. Outside, rain lashed the windows and a branch, growing from the outer walls of the Mansion, scraped against the glass. It should have been better without the singing, but it wasn't. She felt watched, and not by anything friendly.

"It's just a song," she said firmly. "It can't hurt me."

The roar came suddenly. One minute the place was quiet, the next it was filled with a top-of-the lungs howl that Nin could feel vibrating in her bones. She screamed and ran, panic taking over in earnest. The roar echoed from room to room, rising in volume, sometimes in front of her, sometimes behind, driving her this way and that as she fled through room after room until . . .

She jolted to a stop, frowning. Blue and yellow light surrounded her, dappling the walls with the glow of late afternoon. It was familiar. She was back where she had started.

Nin walked farther into the room and something caught her eye, something scrawled on the polished floor in chalk. It said: FOR HEAVEN'S SAKE STAY HERE.

Relief flooded through her. Jonas was nearby and he would come back and find her. He had a better sense of direction than she did.

She settled down to wait. The room was peaceful now, the singing had stopped, and the voices had taken up again, chattering on about Galig's Hall, whatever that was, and how magnificent it looked. They seemed close, so close she began to imagine they were coming from the room next door.

There were four archways out of the blue and gold room. The smallest and narrowest was on the opposite wall to the others, the same wall as the window. In fact, the reason Nin hadn't registered it straightaway was because she had thought it *was* a window.

She frowned. Surely that was an outside wall and there couldn't be a room there? The arch should open onto empty air. Curious, she walked over to have a look.

There was a room all right.

It was lit by four great windows of stained glass, one in each wall, including the wall behind her, which shouldn't be possible because that was the window wall of the room she had just walked out of. By rights it should have three windows, not one. "Magic," said Nin softly.

It wasn't just the room either. In front of her hung a spiral made of something soft and supple, like a twist of ribbon with colors coming off its glowing surface in silky veils. There was nothing visible supporting it; the thing just hung there, turning gently in an unfelt breeze.

Nin stepped closer. The colors were shadowy ones, purples and blues and deep grays, but they gave off a glow like moonlight. Nin's fingers tingled and electricity crackled over her skin. This had to be the clue!

She wondered what to do next. She should go back into the other room and wait for Jonas, but . . .

Frantic that the other room would have gone, Nin spun around. It hadn't; she could still see its blue and yellow light through the doorway. She was about to head back in there when she hesitated. That room hadn't vanished when she went through the arch, but what if this one, the one with the clue in it, did vanish? They might never find it again.

Simple, she thought. *I wait here, just inside the arch, and when Jonas comes back I'll call.*

Picking a spot where she could see through into the other room, she settled down, sitting with her back against the wall. To pass the time she busied herself looking around the clue room, then wished she hadn't.

The windows were staring at her. The four panes

were each filled with the image of a lion. The rain had stopped and the late afternoon sun breaking through the clouds brought the colors vividly to life. The yellow lions had red manes and their scarlet claws and teeth were bared as if ready to attack. Their eyes were emerald green and were watching Nin carefully.

Spooked, Nin switched her gaze back to the softly swirling colors of the ribbon, noticing that faint shadows hung about it, shifting against the glow. Even so, she could still feel her skin prickling under the lions' emerald gazes. Trying to ignore them, she concentrated on her inspection of the clue, but the lions kept distracting her. Their stares seemed just as penetrating when she wasn't looking at them. She began to feel clammy; her scalp prickled and a thin trickle of sweat ran down her spine. She was suddenly aware that all the voices had stopped.

They're listening, she thought, *waiting for something to happen.*

From the windows, four sets of emerald eyes raked over her hungrily, like she was dinner or something. She looked at them, thinking that she might see them move, but they didn't. Then she thought they might move when she *wasn't* looking, so she studied the ribbon, then looked back quickly at the windows to catch them in the act. Nothing had changed.

"This is ridiculous," snapped Nin.

With one part of her brain she heard movement in the other room, a firm tread.

Jonas, she thought, *thank goodness for that! I can get out of here.* She got up and stepped forward, reaching out for the clue.

A boy stepped through the arch into the room. He was about the same age as Jonas, though taller, and was wearing a green jacket, brown trousers, interesting boots, and an awful lot of jewelry. His dark curly hair was tied back with a green handkerchief.

Before she had time to register that it wasn't Jonas and to stop herself from doing what she had started to do, Nin's hand closed over something cool that seemed to stir and shift against her skin. She pulled the clue down, holding it in her palm where it swirled gently, as if deciding what to do next.

The boy drew in a breath. "Oooo, big mistake that!" he said. "Let's hope it's not fatal!"

There was a moment of utter silence while Nin stared at the new boy in astonishment, and then the windows imploded, their stained images splitting into a thousand fragments that whirled about the room in a storm of splintered light and jagged sound.

Nin screamed as the boy stepped forward, grabbed her, and pulled her down below the level of the flying shards. Even so, the whirling glass was dangerously close and she felt a splinter brush across her wrist, drawing a line of blood. Then the whirlwind calmed and she could look. It wasn't good.

The shards were coming together again, but not as a flat image in a window. This time the lions were in three dimensions, formed of crystal slivers sharp enough to spill blood.

Nin shivered. The lions shone like jewels in the light, sending diamonds of color glancing off the walls. One of them moved, tinkling faintly. Its emerald eyes found Nin. The others followed its gaze. Nin wondered why they didn't pounce.

"It's a cat thing," said the boy. "As soon as you start running, they'll chase, right? They're just waiting for you to move, so keep still!"

"I didn't mean it," said Nin trying not to panic. "Here, have your silly clue!" She threw the shadow ribbon into the room. Or at least she tried to. It wouldn't leave her hand. Not panicking got suddenly harder. The ribbon shifted, twining its silky length around her fingers.

"You've got it now," the boy said. "It's a spell of some sort and I'm betting it won't leave you till *they* take it back. Name's Seth Carver, by the way, I'm a treasure hunter. You're Nin."

"How . . . ?" Nin sent him a look, still trying to untangle the spell. It wouldn't let go, and taking hold of it was like trying to pick up water. Every time she went to pull it free, it slipped out of her grasp, slithering up her wrist and forearm to weave itself even more tightly around her. "Oh, come on! You're famous," he said cheerfully, getting between Nin and the glass guardians. "Stories about you are halfway round the Drift."

One of the lions took a step forward, its ruby-tipped paws clinking on the ground. It opened its mouth and gave a snarl like grinding glass. Its emerald gaze was cold, fixed.

"See these boots?" he said calmly.

Nin glanced at the cracked leather bands strapped around Seth's calves, ankles, and feet. The hide looked as if it had been dipped in tar and was scored and scratched with a dozen symbols. "They're traveling magic, but they won't work unless I'm on open land. So what we have to do is get out of here and then we're away."

"But . . ."

"We can come back and find your friend later. And don't worry about these, these are only after YOU. You're the one who picked up the spell."

Seth pushed her backward to the door. The lions

followed, pacing them. The second one gave a low, grating growl. "When I say go, you run, right? Listen to me, I'll tell you which way to go, got that?"

Nin nodded.

"Right," said Seth. "Now RUN!"

Nin ran. So did Seth.

So did the lions.

They thundered through the Mansion, diving through arches, skidding across rooms, and trying not to crash into walls and pillars. Behind them came the lions, one after the other, their manes and paws scraping against the arches as they ran, their tread like breaking glass.

Nin tumbled down a flight of stairs, past tall windows but no doors. She could sense the lions at their backs, pausing, catlike, at the top of the stair. Then taking a step. And another. Then bounding on after them, splintered color swirling in the air as it caught the light of the windows.

They'll tear us up like rags, Nin thought, suddenly knowing why some of the skeletons had been scattered and broken. They were the ones that had found the clue.

She was used to running, but that didn't make it easy. Her breath was already rasping in her chest and her heart thumping madly. Her bangs kept getting in her eyes and her hand was raw where she was running it along the stonewalls for balance as they hurtled down stairs.

She plunged on through a maze of rooms, one leading into another, with Seth behind her shouting directions to tell her which arch to take or corner to turn. As they hurtled past one archway she saw Jonas, running to see what the noise was.

"Can't stop! Trouble!" she yelled to his startled face, and flew on past.

A moment later they burst out into a round room with three exits. Through one of them she could see open air.

"We're out! she yelled, diving through it. She didn't stop to listen for a word from Seth, she just went. With a groan, Seth followed.

Nin had only run a short way across the grass when she realized her mistake. For a start, they were still high up, she could feel it in the clear, sharp air that took her breath away. The clouds had vanished with the rain and the scene was bathed in early evening sunlight. In front of her was a stretch of emerald lawn, rimmed with flowerbeds gone wild. Roses grew in heavy-headed clusters of yellow and dark orange, and even though spring was long past, the trees were rich with pink and white blossoms. Her heart sank as she realized that she had come out into Dark's garden.

Glancing back, she saw the guardians crashing into the round room in a furious blaze of color.

Seth grabbed her. "Wrong door!" he gasped, unnecessarily.

"Come on!" yelled Nin, as she turned back to the garden. Before her, a path of amber cobbles led past the trees, down the slope of lawn, and over a stream to a low wall and some steps leading down. There was only one problem. Beyond that there was nothing but the sky.

Still, there was nowhere else to go; they just had to hope the steps at the end led somewhere helpful.

It wasn't far to the wall. Nin skidded to a halt and gasped, her head spinning at the sight before her. Far below, the Land unrolled in a carpet of vivid color. She had only a moment to take in its green meadows, purple hills, silver rivers, and dark woods, but it was long enough for her to realize that something was badly wrong. In every direction the color was spotted with patches of dense white fog that spiraled up in cloudy funnels reaching to the sky. In one place, the Raw was so bad that only a hill remained, like an island rearing up in a lake of mist. Even as she turned her head to look for the steps, she saw one stretch of Raw explode upward and outward, devouring another wood and a hillside clad in purple heather.

She felt Seth at her side and turned to look at him, the lions forgotten in the moment of realizing something terrible.

"The Land is dying faster," she said, her voice tight with fear. "Not slowly but now, right NOW. There'll be nothing left in a few days!"

"He's attacking the Seven," Seth whispered in her ear. "The Fabulous, the Land, they're all part of the same substance. Everything's twined up together. You can't kill one without killing the rest."

Behind them, the lions bounded down the lawn, scattering light like jewels in the evening sun. One of them roared, a crashing, grinding roar that split the air in knives of sound. With a scream of fright, Nin turned to the steps. There were two of them, the rest had crumbled away. There was no way out. Except one.

"Well," said Seth. "It was nice meeting you, Ninevah Redstone. Sorry it had to end so soon."

He grabbed her hand and pulled her onto the parapet. A long way down, at the foot of Dark's Mansion, she could see a steep hill tumbling away in a series of rocky ledges to end in a deep blue lake.

Just a leap away, a lion gathered itself to spring, its emerald eyes still fixed on its target.

"Let's put your luck to the test, eh?"

"What?" said Nin, bewildered. Before her the

landscape reeled. Far below, trees looked like tiny sprigs. Far, far below. The wind whipped her hair across her face and stung her eyes.

A kaleidoscope of gold and red light broke around them as the lion sprang, its grating roar slicing the clear air like daggers, its ruby claws outspread.

Holding tight to Nin, Seth jumped.

Screaming, they plummeted down toward the rocky hillside.

10

NINEVAH'S LUCK

The world was nothing but a swirl of twisting color and wind roaring in her ears as she fell, tumbling like a rag doll toward certain death on the rocky land far below. She had lost her grip on Seth's hand and fell with her arms outspread, as if trying desperately to catch hold of something. Anything.

The land whirled giddily, now above her, now below, a glimpse of grass and rock, then of evening sky. It seemed to last forever, but then suddenly the grass and the rock were gone and Nin could see only a pool of dense shadow stretching out beneath her, a blue-black darkness that blotted out the ground as she hurtled toward it.

As she plunged headlong into the depths of the shadow, the falling ceased. In fact, she not only stopped going down, but started moving along, flying through the air, wrapped in darkness. Below her, Nin could still see a hint of ground though it was veiled in shadow. Soft, cool air rippled around her from head to foot. It sent a shaft of joy into her heart that was both wonderful and painful. The falling was over. It seemed that certain death was not so certain after all.

Near her, she heard Seth laugh and say something about Ninevah's luck coming through, all right. She joined in, reaching out to find his hand again.

The air around her rippled, and suddenly she felt as though eyes were watching her. Eyes that were curious, but not very friendly.

"What's happening?" said Seth, his tone changing to one of alarm.

Nin gasped as the darkness shifted, altering its whereabouts so that it kept hold of her, but no longer supported Seth. For a second he hung there, still carried by the forward momentum, and now she could see him through the edge of shadow that still wrapped her. He was an arm's length away, bathed in the glow of evening light, his black hair tossed by the wind. His eyes met hers. He grinned.

"It was fun while it lasted, Ninevah Redstone," he said, and began to fall again, the force of his plunge ripping his hand from hers. And then he was gone.

While Nin's head reeled with shock, a soft voice spoke in her ear.

"That's better," it said. "Now it's just you and me."

Jonas was hard on the heels of the glass lions, following them as they tumbled down the slope and bounded on to the few crumbling steps toward Nin and the new boy who were . . .

Jumping!

Without so much as a pause, the lions went over the parapet after their prey, glinting fire-bright in the evening sun.

Breathless, Jonas got to the wall in time to see a stretch of shadow far below him swarming over the land and disappearing into the distance. As he watched, a shape—too big to be Nin—fell out of it, plunging to the ground. From this high up it didn't look as if the body had far to fall, but he suspected it was still enough to kill if the victim landed on the rocky hillside. He held his breath, heart hammering, waiting to see Nin follow. She didn't.

He looked down.

The lions hit the ground and shattered, glittering in fierce sparks of light as the impact flung them across the hill.

Hurrying back up the slope of the garden and into the round room, Jonas paused, sensing the air. He ignored the arch they had used to enter the room in the first place, and studied the three exits. The middle one was the way to the garden and the other two looked as if they opened onto other rooms, but he could feel a draft blowing from the one on the left. Jonas smiled grimly. If the 3-D maze effect of Dark's Mansion had anything to do with it, that thin current of air meant that the archway on the left would transport him to the ground floor and the way out.

It's like a great big game of Chutes and Ladders, he thought irritably as he went to look.

He found himself in a vast entrance hall. In front of him, standing open, was the main door out of the Mansion and through it he found the hillside he had been looking at a moment ago from so high up. The grass was scattered with colored glass so he picked his way over it, heading down to the lake. From Dark's garden it had looked like the dropped body might have fallen straight into the water. As long as it didn't hit the surface in a belly flop it would probably survive.

At the lake he glanced back to look at the Mansion, which rose from the Land in a vast and ragged tower

of earth and rock. Its lower slopes looked almost climb-
able, but farther up it became a sheer face that plants
and even small shrubs clung to against all the laws of
gravity. Far above, though barely a fraction of the way
up the tower, he could see the garden sticking out, supported by the branches of a great tree that formed part of
one side of the Mansion. He looked toward the top of the
Mansion, straining to see the even greater tree that grew
on its summit, but it towered so high above the land he
could see nothing save the clouds that drifted around its
walls. So he turned back to the lake where a figure was
splashing out onto the shore.

Seth collapsed in a breathless heap. "That was
lucky," he gasped. "It dropped me right over the water.
Not that it meant to, I don't suppose. You must be
Jonas."

Jonas nodded briskly and crouched down beside
him. "Nin?"

"Whatever it is, it's still got her, but my feeling is
she'll be all right."

"And who are you?"

"Seth," he said. He looked up at Jonas, smiling. His
eyes were an odd green-blue. "I'm a treasure hunter,"
he went on. "Well, thief some would call it. I search for
magical artifacts and sell them, or trade them, for food
and so on. Some I keep to use, though." He was getting
his breath back by now. He stood, stretching and flexing
his arms.

Jonas stood too, studying him. His eyes flicked from
Seth's necklaces, rings, and bracelets, and then to the
traveling boots. Something wasn't right.

"It's amazing," he said, almost before he realized it,
"how you turned up just when Nin needed you. With a
faerie compass." He nodded at the thing hanging from

Seth's belt. "And a pair of traveling boots." The words hung in the air between them.

Seth laughed. "Isn't it just like I came looking for her? Using the compass. And the traveling boots. Funny how I knew the way out, too. You'd almost think I knew that old place."

"Who are you?"

Seth leaned close. "Work it out, boy," he said softly.

Jonas looked into eyes the green of shallow water and felt the blood drain from his face. He knew the spirit hidden in those eyes. Ava Vispilio, the once-sorcerer whose spell gave him the power to steal the bodies of the Quick so that he could live in them and use them and even kill them. And then move on.

"You're dead!"

"Not dead, boy, never dead. You should have stayed to find my ring."

Jonas dropped his eyes to the once-sorcerer's hand and the ring that glowed on his forefinger. It stood out from the others like gold stands out from clay.

"You should never have left it for poor Seth Carver to pick up." Seth laughed, seeing his glance. "Someone will always come by, you know. The ring calls them. It's part of my spell." Out of Seth's captive eyes, Ava Vispilio smiled and reached for one of the amulets hanging around his neck.

Jonas sprang back. He was too late. Crackles of light leapt from the amulet, closing him in a net of lightning. "The best thing about the sorcerer magic in all of these," said Seth, jangling his collection of jewelry, "is that it's so *specific* about what it does. Much better than all that unformed power in a staff. That will take . . . oooh, let's see . . . around seven hours to kill you. Seven hours of agony as the sparks burn their way through your skin.

Giving you a few minutes' break every so often, just in case you pass out and need time to recover consciousness. Nice, eh? I made it myself, back when I was a real sorcerer, not just a passenger in some stupid Quick body."

The net of sparks closed and Jonas choked back a scream as the lightning began to worm its way under his skin, burning through him in jagged, fiery threads of pain. "Sorry I can't stop and watch, but it takes too long and I've got plans. Strood means business and I'm thinking that brains and cunning aren't enough to keep me safe right now. The only thing that's outwitted him so far is Ninevah's luck, and now that I've seen it in action, I'm inclined to agree. With the world about to end, she would be the safest place for me."

He glanced up at Dark's Mansion towering over them, the wall of the garden so high that it blended into the distance. Then he grinned at Jonas. "She trusts me already. Shouldn't be too hard to get her to put the ring on."

Jonas staggered, dropping to his knees. He opened his mouth to yell back, to curse the once-sorcerer, but pain twisted his words into a scream. Flashes of lightning glimmered in his eyes, dazzling him.

"Especially after I break the news of your death," went on Seth, "and she sobs on my shoulder. I might even cry with her, show my sensitive side."

Overhead, the sun was sinking into a pool of light. Purple clouds like great sharks swam along the horizon, but above them the sky was clear and the first stars were beginning to show.

Seth took the faerie compass from his belt—a flat ring of gold with a single ruby bead on its surface. The ring was edged with an intricate design that made it look like a golden snowflake and it shed a soft light that poured over Seth's hand. "Pretty, huh?" said Seth to the choking Jonas. "Faerie things were always pretty. Usually nasty, of course. But certainly pretty."

He held it up.

"Find me Ninevah Redstone," he said, and the red bead rolled along the rim of the compass. It stopped, pointing north.

"There you go! And the boots work on a state of mind," he explained cheerfully to the writhing Jonas. "All you have to do is think FAR." He raised his right foot to step forward.

The air blurred, and then he was gone.

11

KNOWLEDGE

Back at the Terrible House, Mr. Strood was settled in his chair, hands wrapped around a well-earned cup of coffee. He was in a very positive frame of mind. The House was full to overflowing and his servants had been kept busy finding spaces for his growing army of tiger-men to sleep in. Now the sun was dipping low in the sky and soon his bogeymen would be up and about again. Strood thought fondly of his BMs. They were doing very well, though he hadn't bothered to try persuading them to go out in the daylight. Skerridge might have thrown out the rule book, but that didn't mean the others could do the same.

Strood smiled. Speaking of which.

"Bogeyman Skerridge," he said, "you can come out now."

There was a long silence, then the air shimmered over to make way for a familiar shape. "Ya spotted me, then? No foolin' yew, Mr. Strood, eh?" Skerridge grinned cheerfully.

"Not for a moment," said Strood smoothly. "And don't worry, I won't send for the guards. I don't want them fried. Which reminds me. I take it that the little disturbance in the main hall this afternoon was you? The one where somebody tried to cook my tiger-men?"

Skerridge looked innocent.

"And you wouldn't happen to know anything about the desertion of ex-Guard Floyd, I hope?"

Skerridge beamed. Innocent didn't come close.

"I see." Strood smiled indulgently, looking almost affable, even allowing for the quartz eye. "Well, it won't get you anywhere. Ninevah Redstone is going to die and everyone else with her. I believe people are gathering at Hilfian? Well, my army will start there. And once they've torn Hilfian apart, they can sort out the rest of the Drift."

Skerridge opened his mouth, but Strood put up a hand to stop him.

"Don't talk to me about consequences. I'm well aware that killing the Seven will reduce the concentration of defined magic and so undermine the integrity of the Land, thus inducing it to collapse into its Raw state at an accelerated rate."

Skerridge glared, his red eyes burning like coals as the evening light began to fade. "And the weaker the Land gets, so the weaker the last remaining shreds of the Seven will become, and so the more Land will die. It's a perpetuating situation, a circle of death, see? Or hadn't you worked that bit out yet?" Strood smiled. "And there's more, of course. Even consequences have consequences and the death of the Drift will have its own, too. Look at it this way, if the Raw has been shaped into the Land by all the desires and dreads of the Quick, uncovered from their deepest hearts over millions of years, then what will happen when it is taken away?"

Skerridge looked blank. Deliberately. Inside he was

struggling to imagine what would happen to a world where all the agonies of hope and love and hate and fear had nowhere to go. All that electric emotion hanging around with nothing to do except . . .

It would be like a steam pipe with no vent. He shuddered. "She'll stop ya," he said, his voice heavy on the evening air.

"She's already too late," chuckled Strood. "Bogeyman Rainbow has made a fine job of frying Quick in the Widdern, and the sanctuary must be hanging on by a thread. Bogeyman Rope is wiping out Senta Melana's remains and should be finishing the task very shortly. . . ."

Skerridge kept his face as deadpan as possible.

". . . and Bogeyman Pigwit has dealt with Nemus Sturdy—oh, by the way, I made him Chief Bogeyman you know, he did such a fine job. So all in all it's looking good."

"Azork . . ."

"Won't last the night," said Strood airily.

"Vispilio?"

"Oh, I'm leaving him be for the moment; after all, he's hardly a threat. But I have plans."

"Simeon Dark?" Skerridge grinned. "Yer carn' do a lot about Simeon Dark 'cos first off 'e's a livin' sorcerer. . . ."

"And how much use is a sorcerer if he doesn't know what he is?" Strood leaned back in his chair and steepled his fingers. "For Dark to survive the plague that killed every other sorcerer, he must be so well hidden it is as if he has ceased to exist altogether. And no hiding place is foolproof if someone knows about it, and that includes the one who's doing the hiding! Because if *he* knows, then *someone* knows, and if *someone* knows then so does the world. And that would break the spell at once. Clever." Strood sounded almost admiring.

". . . an' second," went on Skerridge carefully, "ya don' know where 'e is."

Strood leaned forward, his quartz eye glittering. "Don't I?" he said softly.

Silence settled over the scene like a blanket. The shadows had deepened now and Skerridge's eyes were red-hot holes in the twilight as he glowered at Strood. His heart sank because in that long moment he knew what Strood had done.

Strood smiled. "I think you will find that knowledge can be an uncomfortable thing. If I know anything about it, which I do, you are now worrying about what happens if I get to the sorcerer first! What's more, you will have to warn your companions just in case it's true, and so you will spread the fear to them."

Skerridge glowered harder. It was true. Strood couldn't know for sure where Dark was—if he did, then according to his theory, the spell would already be broken. But he might have suspicions and that was bad enough. For a start, it was more than Nin and her friends had! It gave Strood a head start in the hunt for Dark. And if Strood found the sorcerer before they did . . . A shiver of fear stirred deep in Skerridge's insides. If Strood found Dark and killed him, the battle would be over before it had even begun. The thought made him feel quite bothered.

"Doubt, fear, panic, despair. They are all linked," Strood smiled again. His eyes glittered, fixed on Skerridge, noting every expression on the bogeyman's face.

"Gotta go," Skerridge said brightly, "fings t' do, people t' save."

The air fizzed and the door banged open and then shut again, closing on the sound of Strood's laughter.

✳ ✳ ✳

In the Widdern, the Little Garden Shop had closed for the day. Jik watched as the young lad who helped out began to tidy up and move the statues indoors. When the boy reached the mudman, Jik fixed him with glowing eyes. The boy decided to forget about that one and leave it outside. With any luck, somebody would steal the thing.

The sound of bolts being drawn, shutters being pulled, and keys being turned trickled down the street from shop after shop. People began to disappear homeward. Silence fell and the long evening drew in.

The air fizzed.

"'Ow's tricks? Anyfin' 'appenin' yet?"

"Nik."

Silence fell. Neither of the Fabulous moved. Jik went back to watching the window of Hilary Jones's flat with silent attention. Skerridge tried not to keep going over what Strood had said. It wasn't easy. And he *would* have to warn the others; Strood had been right about that, too. But not just yet. Right now he and the mudman had other things to do.

One by one, lights went out and stars appeared overhead. The moon crept up the darkening sky, casting its silver veil of light over the roofs and chimneys, and turning the shadows that crouched in doorways and alleys into black ink. In the first-floor apartment across the road the soft glow of TV flickered. Time stretched on, waiting.

12

THE NATURE OF SPELLS

Speeding through the Drift sky in the grip of the Darkness, Nin was struggling to take in Seth's sudden death. "You killed him!" she said again, her voice full of shock and disbelief.

"He was a mistake. I only wanted you. And I didn't kill him. I just didn't interrupt his dying." The Darkness thickened, settling more securely around her. Nin fought, trying to push it away, but it was pointless.

Tears stung Nin's eyes. Seth had been a human being, full of breath and life. By now he would be nothing more than broken flesh. She shook her head, telling herself that he would have survived somehow.

"You are a strange thing." The Darkness chuckled. "Grieving for someone you barely knew!"

Nin ignored the comment. "So," she went on after a pause to choke back her tears, "what do you want with me? And what are you?"

"There is something you should know and I want to be the one to show it to you. As to what I am, I'll leave you to work that out. Just know that I left my natural habitat especially to find you. And let me tell you, I'm not naturally inclined to the light. Even this late in the day, it makes my presence ache. I'll show you where we're going though, if you wish to see."

It thinned again, shifting back into something like transparent silk. Nin gasped at the scene spread out below her.

They were flying over the Land, just higher than the trees, and in this stretch there was no Raw. A river, its silver-blue ribbon glittering in the evening light, unrolled beneath them. A herd of deer scattered and bounced over wide heathland. Broad oaks and tall beeches, golden and coppery in the late sun, clustered in woods or stood alone in meadows thick with clover and buttercups. It was beautiful.

Nin stretched out, spreading her arms like wings. Around her arm the spell stirred, its colors shifting to darker blues, then a purple that was almost black. It tightened and Nin remembered that it was made by a sorcerer and wondered if it was afraid, if a sorcerer's spell could have in it a sorcerer's fear of flying.

Below, wild horses raised their heads to the sky and shook their manes, then broke into a gallop, racing across a plain of emerald grass that looked almost black in the dying light. As they increased their pace, their hooves burst into fiery life, carrying them over the ground at a breathtaking speed and lighting the dark with red flames.

"Fiery Steeds," said the Darkness. "Once there would have been unicorns, too, but they died, like so many magical beasts. Like the Land itself is dying. And faster now, so very, very fast."

"I know." Nin sighed. "First the Fabulous, now the Land. Soon there'll be nothing left but Mr. Strood."

"Ahh. Strood," said the Darkness. There was an edge to its voice.

"Um, what has he done to you?"

"Not just him. There are others to blame as well."

And, suddenly, it let go.

Nin would have screamed, but her breath was snatched away as she fell. The air rushed past her, burning her face with its speed. Her heart lurched, its beat broken by the sudden plunge. There was no time to think, just the wheeling Land as it rushed to meet her. Even before she hit the ground she could feel her bones cracking, her skull smashing open like an egg. See the blood.

And then she was surrounded by the Darkness again. Through its silky veils, grass brushed her face. She sobbed once, choking for breath, her hand stinging where it had hit the ground a split second before her body would have joined it. The Darkness had caught her barely an inch from the Land. She could smell the earth. A beetle squirmed against her cheek.

Gasping, Nin struggled briefly as the Darkness lifted her up. She felt pain in her arm and knew it was the spell, cutting into her skin as it clung tight. Like the spell, Nin didn't want to go. More than anything right now she wanted solid ground under her feet. But there was nothing she could do.

Up they went. Up and up. When it was high enough, the Darkness began to fly onward again. Slowly Nin's heart stopped thudding and her breathing began to steady. She sensed the Darkness watching her, feeling her panic with amusement. Anger swirled out of the fright.

"What did you do that for?" she demanded.

The Darkness chuckled. "To show you how easily I could have my revenge."

"On me? But . . ." Nin frowned. "Have I done something to you? Is that what you meant by there being

93

others to blame? But how can whatever happened to you be my fault? I never met you before!"

For answer it dumped her on the ground in the middle of a land so ravaged it was unrecognizable. Then it drew back and hovered, a thick shroud of darkness behind her, waiting for her to work it out.

Around them columns of smoke rose, spiraling upward to join the pall that blotted out the sky. It made Nin's eyes smart and the bitter smell caught at the back of her throat. Under her feet, the ground was blackened, crumbling into ash as she moved. And everywhere were the ruined, smoldering stumps of trees.

"A burned forest," she said through her coughing, "you want me to know about a burned forest?"

As she spoke her eye was caught by a charred stump in front of her, its blackened remains jutting toward the sky.

She stared at it, fear forming in her heart, making her move forward to take a closer look. There were the last traces of words carved into the wood. She could just make out a couple of letters. They were:

MUS ST DY

"Nemus!" she cried. When she and Jonas had traveled this way before, the shelter offered by Sturdy's Oak had kept them safe from the Savage Forest and all its nightmares. And now, Nemus Sturdy, oldest and most powerful of the once-sorcerers, was gone.

"Got it now, have we?" sneered the Darkness. "Worked out where we are at last?"

"This is the Savage Forest! But how . . . ?" She stared around, bewildered.

"Strood's bogeymen burned it down. Every tree and flower. Every blade of grass. All gone, just to kill the once-sorcerer who turned himself into an oak. I saw it, the bears and the wolves running for their beast lives, eyes full of panic. And the birds, their great black wings flapping so hard they raised a wind, a whole army of them rising into the night sky. And then there was the oak. When it burned, a golden light came off it like steam. This is what I want you to know," snarled the Darkness.

Hot tears began to flood Nin's cheeks. A sob shook her.

"Poor thing," it snarled. "Poor little living legend."

"Why are you being so cruel! What did I do? You said it was the bogeymen."

"But they did it because of YOU. Precious little Ninevah Redstone. She Who Cannot Fail. Lucky Ninevah who skips through danger like it was a picnic while those around her bleed and burn."

"You're the Dark Thing, aren't you?" cried Nin, suddenly understanding. "The Dark Thing That Lives in the Wood?"

"Lived!" it spat. "I think you'll find it's LIVED in the wood."

"I'm sorry!"

"No use being sorry now, is it?" The Dark Thing surged forward, thickening around her; its voice was right in her ear, right in her head.

"I left you alive for a reason. Because even if you started this, I think you earned your legend. And because you are who you are, you may be the only one who can save the Drift."

"What can I do?"

"Don't ask me! Aren't you supposed to be finding Simeon Dark? That is, if he isn't dead of the plague and no one noticed yet." The Dark Thing hissed at Nin, making her flinch and cry out. "Now that there is no more wood, I am free to travel the Drift. So know this, if you don't succeed, I'll come looking for you wherever you are. And next time I'll drop you from so high it'll take you a day to hit the ground. And I really, *really* won't catch you."

And then it was gone and Nin was alone in the ruined forest.

Nin had never felt so alone, so lost, or so scared. She wished desperately for Jonas, but Dark had built his Mansion far southwest of the Savage Forest, and Jonas had a long journey before he could be with her again. Even if he worked out where she was.

And what of her other friends? Jik had always been able to find her in the past, but she hadn't seen him since he had been lying on the beach after their escape from the Terrible House, almost melted away, his fiery red eyes dimmer than they had ever been. She had no idea where Taggit was and as for Skerridge, well, he was a bogeyman, and although he had helped her once, BMs weren't known for their kindly natures. And Enid Lockheart was dying. And Nemus Sturdy was dead.

Sobs shook her. She didn't want to think about the part where it was all her fault—where all this had happened because of her—it hurt too much.

A feathery touch brushed her foot and she raised her head. Something was creeping over her ankles, treading softly on paws of gray ash. Eyes glowed at her like something smoldering in the depths of a smoldering fire. She drew her feet back, fear making her skin prickle. The creature looked like a small stoat made from the ashy remains of the forest, and she could feel the heat of the thing even through her boots. It hissed at her, a spark kindling in the depths of its ember eyes, like it might ignite at any moment.

Glancing around, Nin saw that night was settling in and the ruined forest was wrapped in darkness. There was a faint glow coming from around her forearm where the spell had settled, its shadowy colors giving off a gleam like moonlight. She could hear it whispering softly, but couldn't make out any words. Overhead, lingering smoke hung in great clouds, hiding the stars.

It wasn't good. Even with the birds and bears and wolves gone, even as devastated as it was, Nin had a bad feeling that the Savage Forest was determined not to be friendly. And now there were *two* ash-things, curling around each other, both glaring at her.

She blinked. No, there were three. She hadn't even seen the third arrive; it had just slipped into view from the night shadows. She wondered if her fear was giving them strength to multiply. How afraid was she? One or two of the things she could manage, but what about twenty? A hundred? Panic began to uncurl in her chest. She looked around, but there was nowhere to go. No shelter from the night.

What she needed, what she really REALLY needed, was Nemus Sturdy.

Picking up the blackened remains of a long branch, Nin leaned forward to prod the closest of the creatures, trying to push it away. Its hiss was loud enough to make her yelp. Sparks flew from its eyes, and the branch she was holding sprang into instant, furious life, the flames leaping inches at a time, racing up the wood toward her hand. Nin screamed and dropped the branch, but a spark had already jumped to the sleeve of her jacket and caught.

Flames began to spread on her sleeve, forcing the spell to slither rapidly up her arm and around her neck, murmuring anxiously as it went. Wrenching her jacket off, she dropped it to the ground and kicked it away, pulling her rucksack free as she did so. Shaking and gasping, she watched the garment burn as the ash-stoats swarmed over it.

Backing away from the gaggle of spark-filled eyes, Nin found that she was almost standing on the remains of Nemus Sturdy. The ash-stoats watched her, hissing. Their number had grown. Now, there were too many to count.

Nin sank to the ground, huddling closer to the stump that once was Sturdy's Oak. Thinking of him made her feel a little better. She lay for a while, still trembling but somehow comforted, while the ash-stoats seethed beyond the reach of her feet. One or two of them lunged for her, but they always fell back just short of her boots. She wondered why and the answer came quickly.

The Seven Sorcerers' spells depended on Quick dreads and desires for the power to keep their sorcerers hanging on to existence. Nemus Sturdy had made a spell to give Quicks shelter from all the dread things that the Savage Forest held at night. His Oak, the center of his ring of protection, had been burned back to almost nothing, but now Nin was here, needing his protection desperately.

Maybe even the need of one Quick was enough to save him?

And there was more than that. Nin eyed the ash stoats, thinking over what Enid Lockheart had told her about the nature of spells and how they worked. With the forest burned, there was not so much reason for Quick to need Sturdy's protection. So, if there was not enough danger around, then maybe his spell *was making sure there was more.* Maybe it was taking her fear and turning it into the ash-stoats.

One of the stoats hissed at her and sparks flashed from its body. Nin imagined it growing, getting bigger with the fear from each passing Quick who saw it. Or the bones of its victims. And they would wish Nemus Sturdy was there to protect them. And the more there were, the more the Oak would grow, provided the Drift didn't go completely to the Raw before it got the chance. She sighed. It all came back to Strood and what he was doing, and whether or not she could stop him.

Her face still wet with tears, Nin put her arms around the foot of the stump, laying her head amid its rough, cindery, still-warm roots, making the most of what little protection still remained. And, after a while, she fell asleep.

13

THE KILLING OF HILARY JONES

While Nin slept, not far away but in a whole different world Hilary Jones was reaching the end of the worst day of her life. Inside her small apartment in the Widdern, unaware that two sets of fiery red eyes were watching over her (three sets if you counted Strood's assassin hiding in the garden under a lilac tree), Hilary sat in the dark in front of the TV, watching the late news about Britain's Blowtorch Butchery and crying quietly into a mug of hot milk.

She was crying because earlier today she had been called to identify three bodies. Well, one body actually, because the others were in too many pieces to be called a body as such. The whole one had been her sister and had been removed from a car just before dawn. A car that had inexplicably turned itself into a smashed-up wreck without even going off the road as her sister was coming home from working the night shift at the local hospital.

Hilary shuddered and put down the hot milk—by now getting cold and rather salty—and rubbed her left wrist. At 4:15:23 that morning, the exact time of her sister's death, a white ring had appeared around Hilary's wrist. It looked just like the trace of an old scar. It also looked just like a mark that her aunt used to have around *her* wrist.

Something has been transferred, Hilary thought fuzzily. Inside her head, pieces clicked together to form a picture. The scar, and whatever went with it, had belonged to her aunt. When her aunt died, it had gone to Hilary's sister, because Hilary's aunt had no children and Hilary's mother was already dead. It had belonged to Hilary's sister for barely two hours and then . . . then it had come to Hilary.

She felt her skin crawl, suddenly aware of a whispering in her head, like a distant voice calling her. *"Hiiilary . . ."*

"I need to sleep," she told herself firmly. "I need to stop thinking about all this for just a little while or I'll go mad with it."

Leaving the television to babble, because she didn't want to be alone right now, Hilary went to lie down on the bed. She kicked off her shoes, but was too worn out to get undressed and fell asleep the moment her eyes closed.

While she slept, nightmares tumbled about in her head like clothes in a washing machine, mixed up and running into one another as they churned. There were flowers that ate people, a mansion so tall it touched the heavens, houses that burned in towering flames against a sky of thunderclouds, and a beautiful golden-eyed woman surrounded by lightning that danced in the air around her like snakes of fire. Hilary cried out in her sleep when she saw that the woman's left hand was just a stump. *"Hiiilary!"*

The woman leaned forward and suddenly she was close, eye-to-eye with Hilary, her face filled with something dark and powerful. From nowhere, a name arrived in Hilary's head: Senta Melana.

"The spell, Hilary," Senta whispered, and even though Hilary knew she was dreaming, the woman's voice was real. *"The spell will keep you alive. It can't offer you magical power, but it has knowledge that will help you survive. And it WILL help you, because you are the last, and you must live. For all the lives to come. For me."*

Hilary sprang awake with a gasp. The bedroom was silent and dark but she knew, she just KNEW, that whatever had killed the rest of her family was here, IN THE APARTMENT WITH HER. *"Go,"* said the soft voice in her head. Only now it was no longer just whispering but clear as a bell. *"GO NOW!"*

Barefoot, Hilary crept silently to the bedroom door and peered through. The hallway was empty. Nothing stirred. Through the half-open door to the living room she could see the flicker of a late-night game show on the television. And then, down the hall, in between her and the front door, she heard a noise. The fridge door opened and there was a sound of rustling. Hilary raised her eyebrows in amazement. Her assassin was stopping for a snack before he got on with the job!

Swiftly, she slipped around the bedroom door, crossed the hallway, and went into the living room, thankful that the chattering TV would cover any small sounds. She picked up her car keys and headed back into the hall. The kitchen was silent. Alarm bells rang in her head and she looked up and down the hall. There was nothing there.

"Look!" hissed the voice in her head.

Hilary blinked. She felt a change inside, as if something had rearranged her vision to show her what was really there. She drew in a horrified gasp.

Standing outside the kitchen, in between Hilary and the way out, was a scaly, green, hunch-backed, one-eyed monster with fanged teeth, huge talons, and bulging muscles that looked designed for tearing people apart. Its eye glowed red and it was clutching a chicken leg in one hand and a lemonade bottle in the other. It was wearing a pair of torn red trousers held up with rope.

It snarled.

Hilary screamed and dove into the bedroom, slamming the door behind her.

The thing in red trousers threw the chicken leg and the lemonade bottle after her, and lurched into motion.

Running to the window, Hilary pushed it open. Outside, the night was quiet. The bedroom looked out at the back of the apartments, and below Hilary was a paved path that ran across the lawn and over to the car park. At her back the door juddered and split, and Hilary screamed again as Red Trousers smashed through it, tearing the wood into splinters. It opened a mouth fringed with knives and gave a screeching roar that froze her blood. It leapt. That one bound should have brought it down on top of Hilary, where it could shred her tender Quick body like paper and scatter her bloody remains around the room. A bit like her aunt. And her mother.

But then a miracle happened.

There was a sound like a thunderclap as the front door exploded and something tore through, setting fire to the wallpaper as it went. It hurtled into the bedroom, moving so fast it made the air spin. Just before it whacked into Red Trousers—right in the middle of its leap—and sent it smashing against the wall, Hilary caught a glimpse of something wearing a fancy waistcoat.

In a bundle of claws and teeth, Red Trousers and

Fancy Waistcoat slithered down the wall and rolled onto Hilary's bedroom floor, snarling and screeching as they slashed at each other. There was a sound of splintering wood and claw marks appeared in the wardrobe. Then the bedside lamp crashed to the floor and the duvet caught fire. The racket was horrible.

Hilary didn't wait to see any more. She scrambled out onto the window ledge and took a breath.

Just as she was about to jump onto the paving stones two floors below, hoping she didn't break any bones, her eyes focused on something standing there, lit up by the garden lights. It looked like some kind of weird, glittery mud statue and it was holding out its arms as if to catch her. She blinked, hesitating for just a moment.

"You have friends," said the voice in her head. Hilary now knew that it was the voice of a spell cast by her sorceress ancestor, Senta Melana. She also knew that it was trying to help. So she went.

The night whirled around her as she fell. Hilary was glad that she had put on a pair of trousers that morning instead of a skirt. It only lasted a second, but it was still long enough for Hilary to feel the dewy air slipping past her, and to see the lawn and the path rushing up to meet her. And then it was over and she was hanging safely a couple of feet off the ground, held in the arms of the weird mud-thing.

"Jik!" it said, and to Hilary it sounded pleased at a job well done. It dropped her gently to the ground. "Bikik gik qwik!"

Hilary scrambled to her feet as some horrible ear-splitting howls rained down from her window, closely followed by most of her wardrobe.

She ran for her car and the mud-thing followed. Behind them, flames licked the walls, billowing out of the ragged hole where the window had been. Glancing back, Hilary saw Red Trousers bursting through the flames as it leapt to the ground after them. Only, as it hurtled through the air, it CHANGED SHAPE. *"Going back to Natural Bogeyman,"* murmured Senta's Spell. *"Now we've got trouble!"*

Red Trousers hit the ground running, moving so fast it was just a streak of blurred air. Hilary yelled as it hurtled past her, knocking her to the ground, then fizzed back into view, landing on top of her car with a loud *CRUMP*. It stood there, scanning the area for any sign of Fancy Waistcoat. The car began to buckle under its weight. With a snort of satisfaction, it decided it had won the fight and turned its attention back to Hilary. It grinned horribly and drew in a long, deep breath. The mud-creature threw itself over Hilary, flattening her to the ground.

"Firebreath," hissed Senta's Spell, *"keep down!"*

But before Red Trousers could breathe out, Fancy Waistcoat got there first.

A tornado of fire ripped over Hilary's head and caught Red Trousers full on. It gave a last furious howl and exploded, along with the car. For a long moment the air was filled with nothing but the sound of roaring flames and the stink of oily smoke.

When Hilary finally peered out from behind her hands, the night sky was filled with black smoke and red flames. In addition to the burning wreckage of the car, the fire in her bedroom had spread to the rest of the block and people were milling about outside, dressed in their nightclothes or wrapped in blankets. Sirens echoed through the air, growing steadily louder, and flashing lights fought with the glare from the fire.

Hilary got to her feet. Her blue eyes were wide in

her heart-shaped face, what you could see of it under the dirt. She was battered, bruised, and not a little scorched, and her hair looked like a pale gold bird's nest. Her clothes were torn and covered in mud and oily smudges, and she badly needed a wash; and on top of the loss of her aunt, her mother, and her sister, she had just lost her home and all her worldly goods. But through it all her beauty shone like a beacon.

She stood looking thoughtfully at the two strange creatures in front of her. In the background someone from a neighboring building was handing out tea in chipped mugs to the refugees. Fire engines and police cars pulled up. People in helmets began running about and shouting. "You know," Hilary said at last. "I think Hilary Jones died today, killed in that burning building. And I don't know what's going to happen next." She pointed a finger. "But I do know that you two have got some explaining to do. So let's get on our way, shall we? You can fill me in as we go. And it had better be good!"

A broad smile stretched across thing number-two's face, revealing a row of mismatched and very jagged teeth. His red eyes glowed. "It will be," he said. "Don'chew worry about that!"

Skerridge was getting more and more bad tempered as the night wore on. It was something to do with the way they kept running across new patches of Raw. It gave him a doomy feeling inside and he didn't like it one bit. Without Jik, who instinctively knew the lay of the land, they would have been hopelessly lost by now.

"Blimmin' Strood," muttered Skerridge. "Rippin' the Drift up like a piece o' paper."

"Wik gik nik-nik-wik," said Jik, studying the Land ahead.

Skerridge gave him a look that would have cooked a steak in seconds. "Whadya mean, norf-norf-west. Wha's that when it's at 'ome? We jus' wanna get ter 'Ilfian!"

"He's taking us to Hilfian," said Hilary patiently, "we just have to go round all this freezing misty stuff."

Jik set off, leading them through a patch of dense woodland. Hilary followed with Skerridge coming last and grumbling busily. He was finding the journey hard going. Not just the strange zigzag path they were having to take to avoid the Raw, but also having to do it all at the painfully slow pace that Quick always used. He kept having to remind himself not to break into superspeed. He grinned and brightened up a little. At least there was something he could do about *that*.

"So," asked Hilary, wanting to get things straight in her mind, "this weird mist that keeps sending us out of our way is the Raw, the basic stuff of magic that the Land was made from and is now going back to?"

"That's it," said Skerridge. "It's lethal to Fabulous because they too are made from Raw magic and it dissolves them on contact, taking all that they are back into itself so that they cease to be. It's also lethal to Quick, because its subzero temperatures freeze their socks off in next to no time. That's why we all have to go round it, not through."

Hilary spun around. Behind her an evil-looking kid in a duffel coat stared back from the depths of a hood pulled forward over its pale, dead-looking face. Its eyes glittered menacingly.

"You changed shape," she said accusingly.

"I'm entitled. It goes with the territory; it's what bogeymen do. And this way I won't miss superspeed so much." Skerridge grinned, showing a neat row of small, pointed teeth.

"Even your *voice* changed."

Skerridge giggled horribly. "Evil Kid With Duffel Coat doesn't speak the same as Natural Bogeyman, see," he said with exaggerated patience. "You have to be consistent to change shape properly. Anyfin' else just ain't done." He blinked. "Oops."

Hilary shook her head and turned back to the path. "I wish we could all superspeed." She glanced up at the sky where the moon hung, half covered by clouds like giant crows circling around its pale globe. "If I've gathered anything at all about the Drift, I'm betting that night in the open isn't recommended."

"Not recommended at all," said Skerridge. "But then you've got us to protect . . ."

The air blurred. There was a brief yelp from Hilary, then silence. ". . . you," Skerridge finished.

The two Fabulous stopped dead in their tracks. They swapped a glance.

"Erm . . . where'd she go?"

Jik shrugged.

Skerridge sighed. "Blimmin' BMs," he muttered, swapping back into Natural Bogeyman. He brightened up. "Still, time fer a bitta superspeed, I'm guessin'. Did ya see which way 'e went?"

14

CLOTHED IN THE ARMOR OF DREAD

U p on the top of the hill, clustered together in the middle of the clump of trees, two bogeymen watched the sky.

"'Ere, take a look at THAT," hissed Bogeyman Rainbow. He straightened his brightly colored tie, the movement causing the jacket of his too-small checked suit to tear a little more down the back seam.

"THAT" was a strange wobbly effect on the horizon, like someone had drawn a veil over the sky and it was rippling in the breeze.

"Uh-oh," muttered Bogeyman Polpp, his heart sinking in his chest. "Yer right. Looks like tombfolk t' me. Which way are they goin' d'ya fink?'"

The air fizzed. "Over 'ere I woulda fort," said Skerridge, popping into view, "what wiv you wavin' that about under their noses." He nodded at the trussed-up bundle at their feet.

"Strood sent us t' sort out Azork an' the tombfolk," said Bogeyman Rainbow cheerfully. "So maggot 'ere's our bait. I caught it 'angin' about in the woods."

Maggot, also known as Hilary Jones, scowled over the

top of its gag made of an old, not too clean handkerchief.

"S'yer nickname. I chose it," said Rainbow proudly, seeing the look. "S'like, yer bait, see, an' when someone goes fishin' . . ."

Polpp snorted irritably. "Blimmin' Strood," he muttered, "didn' used ter do stuff like this in the old days. Snatchin' Quicks fer bait, assassinatin' people, takin' orders."

Skerridge eyed Polpp thoughtfully, wondering what was going on in his head, until Rainbow grabbed everyone's attention.

"They've got maggot's scent, look!"

On the skyline, the soft ripple effect had changed direction and was headed right for them. At once, Polpp and Rainbow nipped behind the trees to wait. Skerridge went with them. Now, the hilltop looked pretty much empty of everything but one trussed-up Quick female and a few trees. Bogeymen were good at hiding and it was amazing how a large, hairy, bony bogeyman could fit neatly behind a slender tree trunk.

"When I give the word, we're out an' breavin' fire, right?" whispered Rainbow. "No 'angin' about. No givin' 'em time to fan out or go up. An' certainly no givin' 'em time t' land!"

There was an outbreak of muttered yeps from Polpp and Skerridge. In vapor form the tombfolk would be vulnerable to fire, but if they touched the ground and took solid form they would be indestructible.

Silence fell as the tombfolk billowed toward them.

From inside the hill, looking out through a thin layer of topsoil, Jik watched. As soon as Skerridge had gone to look for Hilary, he had dove into the earth and swum through it until he was just below the surface right next to where Hilary was lying.

The turquoise streak at the edge of night rippled as the Hive swooped lower. The trussed-up Hilary shivered as she watched, hoping that she hadn't come all this way to help a girl she had met only once, to save a world she didn't know, just to end up dying horribly at the hands of the vampire tombfolk.

"Azork's spell was really very brave," said the voice in her head, sounding almost dreamy as it watched the rippling horizon with her. *"Sorcerers can't break their contact with the Land. If they do, then they become a thing of the air, a wind spirit. They have a choice: either they can spend eternity driven by the gale, or they can become a tombfolk, a creature of darkness and death that feeds on the lives of others. It's the oldest, most basic power. 'Clothed in the Armor of Dread,' we used to call it, when a spell depended on sheer blood-deep terror to keep it alive."*

Hilary watched as the ripples drew closer. She could see them now, their lovely forms almost part of the night air as they swooped low. Something tugged at her hands and the ropes began to loosen.

"Gik rikik," whispered a voice in her ear.

"I'm ready," she said, as the tombfolk circled down toward her, their night-filled eyes glowing with hunger, their graceful vapor forms billowing on the air. There was a female in the lead and she was so heart-achingly lovely, with her silver hair floating around her and her moonlight skin, that Hilary stared with humble amazement.

"GETTEM!" howled Rainbow.

Hilary screamed as the tombfolk exploded in blue and silver flames so bright she had to shut her eyes or lose her sight forever. The bogeymen blew their fire-breath in sequence, so that there was always one of them breathing fire out while the others breathed air in. Screams that were more rage than fear or pain echoed through the night, blending with the crackle of wood as the nearby trees caught fire. Doubled up with her arms around her head, she felt Jik next to her, shielding her from any flames that came her way.

At last it was over. Hilary nervously opened her eyes, feeling sick and with her breath rattling harshly in her lungs. The fire and light were gone and the air was filled with smoke spiraling up from tree stumps.

In front of her, the bogeymen stared around anxiously. Skerridge inched closer to Hilary, ready to grab her and run when he got the chance. There was a moment of silence and then . . .

"Were you looking for me?"

Azork, Daemon of the Night, King of the Tombfolk and once a sorcerer, stepped out of the darkness. His tall figure was dressed in close-fitting purple, studded all over with tiny diamonds like stars in a night sky. His skin was ebony, his eyes were silver whirlpools, and Dread clung to him like a living shadow.

Skerridge's heart sank. Things had gone horribly wrong. The Tombfolk King should have been at the center of the Hive. He should have been so much scorched air by now. But clearly Azork had worked out that Strood was after him and so it would be much more sensible to keep a little way back from the Hive. So now, instead of being vaporized as per Strood's instructions, he was there in front of them, standing on the ground and indestructible.

The night air shimmered and other tombfolk stepped forward out of the darkness, tombfolk who had stayed behind with their leader. Skerridge's heart sank even further as he realized that there must be at least half the Hive left. Suddenly things had gone from horribly wrong to almost unimaginably terrible. In fact, things were so completely awful that he became quite wobbly with fear.

On the ground the tombfolk moved with the easy grace of panthers, swift and sure toward the kill, and their beauty was almost as frightening as the hungry look in their eyes. For a moment, even the bogeymen were paralyzed with fear, and a moment was all it took for the tombfolk to form a circle, a wall of death to enclose their prey.

"Don't bother with superspeed," said Azork gently. "You'll only run up against us. And if we catch hold of you, don't bother struggling, because we are far, far stronger than any mere bogeyman and will rip you limb from limb."

Huddled next to Jik, Hilary was pulling off the last of her bonds. She had a distant look on her face as she listened to Senta's Spell, whispering urgently in her head, telling her anything it could remember about Azork. Anything that might help her survive. In the middle of the vampire circle, the three bogeymen huddled together looking miserable.

The Tombfolk King curled his lip. "Call yourselves Dread," he hissed. "I'll show you DREAD."

Slowly the tombfolk moved forward, shrinking the circle. Skerridge looked around the ring of star-filled or moonlit eyes, of tall, strong bodies all the colors of nighttime and darkness. They looked so hungry, but then they always were. However much life they had to drink, it was never enough. And the power that drives the living—that keeps hearts beating, bodies warm, and brains ticking over—is in the blood.

Azork raised his hand toward Rainbow's ugly face and the bogeyman howled. His eyes bulged and a scarlet haze began to drift from them, twisting in the smoky air as thousands of tiny droplets of blood were drawn out of the bogeyman's body and toward the King like iron filings to a magnet. The other tombfolk followed their leader and the meal began.

Almost at once, Skerridge felt his eyeballs begin to swell and suddenly his limbs felt like what they were, lumps of useless meat and bone. All the power, all the LIFE, was running out of them, surging up the complex net of his veins to boil out through his eyes and skin like fine, hot tears.

One of the tombfolk women laughed. A light laugh, pleased. People, Quick or Fabulous, are never as fully alive as when they are fighting not to die, and so blood was all the more flavorsome if it was torn out slowly and painfully. "Azork," said a voice so soft it was amazing that anyone could hear it over all the racket.

And suddenly everything stopped.

In a heap on the ground, three pairs of bogeyman eyes opened cautiously. The tombfolk were still there, but now their attention was focused on Hilary. She was untied and standing, tall and straight in spite of the haze of blood that had risen to her face and arms, her blue eyes fixed on the night-filled ones of the Tombfolk King.

A faint tremor ran through Azork's elegant frame. For a moment the air shimmered as if the world had been shaken.

At the same time, a small gap opened in the ring of tombfolk bodies. There was an outbreak of nudging from the three bogeymen. Smeared all over in their own blood and feeling horribly weak but more hopeful, they shuffled back onto their feet. Bogeymen were good at small gaps. One of them inched slightly left.

Hilary smiled at Azork while, inside the circle, the remaining bogeymen watched unblinkingly. Polpp took a small step toward the gap.

"Remember me?" said Hilary.

Seeing the look on the King's face, the last remaining bogeyman in the circle swallowed nervously and straightened his waistcoat. "It was Senta I loved," whispered Azork, his words hanging on the air like frosty breath. "*You* are not *her*."

He raised a hand to continue draining Hilary's blood, to suck every last drop of it out through her delicate skin and leave nothing but a useless lump of flesh. Then, for just a moment, he hesitated.

Everything went mad.

Skerridge shot into action, grabbed Hilary, and kept going while she yelled "Let me go!" in his ear as he barged through the startled tombfolk. Jik did an amazing somersault and dove headfirst back into the Land, burrowing away in the same direction. With screams of rage, the Hive launched themselves into the air to give chase to their prey, which were now escaping all over the place, in every direction.

"STOP, FOOLS!" snarled Azork.

For the second time that night the sky filled with blue fire. It surged around the King and the six of his Hive still on the ground with him, outlining them in brilliance, reflecting in their star-filled eyes as all the other tombfolk burned.

At last, left on the hillside, Azork stood gazing into the sky. The blue fire had burned out, but its trace could still be seen as a silvery stain in the air that hung about the remaining members of the Hive like a halo. There were now only seven tombfolk left in the whole of the Drift. It was a sad echo of the Seven Sorcerers, and Azork smiled bitterly.

He looked down at his hands. Was he imagining it or were they fainter than before, less *there*? He knew one thing, he felt different. He felt WRONG.

"What is it?" asked a female with star-laced hair that floated behind her, even though the air was still.

Azork didn't answer, though he had already realized what was happening to him. For a moment, seeing Hilary standing there, he had been surprised into remembering Senta. He had loved her with all his heart, though she had never cared for him. And in that moment, all the pain of unreturned love had swept over him just as strong as when he had been alive and a sorcerer.

As part of his spell to cheat the plague, Azork had clothed himself in the Armor of Dread, but Dread Fabulous weren't supposed to feel the way that Senta made him feel. And so if the Daemon of the Night *did* feel like that then he couldn't be Dread, and without Dread he was nothing. Already, he could feel cracks in his Armor. His spell was breaking.

He drew himself up to his full height and focused on the horizon. There was time yet before he died, time in which he could have some measure of revenge on Strood for the death of his Hive, for sending the bogeymen and bringing all this about. He smiled. Perhaps in doing so he might even be able to repair the damage that had been done and save himself.

Azork started to walk and the rest of the Hive fell into step beside him. It might be slow compared to flying, but flying was too dangerous—there were other bogeymen. "Where are we going?" the female asked.

"We are going to a place where we can feed," Azork said, his voice soft as a night breeze.

"Yes!" The female laughed softly, understanding in her eyes.

The King smiled coldly and his whirlpool eyes glowed as he walked on. "We are going to Hilfian."

15

SKIN AND BLOOD
AND BONE AND MUD

The Sunatorium was quiet now, save for the soft rustle of growing crowsmorte. Through the crystal walls the moon shone, casting its silver light over the carpet of flowers that blanketed the woodland. Strood steepled his fingers thoughtfully.

He wasn't daft. He knew the sorcerers all right; after all, he had been there and understood that finishing them off altogether wasn't going to be simple. He suspected that the BMs hadn't been totally successful in their efforts at wiping the once-sorcerers out. But the point was that they would be hanging on only by the barest thread, and that was enough for now. On top of that, his army would be leaving in the morning and they would sweep across the Drift like a tide of golden darkness, wreaking horrible death on any Quick they found. Hopefully, that would include most of the Redstone kid's friends. And possibly the girl herself, though he would prefer to capture her alive.

Strood smiled grimly, his quartz eye glittering in the cold moonlight. He had everything covered. Except . . .

Except Ninevah Redstone's luck.

And even there . . .

Strood reached out and rang the small bell perched on the table beside him. High above, using the net of crowsmorte that spanned the gaps between trees as a roost, Jibbit woke up and peered down.

Almost instantly a servant scurried into view and bobbed a curtsy. "Ah now, my dear, what is your name?"

"S-Samfy, s-sir."

"Still alive, eh? Well done."

Samfy bobbed another curtsy.

"Now, I want you to fetch me a few things. . . ."

Generally speaking, Strood didn't use Land Magic. He didn't need mudmen or bouldermen to fetch and carry, or mist dogs to track things down, or silt cats to guard, because he had servants and goblin-Grimm to obey his every command. He didn't even need fire-monkeys to wreak havoc on his enemies, he had bogeymen for that. Besides, he thought Land Magic was a little old-hat and much preferred the more creative methods of Distillation.

But right now, because of Ninevah Redstone, he was about to break the rule of a lifetime.

Strood was going to make a skinkin.

It took a couple of hours for the servants to find and prepare everything that he needed, and by the time Strood was ready to start, it was almost Dead of Night, the point in any nighttime that is the furthest away from both sunset and dawn. This was the only time that someone could make a thing so dark and nasty as the skinkin.

"Did you know," he said cheerfully, as he examined the items brought in by Samfy and laid out on the table, "the Dead of Night lasts a lifetime and yet is over in a matter of seconds. During it, the world is ruled by hopelessness and Quick hearts are at their most vulnerable.

It's the time that many people die, the time that others lie awake fearful and alone, ripe for despair to chill their blood and stop their hearts."

"Why aren't lots more Quick dead then?" asked Jibbit, creeping closer down the netting as curiosity got the better of him.

Strood chuckled. "Good question. Fortunately, most Quick sleep through it or the world would be an emptier place. And stopped hearts can start again."

"Fortunate indeed!" mumbled Scribbins, writing "despair" in his notebook and underlining it. He was wearing a crumpled suit that looked as if it had been slept in (which it had), his eyes were red-rimmed, and he trembled constantly.

Mrs. Dunvice said nothing, but watched Strood closely. She had cast off the Housekeeper's dress and pinafore, changing them for a tough armor of beaten leather, along with some solid spiked boots. Her hair had been cut to a skullcap of iron gray. She would have been pleased to know that she looked more like her werewolf mother than she ever had before. Needless to say, she looked absolutely nothing like her very dead Quick father. Not that she ever knew him. He hadn't lived long enough to see her born.

At the table Strood took up a bundle of slender cat bones, their delicate shafts scraped and washed free of any trace of meat. The bundle included a skull, also scoured to clean bone, its empty sockets staring at nothing. Then he turned to a bowl filled with blood from the freshly topped-off barrel, and a pile of carefully sieved earth. Using the blood to mix the earth into sticky mud, he rolled the mixture and the bones into a small log shape, the white bone gleaming amid the dark mud. But not much mud, just enough to hold it all together. Then he stuck the skull on top of it, neatly wrapped the whole lot into a tidy bundle using the skin of a hare, and placed it on top of a silver plate on the table.

Jibbit cleared his throat. "I thought yoo wanted her alive?"

"Oh, I do." Strood smiled. "I most certainly want the girl alive because then the manner of her end will be in my hands. And I have some very . . . interesting . . . ideas about that. So, the skinkin will not be unleashed unless it becomes necessary."

He nodded toward a cage sitting on the ground, or rather the crowsmorte carpet, to the left of his armchair. It was a fine mesh of silver with a handle on the top and a detachable bottom, so that it could be lifted, placed over something to confine it, and then lifted off again at the proper time. There were a series of clips that could be snapped shut to fasten the cage to its base. The base, Jibbit realized, was the flat silver plate under the bundle of bones.

"Dunvice here will keep the thing caged until the moment that she knows all is lost. *If* that moment should come, which it will not. But then we are talking Ninevah Redstone here." Strood's quartz eye glittered horribly. "If it does, however, then Dunvice's dying act will be to release the skinkin. You understand, of course."

The last part was addressed to Dunvice along with a smile that made her want to run and scream, half-werewolf or not. "The skinkin has only one desire. It cannot stop or rest until it has killed the victim I choose for it." He chuckled. "I think you will find that even luck won't stop a skinkin."

"Is clever," said Jibbit, but he inched away again. He was beginning to get a creepy feeling and he didn't like it.

By now Strood had arranged the bundle so the head

of the hare skin was roughly placed over the cat skull. He paused, waiting, sensing the air.

"Aha, here it comes. The Dead of Night is just arriving."

Nothing changed. The moon went on shining, the dark didn't get any darker or any colder, and yet . . .

Jibbit whimpered and Dunvice shivered, her heart turning over with dread. Scribbins shuddered. His eyes went distant and his face paled to the color of putty. Sweat broke out on his skin. He dropped his notebook, his hands fluttering over his heart.

Leaning toward the bundle on the table Strood paused, then smiled. He breathed into the thing's mouth the words: "The legendary Ninevah Redstone."

Dunvice gasped, her luminous eyes darted from Strood to the skinkin and back again. There was a sound like a drawn out, strangled scream and for a moment she could have sworn that the Land shook beneath them.

Then came a strange cracking sound like small bones breaking and rearranging. The bundle heaved and twisted, the hare-skin legs pushed out, the head settled on the neck, and the whole thing sat upright. It paused, then twitched its long ears and turned its head to look at Strood, the empty sockets showing through the eye holes. It gathered itself to leap, its thin flanks quivering.

Strood slammed the cage lid over it and snapped the clips shut.

The skinkin snarled at him, letting out a sound that made Dunvice's blood tingle. A sound like screams in the night. Its empty sockets shone with a dark kind of light.

"Excellent," said Strood.

There was a soft thump. Both Strood and Dunvice turned to look.

Strood sighed. "Has Scribbins fainted *again*? Really the man is becoming quite unreliable."

"I'm afraid he's dead, sir," said Dunvice, who had gone to see. "Of terror, judging by the look on his face."

"Oh well, never mind. I think the time for note taking is past, eh?" Strood beamed at her. "It's all action from here on in. Better make sure everything is ready to leave at dawn, hmm?"

Mrs. Dunvice reached up for Jibbit, who didn't object at all, gave a strangled "yes, sir," and left the Sunatorium.

Peace descended, or at least something pretending to be peace. Strood settled back into his armchair, checking over his plans while the crowsmorte quietly finished up the body of Secretary Scribbins.

And in the cage, the skinkin waited.

16

UNEXPECTED HELP

Floyd was running for his life. His breath came in gasps, the air raking in and out of his lungs like cold fire. His legs hurt. His chest hurt. In fact, most of him hurt, but he kept on anyway. He was a goblin-Grimm and it was amazing how much a goblin-Grimm could endure when the chips were down and time was running out like sand in an hourglass.

Because time *was* running out, the Drift's days were numbered and that number was shrinking, hour by hour, minute by minute. The farther Floyd got from the Terrible House, the more Land he passed that had gone to the Raw, and the larger those stretches of Raw were. As far as Floyd could see, the Drift's only hope lay in a small Quick girl and her friends. So, he was going to Hilfian to find her. If he could survive the horrors currently jumping and tumbling at his heels, that was.

Under his heavy tread, cinders crunched into gray dust. On either side of him were blackened stumps that used to be trees, some of them still smoldering even so many hours later. The moonlight-silvered ruins were strangely quiet. No birds sang, no wolves howled, and there was certainly no screaming from the Dark Thing. The only sound was the hissing of the ash-stoats as they tumbled along behind him in a wave of fire-seamed gray, their eyes glowing with ill-will.

A Quick would have been caught by now. A Quick would have been so much smoldering ash with maybe the odd bone left over to strike dread into the hearts of other travelers. But Floyd was a Grimm.

Glancing up at the sky, Floyd saw a line of light run across the horizon, so bright he could easily see the glow of it though the drifting smoke overhead. A moment later, dawn ignited, racing across the sky in a tide of bloodred flames.

Floyd risked a look back. Behind him the ash-things raised their heads to the day, but not in welcome. With a long hiss, rising as one from many throats, they exploded, bursting into a flurry of ash that spun and whirled across the ground, then fell still.

"Thank Galig fer that," gasped Floyd. They were only night magic and would be back as soon as darkness fell, but he'd be well away from the forest by then.

As he turned to face front again he saw something. A Quick kid, thin and gawky with a straggle of brown hair flopping over her face and wearing ash-covered, too-big clothes. At her feet, for it was a her he was certain, drooped a battered pink rucksack. She was waving at him, jumping up and down with excitement or relief or something.

Floyd had never had anyone be so pleased to see him before and found himself grinning back and running all the faster, even though his legs felt like burning stumps. "I never expected any help," she called as he covered the last few yards, "but I guess my luck came through again!"

And then, through all the dirt and the old tearstains, Floyd recognized her. "Ninevah Redstone!" he croaked and crashed to an exhausted heap at her feet.

The scarlet dawn that had put an end to the ash-stoats, for now at least, washed around Dark's Mansion like a sea of blood.

On the shores of the lake below, a ragged pile lay huddled. Sparks crackled across its skin and winked out with a sizzle. A wisp or two of smoke drifted away from its burned remains. There was quiet for a while. Maybe a bird or two sang. A light breeze got up and ruffled the surface of the water.

The ragged pile heaved and sat up. It shook itself into the figure of a boy, his face hollow and darkened with pain and his eyes flashing with white fire that burned in their depths like lightning in a stormy sky.

Jonas grinned a grin that would have made Nin shiver if she had been there to see it.

"You shouldn't have tried to kill me with lightning," he said to the empty air where Ava Vispilio had stood in Seth Carver's body. "Lightning is something I know about."

He sat for a while, waiting for the Hound inside him to settle down. Once he would have been in danger of it taking him over, but he had won that battle long ago, and, against all the odds, the Hound was tame. It had been an unexpected help, and without its strength to fight the lightning raging through his body, Jonas would have been dead.

He looked down at his hands and the shadow of the magic bolt from the amulet flickered over his skin. It stung, a faint reminder of the night's pain, but that was all. "Time to get moving," he said firmly.

It took him a few tries, but soon he was back on his feet. He faced northeast and set off, heading toward Hilfian. It was where they had planned to go and if Nin could, he was sure she would get there somehow. And if she wasn't there herself, then someone would have heard something about her. Bound to.

He knew that with the traveling boots, Vispilio would catch up with Nin long before Jonas had even cleared the hills he could see on the horizon. Might have caught up with her already, for that matter. But he had to try and warn her; there was nothing else he could do. Giving up was not an option.

Staggering a little, but gaining speed, Jonas headed into the day.

Elsewhere, others were facing the day too. It was a strange day, a day in which the balance tipped and the Drift was now more Raw than Land.

Skerridge knew it. He could sense the change like a cold breath on his skin. It gave him a doomy feeling that wouldn't go away. His bones could feel it, even when he was doing Evil Kid. He tried One-Eyed Hump-Backed Monster, Twisted Tree Man, and even Mad Clown, but it was no good. He went on flicking dolefully through every shape he could think of until Hilary refused to go any farther if he didn't quit.

Jik felt the same as Skerridge. The mudman's glowing eyes had a hot, fevered look. He was of the Land and the Land was dying, and Skerridge couldn't help but wonder just how nasty that must feel.

They kept on walking, Jik in the lead with Hilary next, her feet bleeding from the long, long trek. Skerridge brought up the rear, still feeling helpless in the face of all this doom.

He just wished they would make it to Hilfian.

Some miles to the east, Azork kept on walking too. Even when the few remaining members of his Hive wanted to sleep. Even when they complained that their feet, unused to the hard earth, were aching with the journey.

Even when the sun rose.

"Indestructible, do you know what that means?" he said to his cowering Hive as the line of fire ran across the horizon. "In the air, in vapor form, we are vulnerable and the fires of dawn would burn us up like so much morning mist. But here, with our feet on the ground, we are strong. Our glamour is part of the night and so the light of day will show us up for what we are, but it cannot kill us; NOTHING can kill us. Walk on."

As dawn tore across the sky, their beauty vanished like the night it came from. One of the females, her long hair now just white and thin and her face little more than a skull with eyes, began to cry. The males, skeletal now, with skin stretched so tight over their bones that it hurt, sent nervous glances at their king. "Trust me," Azork said, "it will all be right again, soon." He smiled, and deep in their sockets his eyes flashed with dying stars. "When we make it to Hilfian and feed."

And back at the Terrible House, Strood's army got on its way.

PART
2

A TIDE OF GOLDEN DARKNESS

17

RAW

It was still early morning. Nin had been riding on Floyd's shoulders since they had set out at dawn around four hours ago. They could travel faster that way, and to a goblin-Grimm the weight of a Quick was thistledown. Floyd's sturdy legs had been eating up the miles at a terrific pace, and although they had seen a lot of Raw, luckily none of it had been in their way. They had also seen a horseman in the distance, heading in the opposite direction, toward the Heart. The dark shape had been riding along the top of a hill and had looked huge, a menacing hulk on the back of a black horse with hooves that flickered with red flames. "Gotta be Fabulous," said Floyd, "if 'e's ridin' a fiery steed. Only the Fabulous can do that. 'Ope e's not off t' join Strood's army!"

Other than that the journey was uneventful and Nin was beginning to think they would make it to Hilfian by breakfast. She hoped her friends would turn up there too, and soon. She couldn't afford to delay too long in her search for Simeon Dark, but she knew she would need their help in finding the last sorcerer. Lucky or not, she couldn't search the Drift alone.

It had been a comfortable trip so far because Floyd's shoulders were broad, but now she wanted to stretch her legs, so he set her down and they walked at a slower pace, following the ragged edge of a wood bordered by a field of daisies and clover. There was a smell of old iron in the air that Nin was sure came from the band of Raw just the other side of the trees. Shadows lay across the meadow grass, even though there was nothing to cast them. They seemed to shift, too, stirring restlessly as if disturbed by the nearness of people. Even so, bees the size of Nin's fist hummed from bloom to bloom. According to Floyd, Hilfian farmed bees and exchanged the honey for goods and food.

Also according to Floyd, the town should be very near by now. "Y'know, we might even 'ave gone past," he said anxiously. "S'ard t' tell. The Land's changin' so fast."

Nin looked up at the cornflower-blue sky that was too peaceful to be hanging over a world on the edge of death. She was conscious of Dark's shadowy spell twined about her forearm. Occasionally it moved, stirring against her skin as if getting more comfortable, and one or twice she caught it humming to itself. She could still see the colors in it, purples and midnight blues and iron grays, all swirling together. Sometimes a touch of vivid rose would swim to the surface.

"If we find Simeon Dark, he might be able to do something about Strood," she said. "Then Strood will stop killing the last remains of the Seven and the Raw will stop spreading so quickly."

"Yew fink?" Floyd didn't sound convinced.

"I do," said Nin firmly. "What do you think he did to stay alive? As a sorcerer, I mean." If he is alive, she added privately, remembering what the Dark Thing had said about the sorcerer having died of the plague and nobody knowing. She supposed it was possible, but she decided not to believe it anyway.

Floyd shrugged. "My favorite story is that 'e lives in the woods as a great bear and 'unts Quick fer food."

"Jonas told me it was his favorite too! Only without the hunting Quick part. Enid thinks he's disguised as a Quick, that he married one and had a family."

"So there might be some Quick kid runnin' around wiv a bit o' Dark in 'im? Or 'er?" Floyd looked at Nin speculatively, wondering about her father. She didn't notice.

"They wouldn't be Quick though, would they? They'd be Grimm. I mean, Dark'd only be pretending to be Quick, not *really* being Quick like Senta."

Floyd thought about it. "True, but magic is a funny thing. Sometimes it can be tricked, so if 'e was pretendin' to be a Quick so 'ard that everyfin' believed it, then 'is kids might be . . . not Quick true, but not Grimm eiver."

Nin was still trying to puzzle it out, wondering if magic could be tricked enough to allow Dark to live in the Widdern, when the air began to tingle with something electric, like the feeling just before dawn. For a moment the iron smell grew stifling and all the birds stopped singing. In the eerie silence, Nin shivered and reached out to find Floyd's hand. But before she could take it, something horrible happened.

With an inner lurch, she saw the distant wall of Raw expand, exploding outward, its thick white mass rushing toward them as swift and overwhelming as a slow-motion tidal wave. As it poured through the wood, trees began to twist and buckle, their trunks screaming as they split, the terrible shrieks filling the air. In seconds they were gone, bursting into vapor and swallowed by the Raw as it swept on.

It all happened so fast, and although Floyd was calling to her to run, Nin couldn't help but stare for a second longer as a rabbit tumbled out of a clump of bushes, its eyes stark with fear and its ears laid back. It took one huge leap into the field and then stopped in its tracks, caught by a thin tendril of Raw running ahead of the flood. At once the creature began to tear apart in front of her, its fur and flesh shredding away from its skeleton. Nin screamed, horror finally taking hold as the filigree of bones split and crumbled, dissolving into a fine mist.

Floyd grabbed her arm and pulled, jolting her to life. "I said run, kid. Run!"

They ran, clover bursting into swirls of mist under their feet, but it was no use. The Raw flooded over and around them, drenching them in chill cloud that smothered sight and sound in a dense blanket of luminous white.

Nin's feet thudded on stones now, even the soil was turning to mist. The Raw was everywhere, surrounding them, filling up her vision until there was nothing left but the curling fog and the dark bulk of Floyd leading the way. She followed him until he stumbled to a halt.

"Dunno where we are!"

Nin's heart sank at the sound of his voice. It was faint, threaded with panic. "What does the Raw do to Grimm?" she asked. "I know it dissolves the Fabulous, but you are only part Fabulous."

The ex-guard's bulk sagged. Nin grabbed his arm and shook as hard as she could. "Floyd!"

"Dunno. Went froo the 'eart on the river an' it was movin' so fast the Raw didn' get an 'old. This is different. Feels like . . . somefin' in me is . . . kinda . . . gettin' lost." His voice slurred. He shook his head, as if the fog was trying to get into his mind, then sat down suddenly. "Legs don' work no more."

"Get up, Floyd." Nin pulled, but she might as well try to move a mountain. "GET UP!" she yelled. "'Cos if you don't move, then I don't move and we're both dead."

Floyd mumbled something like, "nah, save yerself, kid," and slumped a little further. Nin hurled herself at him, pushing and heaving and pummeling until he staggered back to his feet. He had as good as saved her life once, when he had let her get away in Strood's laboratory, and now she was going to repay him. Gathering her strength, she rammed him, pushing him on, and together they lurched further into the mist. She was shivering as the cold seeped steadily into her skin; her feet were going numb and her hands were frozen. She prayed they were going in the right direction, though there were no landmarks to see. For all she knew they could be wandering round in circles.

Floyd stopped again, jerked into movement for a few steps, and then crashed to the ground, sending coils of Raw spinning around him. Nin screamed and dropped to her knees, shaking him hard. He didn't stir. She grabbed his jacket and tried dragging him, but it was hopeless. Sobbing, she leaned against the mound of his body and realized that the only way she could repay his kindness was to stay with him while he died.

Skerridge eyed the way ahead gloomily. Their haphazard path to Hilfian had taken them all the way around one block of Raw, only to be stopped by another. According to Jik they didn't have far to go now.

"Tik wik," said Jik, pointing with one stubby arm to a rise of hills on their left.

"Yew 'ope," snapped Skerridge. "Wha's t' say the 'ole town isn't surrounded by Raw? Wha's t' say there's a way in at all."

Jik gave him a look. It was the sort of look that was running out of patience.

"What on earth is *that*!" gasped Hilary, her eyes watering as they tried to make sense of a blur streaking across the landscape alongside the bank of Raw. It looked like a pulled thread in a tapestry, only moving. Even before she had finished speaking, the blur stopped being a blur and became a boy wearing a lot of jewelry and some interesting boots.

He looked them over and said, "Bogeyman Skerridge, I believe. And the new Fabulous, too." His eyes shifted to Hilary. Then away. Then back again. His face reddened slowly.

"Hilary Jones," said Hilary, who was used to people getting overcome when they first met her.

"Um . . . Seth Carver," said the boy, looking overcome. He got a hold of himself and grinned back. "Took my breath away for a moment there," he confessed.

Skerridge was eyeing the thing in Seth's hand. He sneezed. "Faerie magic," he said by way of explanation. "Gets up me nose. Where's it leadin' ya? 'Iilfian?"

"Ninevah Redstone," said Seth. "Thing is, it's been taking me round and round this . . ." He nodded at the curtain of Raw. "And I'm getting the bad feeling that the reason is, it's protecting itself, see. If it goes into the Raw then it will be undone."

"An' if it's takin' yer to Ninevah Redstone and it don' wanna go in the Raw, then . . ."

Eyes turned to the curtain of cold mist in front of them.

"Then it means she's in there," said Hilary.

✳ ✳ ✳

The tears were freezing on her face and her brain was full of stars that exploded in showers of silent white. She felt as if the world were growing smaller, drawing in on her and binding her in cold bandages of mist. She coughed and a spot of blood appeared on her chin, bright in the colorless Raw. Floyd did not move and she thought he must be dead. Nin knew she should get up and go, but she was so frozen that she could barely shift her position, let alone stand or walk. Her ears were playing tricks on her too, because she thought she could hear voices, which was stupid. There was no one here but her and a dead Grimm.

She felt so horribly tired that all she wanted to do was give in and sleep, but she tried again to struggle onto her feet. Her limbs just wouldn't do what she told them and she fell back with a cry as pain stabbed through her arms and legs.

The voices went quiet, as if they had heard her. A shape loomed out of the curling white. A dark shape, a slash in the white. "Nin!"

"Mirage," she whispered. "Seeing things now. You're dead."

More tears leaked out and then someone put their arms around her and lifted her up. A voice that sounded just like Seth said, "All right, Nin, we've got you now."

Then another voice that sounded just like Skerridge said, "Galig's teef, if it isn't Guard Floyd!"

Cuddled against Seth, Nin gave in and believed. "I'm fine," she murmured, only it was more of a croak.

"We'd better get her out of here," added a third voice, a female one that seemed familiar.

"Senta?" mumbled Nin.

"'Ow's that compass?" demanded Skerridge.

"On its last legs, I'm thinking." Seth held out a circle of dulled metal, its surface so corroded and eaten away that it was barely holding together.

"Fikkik mik," called out a voice that nearly made Nin burst into tears to hear it again. "Jik nik tik wik."

"Better hurry. Skerridge and Jik are going all wispy. Look, if we all pitch in and pull the guard, we should be able to move him," said the Senta-like voice. "We've got a bogeyman after all."

There was hasty movement and some grunting, followed by the sounds of hurrying feet and a heavy body dragging on the ground. And then light and a gentle warmth that made Nin gasp and tip her head to try and catch it all.

"We're 'ere!" Skerridge sounded ever so slightly amazed.

Nin turned her head to see life and movement and something like tall chimneys standing against the sky. Someone shouted.

"Hilfian." She sighed and finally closed her eyes to sleep.

18

HILFIAN

When Nin opened her eyes again, it was dark and she was safe and warm under a soft blanket of rabbit skins. There was a fire burning nearby and two red glows made a cozy light next to her bed. She was just trying to work out why they seemed familiar when someone said:

"Jik?"

She pushed back the covers and sat up on her elbows.

"Jik! I missed you."

"Mik yik tik." Jik patted her arm with one dusty hand. It glittered in the dim light of his eyes.

"You're all sparkly!" Nin yawned and flopped back down. "Rock crystals or something I s'pose." The events of the last day began to filter back into her brain. "What happened to Floyd, is he all right?"

"He's fine." A shadow moved in the corner of the room and a light flickered into life. The yellow glow of a lamp showed her the face of an old black woman with bright blackberry eyes and fine white hair. She was dressed in a shapeless cotton dress with a shawl around her shoulders.

"Doctor Mel says all he needs is thawing out, a good meal or two, and a rest. It takes a lot to kill a goblin-Grimm." The old woman got busy over the fire in the middle of the room, setting a kettle and a pan of porridge on a griddle on top of the flames to cook.

Outside, beyond the dark walls, Nin could hear the sound of people coming and going.

"This is Hilfian, right? What time is it and who . . . ?"

"I'm Hen. You're with me because I'm the town witch and everyone else is spooked by the mudman." The old woman chuckled. "Dunno how you did that, girl, but it was a fine job."

"Yik." Jik looked suitably smug about things, making Nin laugh.

"And, yes, this is Hilfian. It's late morning and you've been asleep for three hours. The town is up and about, so I sealed the door to give you some peace and quiet."

Nin sat up straight, pushed the blanket back further, and stretched, rubbing her eyes. She felt warm and clean and noticed that someone, probably Hen, had taken off her jeans and jacket. She got out of bed, and spotted her clothes in a tidy heap in the corner. "You can wash your face in this," said Hen, pouring water from the kettle into a bowl.

By now the pan of porridge was bubbling, and while Hen sorted out bowls, plates, and mugs for tea, Nin pulled on her jeans and took a look around. Set against the curving wall she saw a water barrel, a bucket of what looked disturbingly like blood, a bulging sack, and a twig broom. Apart from the fire and the cooking things, that was about it.

Seeing that Nin was dressed, Hen went to open the door. It wasn't that simple. The walls of the hut were of mud and the door was a wedge of plant life, the stalks so thickly interwoven they made a dense curtain. At the edges of the curtain, the stalks had grown into the wall, sealing the entrance shut. Hen had to cut an opening using a knife.

"Crowsmorte," she said, seeing Nin's look. "Thank Crow for it. Useful for pretty much anything. Smear a drop or two of blood on it and the opening just seals up again."

With the door open, bright morning sun fell in, lighting the earth walls to a rich loamy brown dotted here and there with a crowsmorte bloom. Nin went to get her first look at Hilfian; Jik followed her and they both settled on a bench by the door.

Hen's hut was near the center of the town, not far from a well where people came and went with buckets of water. A range of lumpy constructions clustered around the well—the hut being one of them—all built from the mud of the Land and all covered in grass and wild flowers. Some of them ran into one another, like a long hill with holes for doors.

"Don't they melt in the rain?" asked Nin, leaning to look back into the hut where Hen was dishing out porridge.

Hen laughed. "Oh no, not if they have a good coat of grass. It drinks the water, see. Plus, its web of roots holds the mud together so that even in a real downpour the walls stay up."

As well as people, both Quick and Grimm, wiry goats and skinny chickens ran all over the place, bleating and clucking. And there were mudmen, too, trundling by, usually carrying something balanced on their heads. These mudmen weren't alive like Jik. They were just Land Magic, mindless things created to do the bidding of their maker, and although it was Jik who was the exception, Nin thought it was the normal ones that were creepy.

There was a feeling of anxious movement about the place. The people hurrying to and fro didn't seem to be doing much. Knots of folk clustered here and there, talking. Probably about Strood and the spreading Raw.

Then Nin saw the bees, the same fist-sized ones she had seen on their way here. The low flying ones hummed past, swerving round the townsfolk as they went about their business. High above, more of them flew back and forth in swarms. The sound was everywhere, like fuzzy background music. Now she saw that the strange chimneylike things she had seen on her arrival were the hives. They were golden, shining in the sun, and stood on tall stilts that reared over the town. Their light reflected onto the towering cliff of the Raw that loomed in the background, giving the mist a yellow glow. "It's beautiful," said Nin, and meant it. It made her sad to think that this wonderful and strange place was waiting on the edge of destruction.

"Here." Hen held out a bowl of hot porridge with a dollop of honey in it and a spoon, then sat next to her.

"If you're the town witch," Nin said cautiously, after a few mouthfuls, "you'll know lots about magic and spells, right? So I was wondering if you could help me work out what this does." She held out her arm. "I found it in Dark's Mansion."

Hen nodded. "Hmmm, spotted it when I put you to bed. Powerful." The old woman shook her head. "Many have tried finding Dark before, you know. Some people think it's like a challenge, or a promise. That finding him will somehow stop the death of the Land."

Nin remembered the skeletons in Dark's Mansion. She sighed, feeling sorry for them.

"Look," said Hen. "Truth is, the Drift has been dying ever since the plague killed the Fabulous. Strood is only speeding up the end. You think that Dark will be able to stop him, but what exactly do you think can be done? Dark may be a sorcerer, but Strood is immortal."

Nin put down her empty bowl and leaned to pick up the mug of honey tea that Hen had set down by her foot. "Reverse the spell that separated Strood from his death," she said. "Then he'd be mortal again, right? There must be a way of . . . of putting the Maug back into him. That's what he calls his Death," she added by way of explanation. "The Maug. It's like a big shaggy dog-thing made of darkness." She shuddered, remembering.

Hen's bright eyes watched her closely. "It took seven sorcerers to make that spell. Do you think that one will be powerful enough to undo the work of seven?"

Nin stopped halfway through a sip of her tea and turned a serious face toward Hen. "I didn't think of that. But we have to try; we can't just sit here and watch death racing toward us."

Hen nodded. "Anyway, there's an answer." She leaned toward Nin. "Spells that work against the grain of nature always need more power than spells that work with it."

"And people are meant to die, so putting his death back into him should be a whole lot easier than taking it out?"

"Exactly." Hen chuckled. "So keep on trying. There's hope yet."

Finishing her tea, Nin stood up. "I want to talk some more about Dark later, if that's okay, but can I see Jonas first?"

There was a moment of silence. Jik sent Hen an anxious glance. "I want to see Jonas," said Nin again, a trickle of fear stealing into her heart. "Seth is here, so Jonas must be." For the first time she wondered why he hadn't been part of her rescue party in the Raw.

Hen seemed about to speak, but changed her mind as a shadow fell across them. It was Seth. He must have heard what Nin had said, for he looked worried. His green eyes fastened on hers.

"I'm sorry, Nin. I asked Hen not to tell you until I could see you myself. I thought I should explain."

Nin felt the chill inside her deepen as Jik moved to let Seth sit beside her. "I don't know how to say this, Nin." Seth sighed. "But I'm afraid Jonas is dead."

"There was nothing I could do, it was all over by the time I got out of the lake and back to the Mansion," Seth told her. "Dark must have had a trap set to go off when anyone left by the front door. Of course, Jonas would have been in such a hurry to get out, to find you, that he didn't stop to check."

"It doesn't make sense," said Nin patiently, her head spinning as she tried to take it all in. "Why set a trap to go off when someone's *leaving*?" She was trembling all over and tears were close.

Seth shrugged. "Let's face it, Dark knew that most people who got in would never get out again, they'd get lost or torn up by the lions. But if they were lucky enough to find their way out, then the trap would zap them as they left. A last way to make sure nobody stole the spell."

"That's cruel," said Nin coldly, feeling a stab of hate for Simeon Dark. After all, he was a sorcerer, just like all the others. Selfish, arrogant, and careless of the Quick lives he could shatter with a word.

"It was a lightning spell," Seth said. "There wasn't much left of him by the time I got there. He . . ."

"Then it wasn't him," said Nin firmly. Relief swept through her and she smiled, almost laughed. "He got away somehow; the remains must have been someone else's, see?"

Seth looked thrown for a moment, then gathered himself. "Nin, I understand how hard this is, but I think you have to face facts. It was Jonas, I know."

"You can't KNOW unless you were there," said Nin.

For a flicker of a moment, Seth's eyes slipped away from hers, but she was so filled with gladness that Jonas wasn't dead, she didn't notice.

"You only think it was him because it seems logical," she went on. "It's all . . ." She hunted for a word. "Circumstantial!" she finished triumphantly.

Seth nodded in a distracted way. He looked bemused. The conversation was clearly going in a different direction from the one he'd imagined, the one where Nin sobbed her heart out and clung to him for comfort.

"But I'm as sure as I can be, Nin," he said. He hesitated as if he'd planned something further to say, but wasn't sure he should say it. "I feel guilty. It should have been me dead, smashed to bits when the Dark Thing dropped me, but somehow . . ."

Nin patted his hand comfortingly. "Don't worry, Seth. I don't blame you for thinking he was dead. And if you'd realized it wasn't Jonas, you'd have stayed to find him, I'm sure. As it is, he'll get here somehow, I know Jonas."

The corner of Seth's mouth twitched downward and for a second she thought it was anger because she wouldn't believe him. Then he smiled.

"You're something else," he said, his green eyes glinting with humor. "I admire your faith, girl. You'll find out the truth in time, eh."

＊ ＊ ＊

145

When he had gone, Hen took Nin out to see the town. It was bustling with life. According to the old woman, most of the folk didn't live there. Hilfian had been falling apart as years passed and more and more Quick left the dying Land to take their chances in the Widdern. Suddenly that was changing again.

"For the last couple of days," explained Hen, "Quick, Grimm, and even a couple of Fabulous have been rolling in from all over the Drift, chased here by the spreading Raw or by Strood's guards raiding their homes."

Nin could see it as she looked about her. Hilfian was filling up with worried folk, all looking for company, help, and maybe a plan.

Hen, with Nin at her heels, had barely gone more than a few yards when there was a sound of thundering hooves and something galloped into the center of the village. It was huge and horrible and riding on the back of a midnight black beast with hooves of scarlet fire.

There was a flurry of shouts as people leapt out of its way. Someone screamed and Nin grabbed hold of Hen. She remembered the horseman they had seen on the way here. It had been riding toward the Terrible House then.

A couple of huge Grimm charged out of a hut, both clutching weapons. Hen grabbed Nin and pushed her back, standing in front of her.

The horse reared up, snorting, its flame hooves scattering sparks in the air before they thundered down to the ground again. More screams. One of the Grimm roared a challenge.

And then Nin took a look at the rider. He must have been at least eight foot tall, with a face like a nightmare made real. She saw blue-black skin that glistened in the light, shiny and hard as a beetle's, and yellow eyes that glowed like minisuns. But, most important, she saw a

T-shirt printed with a picture of a grinning skull and the words DID SOMEONE SAY PARTY?

"Taggit!" she yelled, feeling a surge of excitement.

The two Grimm paused, looked at Nin, then lowered their weapons as the Fabulous goblin brought his mount to a halt next to her. He towered over her and Hen like a dark cliff.

"Got meself a fiery steed," he said. "Not many of 'em left, so I reckon some o' your luck musta rubbed off on me!"

The beast snorted and rolled its black eyes at Nin. Steaming sweat ran from its glossy coat, and now it was standing still, the flames had died down, leaving hooves that glowed red-hot.

"I've been to the 'Ouse, but no sign of Skerridge or the mudman so I guessed they came 'ere. Saw Strood's army though!" His Halloween face twisted into a grimace.

The townsfolk had begun to gather, faces gawping at the sight of a real live fiery steed. Taggit raised his voice.

"Right, you lot!" he yelled. "Strood's comin' an' it's about time we got a plan. 'Cos if we're not ready 'e's gonna eat us alive."

More gathered.

"So what we're gonna do is this, we're gonna start the fight now, see? Make sure that most of Strood's army never reaches Hilfian. And then, maybe, we'll be able to fight off those that are left."

Already there was a different feel in the town. Hopeful. Purposeful.

"By the way," whispered Nin to Hen while Taggit barked orders and the town got to work. "Where is Skerridge?"

The old woman winked. "Gone spying," she said. "Won't that be fun for someone!"

147

19

A TIDE OF GOLDEN DARKNESS

Jibbit had found a place in the first platoon, on top of Hathor's helmet. Hathor was Strood's giant-Grimm guard, an armor-coated minimountain, who stomped along at the head of the army, just in front of Dunvice and Stanley.

Turning around carefully on the helmet, Jibbit looked back the way they had come. It had turned into a beautiful day, clear as a bell and full of golden light. By now, the House was a distant smudge, its chimneys, towers, and sloping roofs no more than a blur against the blue sky, and the sea was a line of a deeper hue on the horizon. Between the House and Hathor flowed the tiger-men, a river of gold, the dark stripes on their backs like hurrying ripples.

Although the tiger-men had been fashioned from crowsmorte, they had been grown with Quick blood and so were a mixture of Quick and Fabulous. In Jibbit's view that made them technically Grimm, though it was often hard to tell where Strood's experiments were concerned. He thought their glowing eyes and strong, wiry bodies were certainly Grimm rather than Quick. Though definitely not Fabulous.

Jibbit's eyes flicked to the two Fabulous goblins, at the left and right flank of the horde, that looked like walking slabs of rock. Bristling with axes, knives, and spiked balls on chains, they radiated physical power. And then to Lord Grayghast, the Fabulous werewolf, his yellow eyes like twin fires in his dark shape as he flowed along at the center of the horde, leaving a stain of shadow on the air behind him. As far as Jibbit was concerned, the Fabulous were unmistakable.

There would have been Strood's Fabulous bogeymen too, but it was daylight and no proper bogeyman would go out in the daylight. But then, they had superspeed and could catch up any time they pleased.

Studded throughout the horde of tiger-men, keeping the platoons in order and sticking out like so many sore thumbs, were Strood's goblin-Grimm guards, like Stanley. Stanley had been promoted and was in charge of the whole army—he was now Commanding Officer Stanley—but Dunvice, the werewolf-Grimm, acted as backup and was responsible for getting nasty if anyone didn't immediately do as they were told. Except, of course, for the Fabulous members of the army who could do what they liked with no argument from anyone simply because they were Fabulous.

Jibbit's eyes settled on a figure he hadn't seen about the House before. Which was odd, because he was sure he would have noticed an insane, white-faced, glittery-eyed kid in a duffel coat, who might do nothing but watch you horribly till you were crazy with fear. But then again might do something else involving knives. And who almost certainly *knew where you lived* . . .

Oh well. Jibbit shrugged, shaking off the feeling of stealthy oppression that had crept over him. He went back to viewing the scene.

At the rear of the army, stacks of great wooden rafts were rolling along on beds of wheels, dragged by a platoon of tiger-men. Each pile was stacked up three or four deep. The army didn't have time to go around the Heart of Celidon. It was going to go through it, traveling on the river so that the speeding water would carry them quickly through the deadly fog to bring them out on the other side, hopefully alive.

Altogether it was an impressive sight, but all it did for Jibbit was to fill him with a kind of wobbling sensation in his middle. The truth was that although he could kill people with his freezing rainwater spit, or split their heads open by falling on them, he didn't really want to. Especially not the last thing, because that meant traveling in a downward direction, which meant he might end up on the gr . . . gr . . . really low. He sighed deeply, then realized that Commanding Officer Stanley was staring at him.

"If it's downphobic," said the CO heavily, "why don' it sit on one o' them goblins? They're the 'ighest it's likely to get."

Dunvice shrugged. "Ask it."

"Is not polite tooo talk about people when they are there," said Jibbit crossly.

"Yew ain't people," said Stanley in a reasonable tone. "Yore a carved lumpa stone wiv additions."

The gargoyle hooted irritably. "In answer tooo your question that yoo didn't ask me, I doesn't want tooo go near Fabulous."

Dunvice gave a short laugh. "It's got some sense then."

Jibbit glared at her, clenching his toes in anger and frustration. "Yoo're still doing it!"

"Oy!" Hathor thumped the side of his helmet with

a metal-fisted hand. "Stop wiv the claws or yer gravel."

Jibbit squawked with fright, but managed to hang on.

Stanley chuckled. "It's a bit of entertainment I s'pose. Least it don' give me the creeps." He was silent for a moment, thinking about the tiger-men, who most certainly did give him the creeps. It was something about their eyes, bright and alert with a kind of concentrated desire to tear things apart. It was all they thought about. Blood. Meat. Tearing things. More blood.

"And there are so many things here to give you the creeps," said a voice from about his elbow.

Stanley glanced, then glanced again. The speaker was someone he hadn't seen about the House before. And he was sure he would have noticed someone who looked like that.

"Yeah," he said feelingly. "And yore one of 'em!"

The evil-looking kid in a duffel coat gave him a creepy smile. "I aim to please," he said.

Dunvice sent them an irritable glare. She was worrying about the silver cage and its occupant, currently strapped to the back of one of the tiger-men. Dunvice had made that particular tiger-man walk beside her because she wanted to keep an eye on the thing.

"Not to mention *that*," she said to Stanley, nodding at the skinkin. She leaned closer to the CO. Evil Kid shuffled up a bit. Jibbit listened hard. "Thing is," she said softly, "he didn't make it right."

"Nah! Mr. Strood don' do mistakes."

Dunvice shrugged. "You are supposed to breathe a name into it, the name of the one you want dead. Only thing is . . ." Dunvice shuddered. "He told it to kill the *legendary* Ninevah Redstone."

Unseen by either of them, Evil Kid sent the skinkin a look of alarm.

"And?" asked Stanley.

"How do you kill a legend?"

Jibbit was getting bored. The conversation seemed rather pointless as he had no idea what the half-werewolf was fussing about. Stanley fell silent, thinking. In its cage, the skinkin swiveled its head, the empty sockets fixing on Stanley, then Mrs. Dunvice, and then Jibbit. And then on Evil Kid.

"It does give me the creeps, tooo," muttered Jibbit.

"Understood," put in Evil Kid. "The thing cannot go back to the death it came from until the task is fulfilled. And it wants to go back, so it will be relentless and merciless."

"Do I know yoo?" asked Jibbit a trifle nervously.

"S'easy," interrupted Stanley suddenly. "She's famous fer bein' lucky, right, so all it 'as to do is kill 'er in the normal physical way. If it kills 'er then everyone'll know that 'er luck didn' work, see? An' so bofe she's dead an' 'er legend is dead. They might tell stories about 'ow there was this girl what nearly got away from Strood, but it ain't the same. 'E won in the end. So my point is, yer don' need t' worry. Killin' the girl an' killin' the legend are one an' the same fing."

Dunvice eyed him with something approaching respect. "You know, Stanley, for a goblin-Grimm you're almost bright at times."

Stanley cleared his throat loudly and looked embarrassed. In its cage, the skinkin switched its eyeless gaze in his direction. "Hmm," said Evil Kid. "One almost hopes you are right. Otherwise the skinkin would have a task it could never complete and Strood will have done what Ni . . . the Redstone girl did with that mudman. He will have made a new Fabulous."

Dunvice nodded, her eyes serious. "I was thinking that very thing."

152

Stanley went pale at the thought. He stared at the skinkin. So did Dunvice. So did Jibbit. So did Evil Kid.

The skinkin stared back.

Stanley sighed, watching another tiger-man start to make that horrible hacking sound in its throat that meant it was going to throw up.

When it came to water it seemed that the tiger-men were really just cats. They had barely loaded half on to the first of the rafts and the creatures were already in a miserable state. The raft shifted gently, rising and dipping with the current. It would get a lot worse as the river narrowed, growing deeper and rougher as it poured through the Heart.

Stanley gave an inner groan and got moving, picking his way carefully through the vomit-strewn pile of seasick tiger-men toward the head of the raft. There was a choking sound to his left and one of them threw up on his feet. Stanley kicked the creature. It bit him. Angrily he stomped off, smelling foul and with a sore leg.

At the front of the raft, he stopped and glanced up at the sky. It was still clear save for one white cloud hanging on the horizon like a lonely hawk. He looked ahead and his heart stopped. Just for an instant, but long enough to make its point.

Before him towered the Raw that was the Heart of Celidon. Cloudy snakes of mist coiled and twisted from its surface, groping toward anything nearby. Where it touched the trees, bushes, or the banks of the river, faint wraiths of mist rose into the air leaving dead bark and bare earth behind.

Stanley did not relish the thought of whatever lay behind that vast white curtain. It was beyond imagining.

"Beyond imagining isn't it," said a voice at around the level of his elbow. He jumped.

"Whatchoo doin' 'ere?"

"Dunvice assigned me to your raft," said Evil Kid smoothly.

"I might 'ave somefin' t' say about that later," muttered Stanley. He gave Evil Kid a suspicious look, wondering if he could see a hint of fancy waistcoat in a gap between the toggles of the duffel coat.

Something heavy stood on his sick-free foot. He looked down.

"Oh lor' yew an' all. Watcher doin' down there? Fought yer didn' like ter be low."

"I'm not," said Jibbit calmly. He inched forward until he was right on the very edge of the raft, stone claws dug deep into the planks. "There is lots and lots of downward between me and the gr . . . gr . . . bottom of the river. Is just filled with water instead of air and that's no bother."

Stanley snorted. "It's a big bovver to those of us wiv lungs!"

Jibbit yawned and settled down, opening his stubby wings so that they lay at right angles to his back. It helped keep his balance, and judging by the foamy water dashing ahead, balance was going to be very necessary. Which was fine, because he was good at balance.

Evil Kid settled next to him, eyes glittering in the depths of its hood. "So, when are we going?"

Stanley looked back. His raft was filled to capacity, every square inch lined with rippled golden fur—currently rather foul-smelling and miserable. In some places they were lying two deep. Behind this raft was another, also filled to capacity and watched over by one of the other guards. Still farther upriver, Dunvice and

Lord Grayghast were busy shepherding the next batch of whining tiger-men on to the third raft. Beyond that, Hathor was Grimm-handling the fourth raft into position. And so on.

"Now," said Stanley as calmly as he could, and he cut the rope that tethered the raft to sanity.

20

GETTING READY

Trailing behind Hen and Jik as they walked across the town, Nin found herself lingering to stare. To her right, the view beyond the edge of Hilfian was masked by the wall of Raw, its chilly fingers reaching into the blue sky where they hung, unmoving in the still air. Horrible though it was, Nin knew that it gave Hilfian a protecting wall to hide behind. At least they knew Strood's army wouldn't come that way.

In the other direction were hills, rising in steep mounds of purple and green. At their foot, between them and the town, stretched fields of clover and buttercups. To the south the hills dipped and Nin could make out the green blur of a wood. This wood was the town's weak spot, the point where Strood could break through. So this was where they needed to build their defenses. Even now, pits were being dug in the fields. Set with stakes and covered with grass matting, they would make a fine trap.

Since Taggit's arrival, the town had exploded with busy life. People ran to and fro carrying shovels, lengths of wood, water, and food for the workers. A goblin-Grimm blacksmith had set up a sharpening service and was working his way through an armory of knives, scythes, pitchforks, and a few things Nin couldn't name.

Right in front of the town hall was a stretch of open land where, according to Hen, market stalls selling chickens, chestnut flour, honey, and household goods usually stood. Now it was full of men shaping wood into rough stakes. They were laughing at a joke one of them was telling, something to do with why there were never any bogeymen-Grimm. Nin tried to listen. It sounded rude and she wasn't sure she understood it anyway, so she gave up and hurried after Hen instead.

The town hall was the only wooden structure in Hilfian and even this had a grown-together look about it, with leaves sprouting from its walls and daisies nodding in the mud packed between rough-cut boards. Next to it was a bell tower, built of mud on a skeleton of branches and joined to the town hall roof by a rope bridge.

Inside, the large hall was being turned into a hospital by Doctor Mel, a dark-haired woman with a warm smile that Nin remembered from blurry images of early that morning. She was giving crisp orders to a group of older women as they put together makeshift beds and gathered bandages, bottles of bee venom—a wonderful painkiller, said Hen—and pots of healing crowsmorte paste. Hilary was there too and she broke off long enough to come over and say hello.

The town hall had a cellar, a dugout room of bare, packed earth. In it, around the walls and piled on top of an old table, was stacked a collection of magical devices, brought in by the townsfolk. Jik immediately set to rummaging through them, finding out what they did and how they worked. It was a job nobody else wanted because it could be dangerous and they would all rather keep as many of their body parts attached as they possibly could. For the present anyway.

Leaving him to work, Nin and Hen went back outside. Nin's job, said Hen, was to help her make Land Magic. They settled outside on the green close to the town hall and got to work.

Being busy helped because Nin was worried about Jonas. She didn't doubt that he was still alive. He HAD to be, but she missed him and wondered where he was. She had decided to allow a day here in Hilfian before she went on with her search for Dark, partly to talk to Hen and see if she could help, but mainly to wait for Jonas. Also, she felt a kind of responsibility for the townsfolk of Hilfian. Strood was attacking them because of her, so maybe she should stay and help. And anyway, she had no idea where to look for Dark next. He could just as easily be here as anywhere else. So she would stay for a day, help the town prepare, and find out anything useful that she could. Then move on tomorrow, hopefully with Jik if not with Jonas to help her.

Hen started her Land Magic with heaps of silvery dust—dried-out silt dredged up from the riverbed. She organized it into mounds about four feet long, then used a stick to draw lines suggesting catlike limbs and a head. She put a cord around neck of the first one and told it to guard the hills. The silt-cat sat up and yawned, the sketched outline suddenly very real. It looked at Nin with eyes that glowed yellow-white, then padded away to do its work. It moved like silk, flowing along in an almost liquid way.

Hen handed her more cords. "You heard what I said?"

Nin nodded dumbly. "Then send the others to join that one. I'm going to make smoke-hawks to keep an eye out for the army."

Nin had only just finished the cats, when she got a visit from the doctor.

"How are you?" asked Mel, with a warm smile. "Now, I'm just going to listen to your breathing for a minute. How's the cough?"

"Gone. I feel a bit wheezy though."

"Not surprising, with all that Raw cluttering up your lungs. It'll clear soon." Mel smiled again, a twinkling smile from bright gray eyes. "Now let me see your fingers and toes. People have come out of the Raw with frostbite before now. Those that *do* come out—you're lucky your friends found you." She laughed. "But then you're the Redstone girl, so you would be, wouldn't you?"

Nin made a rueful face. She had already heard a couple of people say things like ". . . but with Ninevah's Luck we'll make it," or ". . . they'll hold—with Ninevah's Luck . . ." She was beginning to feel like some kind of fluffy mascot.

When the doctor had gone, Hen and Nin began piling up the boulders that Seth was bringing them. He was covered in dirt and sweat from digging pits and paused for a moment to give Nin a broad smile and a wink.

"You look better. How's the cough?"

"Fine," said Nin, taking a deep breath to show him how clear her lungs were. She coughed hoarsely, put a hand over her mouth, and gave him a look that made him laugh.

"Look," he said, "come and find me later. I've got a present for you. A bit of magic—you'll love it!"

Nin blushed and went back to helping Hen arrange boulders. The job was made instantly easier when Floyd turned up. He looked gray and somehow smaller, but otherwise fine. He gave her a bashful smile and said, "Thanks, kid."

Nin patted his arm and said, "I'm glad you're all right," and that was that.

At Hen's command, the piled-up boulders stirred into bouldermen nearly as huge as a Grimm guard. Blue-light eyes shone out from crevices where the boulders didn't quite fit. The spaces weren't even either, so one or both eyes could be too far to the side, or in a forehead, or where a nose ought to be. They were to stand guard in the river where they could wait for days, ready to wreck any craft that tried to pass them. Just in case Strood's army thought about sneaking in that way.

Nin and Floyd watched them stride off, the ground shaking with their weight.

"There are times," said Nin thoughtfully, "when I realize all over again just how creepy this world can be."

Next, Hen set her to strip the leaves and petals from piles of crowsmorte flowers to be turned into healing paste. The leaves she put in one pile, the petals in another, and the cleaned stalks she passed to Hen to shred. Floyd went off to join the diggers.

"So," said Hen as soon as they were settled, "you want to find Simeon Dark, eh? Where are you going to start?"

Nin had already discovered enough to know that it was Hen who had found Jonas when he was lost in the Drift four years ago, and had brought him up. Hen had been born in the Drift, her parents having found their own way in without the help of bogeymen. She was one of the few Quick still living who remembered Celidon and the Final Gathering, though she had been a very little girl at the time. And she certainly knew all about magic.

"Enid thinks Dark might be disguised as a Quick," said Nin. "Not stealing a body like Vispilio, just making

160

his own look different. But really he could be anything: Fabulous, Grimm, or Quick. And it needn't be a human Quick. I mean, there's the 'Great Bear in the Wood' idea." She crinkled up her nose.

"But you think there is something wrong with all that?"

"What's he living on?" said Nin at once, suddenly realizing that it had been bothering her for ages, she just hadn't had time to put it into words. "Neither depends on Dread or Desire and he needs that, doesn't he? To keep his spell going."

Hen smiled and her berry eyes twinkled. "He's a clever one, Dark. You're right. The other sorcerers' spells depend on Quick to keep them going. Senta exists in the blood of her children. Vispilio needs a Quick heart to live in. Azork feeds on Quick life."

Nin nodded. "And Enid is a place of safety, and Nemus is shelter in the night. Both things the Quick need."

"But Dark, now what's he done?"

"Huh!" She frowned. "Well, he's become a legend I guess. You know, the mysterious Seventh Sorcerer."

"And why's that so special?"

"All the other Fabulous that are left, they're magical in their own way, but they can't actually *do* magic. Bogeymen can change shape, but just because that's what bogeymen do. They can't fly like faeries, or swim in the Land like Jik. Only sorcerers can cast spells and *make magic*. So a sorcerer could do any of the things the other types of Fabulous could do, but where a BM does superspeed because it's the way they are made, a sorcerer could do it simply because he can do *anything*!"

Hen nodded, smiling. "You're certainly learning about the Land."

"Thanks. Anyway, what I'm getting at is, that's why sorcerers are special. So, because he's the only sorcerer left, Dark is the last bit of real living magic in the whole world. The last bit of that old magical world of Celidon."

Nin's face cleared and her eyes brightened as it all clicked into place. "Of course! Simeon Dark, it's like, he IS Celidon, right? And the Quick don't want Celidon to die. They don't want magic gone from their lives forever."

She looked up at Hen and smiled. "It's perfect. Nemus and Enid give the Quick something they want. But with Dark it's not what he *gives* them, it's what he *is*, that the Quick desire. *Simeon Dark is still alive because everyone wants him to be!*"

"Exactly," said Hen. "And it wouldn't have worked unless Dark was the only one left."

"That's not very nice, is it! I mean, counting on the others ceasing to be sorcerers just so's he could go on living."

"Sorcerers aren't known for being nice." The old woman chuckled.

Nin laughed, then sighed. "Doesn't get me anywhere though, does it? I may know more about how his spell works, but I've still got to find out where he's hidden!"

Suddenly a shout went up from some of the townsfolk and a shadow fell over the square. Everyone stopped what they were doing and looked up.

Over the town, bees were swarming in great clouds, their furry golden bodies clustered so thickly they blocked out the sun. They were pouring out of the hives in streams and their buzz filled the air. Swirling together, the great mass circled the town once and then headed out over the river, disappearing swiftly into the distance. Soon, they were nothing more than a dark strip on the horizon and the sky was clear again, save for the distant, circling shapes of Hen's smoke-birds. A shocked silence fell across the town.

Puzzled, Nin turned to Hen, but one look at the old woman's face told her everything she needed to know.

The bees had gone because death was coming to Hilfian. Strood's army was crossing the Heart.

All morning, while Nin had been stripping stalks and thinking about Simeon Dark, Jik had been finding interesting things in the town hall cellar.

The Quick clearly had a mania for collecting any bits of Old Celidon that they came across, even if they didn't have a clue what it did. In Jik's view, that just went to prove how much they missed it and wanted it back, even the deadly bits.

Some of the items were long dead, their stored magic used up, and those Jik tossed aside. There were also things that were useful, but only if you wanted to heat water, travel fast, see in the dark, and so on. He was more pleased to find three staffs of varying sizes that had firepower left in them, some wands, and a few charms that could be turned to good use as weapons.

Seth had a knack of spotting live items too—after all, it was how he made his living—and once he had done with digging, he turned up, holding a battered old pack that he dropped at the back of the room, then got working alongside Jik.

They were both ignoring the thing in the corner. Neither of them knew what it was and neither of them cared to find out. The four-foot-long item had been wrapped in several layers of thick cloth, but still shone bright enough to remove the need for a lamp. Jik had promised himself to have a look at it later. If he really had to. The steady, golden glow seeping through the cloth made his mud

163

tingle uncomfortably. Seth hadn't given it so much as a glance, but he knew it was there all right.

"Well now! A faerie spindle!" Seth picked up a slender needle wrapped in an old handkerchief. "This is a real find!"

He held it up for Jik to see. The gleam from its elegant shape, etched all over with intricate swirls, looked sharp enough to cut flesh. It was about as long as Seth's hand from his wrist to the tip of his finger, and Jik didn't like it at all.

"Nik mikik."

"True, it hasn't got any magic in it as such, but it's not meant to have. It's a tool, not a device. A spindle is what you use to shape or move other things, things of power. So, unlike those devices full of magic, this will never die."

Seth pointed the spindle at Jik, who backed off. For a moment he could have sworn he felt his inner fires twist, pulled toward the spindle.

"Faeries used to use spindles to weave moonlight or water into beautiful cloth to wear. Or fire. Fire made a lovely cloth."

"Ik!" snapped Jik.

"Well true, but faeries were nasty things all round. Fierce and clever and very, very powerful. As powerful in their own way as the sorcerers. And it takes a lot for me to say that."

Seth shook his head, his eyes fixed on Jik. "You're interesting, I'll give you that." A fierce grin split his face, lighting his green eyes. "But you caused me grief not so long ago, in the Giant's Wood. Do you remember? I do, mud-rat. Time for revenge."

Swiftly, Seth began to weave the spindle to and fro in a complicated pattern. Jik tried to dive into the safety of the earth, but suddenly his limbs felt like lumps of mud and he couldn't move them. A chill spread through him as his inner fires began to flicker, drawn out by the spindle. He felt heavy, crumbly almost. Lumpy. He could see a pattern of golds and reds forming about the spindle, a pool of flame hanging in the air, growing as fast as the fire inside him faded. A crack split across his middle scattering a shower of dry earth on the floor.

"Vikikikik," he said, recognizing his enemy. Even his sight was dimming now. The pool of fire, the essence of his mudman life, seemed further away, its colors hidden by a creeping shadow that filled up the cups of his eyes as their flames dimmed to sparks. And then the sparks flickered and were gone and there was only darkness. Jik crashed backward to the ground. He lay still.

Seth stopped twisting the spindle and reached out with his other hand to catch the cloth of fire as it fluttered down through the air like a dropped handkerchief. The square of colors bathed Seth's hand in golden light, turning the jewels of his many bracelets and rings into small fires of their own.

He walked slowly over to the remains of the mudman and kicked him. Crumbs of earth skittered over the floor. If it hadn't been for the crystals mixed into the mud, the useless body would have exploded back into the dust it really was.

"Perfect," he said softly. And went to wait for Nin.

21

THE HEART OF THE HEART

About the time Nin was waking up, Evil Kid was hanging on to the edge of the raft as it cast off on its journey through the Heart of Celidon. He shivered as the current took hold and the raft began to pick up speed, hurrying toward the blanket of Raw. He was feeling anxious, because even if there were stories about how people had crossed the Heart by traveling on the river, he wasn't convinced it was possible.

All anyone knew for certain was that the river hurtled through the mist-draped Heart until it reappeared on the other side. This meant that there had to be some last dregs of the Land left undissolved by the Raw. Otherwise, there would be nothing to channel the water through the Heart, and it would have rushed into the mist only to fall helplessly through the Raw until the river itself was dissolved. It was not a nice thought, and, generally speaking, anyone wanting to get to the other side of the Heart preferred the long journey around the edge.

As their raft drew rapidly closer to the Heart, Evil Kid's sharp eyes spotted a difference in the thickness of the Raw where it hung over the river. This difference hadn't been all that visible before because of the general surrounding whiteness of everything—like picking out a white hole on a white background. Evil Kid frowned, puzzled.

And then understanding dawned. That difference in the thickness of the Raw had to be the reason why anyone traveling through the Heart this way might just make it out alive! The river's advantage had to be the sheer vigor created by its speed. As the water rushed swiftly through the Heart, the Raw could not settle on it or anything it carried. And if the Raw couldn't settle on the river, and so couldn't take hold of any Fabulous who happened to be traveling on the river's back, then the icy mist couldn't dissolve that Fabulous away to nothing. Or in the case of the Quick, couldn't freeze it slowly to a horrible death. Evil Kid grinned, feeling a moment of triumph at having worked things out. It didn't last.

By now they were so close that the Raw towered over them, filling their world. The tiger-men yowled miserably. It dawned on Evil Kid that even traveling on the swiftly running river, they would still be surrounded by the Raw at its thickest and most terrifying. He wondered if he should swap back to Natural Bogeyman and do a superspeed runner, but it was too late. And he had to admit he was curious. The mudman had done this journey once, not by river of course, but on his own two feet, walking through the Heart. He never spoke about it, apart from hinting at some great horror that lay there, concealed at the very heart of the Heart. . . .

On second thought . . .

Evil Kid looked over his shoulder at the rapidly receding world. No, definitely too late!

He braced himself as the swiftly flowing water carried them across the threshold of the Heart and into a world of eerie white that arched over and around them so thickly, it cut out all light and warmth and air. It wasn't dark though, not at all. The Raw had its own light, an ice-white glow that made Evil Kid's eyes ache if he stared into it too long.

The tiger-men fell silent. Everywhere, purple eyes peered warily at the mist that rose on all sides. One or two of them shifted about, their claws scratching on the wooden planks. The temperature plummeted and Evil Kid could see his breath misting the air around him. He could also see that his theory was right. Where the river rushed through, its sheer speed cut a kind of tunnel through the Raw keeping its hungry mists away from them.

Glancing back, Evil Kid could see nothing. He knew that the next raft would be following a minute or so behind theirs, but it was hidden from view by the curls of river vapor that rose from the hurrying surface of the water. They might as well be traveling through the Raw alone.

"Well, so far so good," said Stanley, his voice sounding strangely dead on the icy air. He was examining the planks of the raft. "Not even touched!"

Overhead, the Raw hung like a dank, icy blanket. Ahead, though not far, Evil Kid could see the river like dark metal cutting through shadowy banks of scarred gray rock.

Now, Stanley was examining the tiger-men. They were in a right state, shivering and whining like a bunch of seasick kittens.

"Oy! If yer gonna chuck, try and do it over the side!" he yelled, forgetting for a moment that they were actually deadly killing machines. "We'll be ankle deep in cat puke at this rate!"

There was a chorus of hissing and snarling, and

many pairs of luminous and angry eyes switched in Stanley's direction, along with a frightening display of teeth, reminding everyone that they *were* actually deadly killing machines.

Something grabbed Evil Kid's sleeve. It crunched, stiff with frost.

"Wha's that?" Jibbit sounded nervous.

Evil Kid listened for a moment. "The Voice of the Land," he said in a whisper.

It rose all around them from the river, in sighing waves that chilled their hearts as much as the Raw chilled their skin. It sounded like someone in the throes of a grief so deep it could never be healed, and as the raft went on, the sound grew and grew filling the air with bitter, heart-wrenching sobs. The tiger-men were silent now, listening, their claws outstretched and ready to attack, their eyes wide with a kind of dark loathing born from fear.

"No," whispered Jibbit, "not singing. THAT!" There was awe in his voice as he pointed ahead and up.

Something reared through the mist, looming over them. It swept up from the banks in a wall of sheer gray. And it must have been as tall as the Raw, too, because it rose up and up in a great rugged mass that went on until it had disappeared in the white clouds. And even then, Evil Kid just knew that it was still going.

Jibbit gave a strange sigh of longing. "Is so HIGH," he whispered, his stony eyes wide and full of desire. "Does it reach the sky? Is it . . . ?" He paused, searching his brain for the right word, a word that conveyed the feeling of great, wonderful, heaven-reaching height. "Is it a *cathedral*?"

"I dunno, do I?" said Stanley. Feeling the raft bob and twist beneath him, he switched his gaze back to the river. His eyes went glassy and he muttered something incomprehensible and probably rude.

"Wha's that mean?"

"Trouble, I suspect!" Evil Kid watched curiously as Stanley lowered himself to his knees.

"'ANG ON FER YER LIVES!" the CO bellowed, then dropped flat on his face and grabbed whatever handholds he could find. And then, suddenly, the river threw them over the edge of the world into darkness.

Skerridge dropped Evil Kid shape like a shot. Natural Bogeyman was always best when it came to survival against the odds.

What got him most was the sound. It wasn't just the inhuman screams of the tiger-men as they scrabbled to hold on, digging their claws into the wood of the raft— or each other, if necessary—nor was it the rushing roar of tons of water as it fell through the emptiness; it was the fact that all this racket barely dented the silence that enveloped them.

They were falling through nothing. Absolute nothing. Here, even the Raw had gone, leaving a darkness so complete it made Skerridge's eyeballs pop. All they had was the sound of their falling, and yet that sound was a tiny scraping in a silence so huge that he felt it was eating into his brain, stifling even the noise made by his thoughts. It was as if everything, even the things inside his head, had gone away and he was an infinitesimally small bit of nothing hurtling through a nothing so vast he couldn't begin to understand it.

He could understand one thing, though. This was the horror at the heart of the Heart. Here even the raw, unformed magic that the Land was made from had died, killed by the plague. And it had left . . . emptiness.

Something cold shoved into his ear and whispered, "Wha's it?"

And suddenly Skerridge's brain clicked back into gear and he realized that he was being drenched in freezing spray, that several tiger-men had their claws bedded in his legs, and that, actually, the racket was deafening.

He also realized that although, here at the heart of the Heart, the rocky walls of the ravine through which the river ran had been eaten away completely, the river STILL RAN OUT THE OTHER SIDE, which must mean . . .

"S'a waterfall!" he yelled over the thundering, which was getting louder and louder. "There's nuffin' 'oldin' the river up 'ere, but furver down there mus' be more rock."

By now, the sound was so loud it shook his bones and the wind rushing past his face was more water than air. "BREEEAAVE IIINNN!" he yelled, then he hauled in as much air as he could find and shut his eyes as the raft plunged deep into the whirlpool below.

For a few moments that seemed to last forever, everything was a turmoil of roaring, swirling water, and scrabbling bodies, as those who were shaken loose tried to grab at those who were still hanging on. Under the waterfall, the raft was tossed and flung around by the force, sometimes upside down and sometimes spinning like a crazy top.

Next to him, Skerridge felt Stanley's arm jerk as his grip slipped. He opened his eyes and saw the goblin-Grimm's face, eyes wide with horror as the swirling water ripped him from the raft. On the other side of him, the gargoyle hooted as a sharp buck to the left shook him loose and tossed him free.

In Skerridge's head everything went into slow

motion. A weird feeling swept over him, as if he were only a bit player in a much bigger story.

This is it, he thought, *this is the moment when* every-thing *hangs in the balance.*

He could let the two of them go and the army would be minus its commanding officer and one small and probably not very significant stone.

Or he could save them.

Any normal bogeyman wouldn't think twice. In fact, he wouldn't think once. It wasn't bogeyman nature to worry about other people. But Skerridge had already chucked out the rule book, so he had options. And for some reason the decision seemed REALLY IMPORTANT.

So he made it.

His shape burst and split into something so weird it was barely recognizable as any one thing. A long, suck-ered tentacle shot out in the direction of Jibbit, a many-jointed arm-cum-leg shot out in the direction of Stanley, and a whole barrage of claw-tipped bits and pieces dug deeply into the raft and hung on tight.

At last the raft surfaced and bobbed, turning gently on the water. "That was fun," said Jibbit, cheerfully, dan-gling from Skerridge's left tentacle. "I liked the rushing into nothing bit, and the falling bit, and the swirling in water bit, tooo."

"Weren't you afraid we'd hit the bottom?" slurred Stanley, trying to get his nerves back under control. It was just entering his brain that he was pinned to the edge of the raft by a long black arm with spiky bits. In the time it took for him to register the fact that Evil Kid was now Unspeakable Thing, he had been dragged safely onto the raft, and Evil Kid was back again, staring at him innocently.

"No. The bottom was so far down we would never get there. Is a lot of water in this lake."

Ignoring the gargoyle, Stanley frowned. "Bogeyman Skerridge," he snapped.

Evil Kid's eyes glittered at him even more innocently.

Stanley sighed, decided not to deal with the problem, shook himself, and took stock.

The Raw was back, but only in thin spirals that hung over the water, giving off a gray-white glow. The raft was in a kind of rocky basin, bobbing about on water that looked like ruffled black silk. They could still hear the roar of the waterfall, but it was receding. The force of the fall must have pushed the raft under and then up, into a swift flowing current that was dragging them on through the Heart. They couldn't see the banks of the river either to the left or to the right.

Surreptitiously, Evil Kid counted the tiger-men. There were less of them. But even without the ones lost on the journey, there were enough on this one raft to cause the people of Hilfian serious problems. "He counted on it, I expect," said Evil Kid out loud. "He knew he would lose a lot of them on the way. That's why he made so many."

"Eh?" Stanley gave him a look. "Now see 'ere, bogeym . . . Evil Kid or whatever yer name is. I'm appreciatin' that yew saved my life, but yer gotta see that I'm in a tricky position 'ere, what wiv you bein' on the ovver side an' all."

"Oh, don't worry, I'll be gone soon enough!" Evil Kid smiled at him. It might have been meant to be reassuring. It wasn't.

The raft sped on, full of bedraggled and battered tiger-men. They hissed and spat at each other every time one of them moved, and their yellow eyes glowed with hate and rage. "It's not so bad," muttered Stanley. "An' at least they don' stink of sick anymore."

"They are getting used tooo it, I think."

Jibbit was right. Even though the raft was bobbing and twisting as it rushed along, the tiger-men were not throwing up anymore. One or two of them were even leaning over the edge to dabble inquisitive paws into the water.

Something hot and wet ran up Evil Kid's leg. Startled, he looked down to see one of the tiger-men licking the blood off his clawed calves. It looked up at him speculatively.

He glared. "Don't even think about it," he hissed, "not if you want to stay whole."

The tiger-man yawned and settled down for a nap on top of one of his comrades. Most of the others were doing the same.

After a while they came to a stretch of the river with walls that towered around them, broken and jagged and half eroded away by the Raw.

Then they came to a stretch with sunlight.

Then they were out.

"There yer go," said Stanley cheerfully. "We made it!"

"Is true!"

The air fizzed. Guard and gargoyle looked around startled, but there was nobody there. Evil Kid was gone.

When they had been carried far enough downriver that they were within a couple of hours' march of Hilfian, Stanley commanded the tiger-men to paddle to the bank. Dunvice and her party joined them shortly after, to be followed by the other rafts. Stanley watched as the horde gathered itself together.

"Reckon we've lost about a third o' the tiger-men in total. Plus two guards. No Fabulous, fank Galig. Coulda been worse."

Dunvice looked pale, her yellow eyes narrowed to anxious slits.

"I don't care about them," she said, dropping an empty silver cage in front of him. "But take a look at this. When we went over the waterfall the catches were knocked open."

A chill ran up Stanley's spine as he took in what she was saying.

"It's gone," she went on miserably. "The skinkin got out and now it's gone to kill Ninevah Redstone."

"Then yer'd better 'ope we get there first," said Stanley, his face grim. "'Cos if we don' then it'll be yew tells Mr. Strood why we failed t' get 'er alive."

22

HARNESSING THE STORM

Having found out enough about Strood's army to give the folk of Hilfian nightmares for a lifetime, Skerridge superspeeded back to the town. He found Taggit in charge and passed his news on to the goblin.

"They'll be 'ere by teatime, count on it," he said warningly. "Once they've got themselves together and got moving. Two hours, tops, even goin' all the way round the Raw on the edge o' town to come at us froo the wood. The plan is to demolish the town and take the kid alive, then the BMs'll turn up after dark an' mop up any survivors."

Taggit was looking grim. "Not likely to be any survivors if they've got the werewolf. 'E'll be on the Quick like a dog on its favorite bone."

"Don' worry," said Skerridge gloomily. "I'll be back by the time they get 'ere an' I'll make sure I keep 'im occupied." He sighed heavily. "In fact, I'm ready t' bet Strood 'as already told 'im t' take me out, so if I'm not around, 'e'll come lookin' fer me anyway."

Taggit nodded. Werewolves could match a bogeyman

strength for strength and speed for speed. It would be a pretty even fight. He just hoped the bogeyman would win.

"Better be off, then," said Skerridge, cheerfully. "Time t' find Jonas. Dead or alive."

According to Seth, Jonas had died at the entrance to Dark's Mansion. So that was where Skerridge looked first.

He found nothing. No burned body. No Jonas. Dead or otherwise. He grinned savagely. Nin was right, somehow the boy had survived. Plus, Seth Carver had lied, which was interesting.

Skerridge got going again, heading in the direction of Hilfian, because if Jonas was alive, that was the way he would be traveling. Moving at sub-superspeed so that he was traveling fast, but not so fast the countryside was a blur, he soon found the boy standing on a hilltop and staring at the sky.

Jonas was watching a bank of dark cloud as it raced along the rim of the world and he was thinking. The problem was this. With each second that ticked by, disaster drew closer to Nin. But Jonas was more than a hundred miles away, and however fast he ran, he could never cover the ground in time to warn her. It might already be too late.

His nose twitched at the smell of scorched ozone as Skerridge popped into view.

"Found ya," the bogeyman said cheerfully, "still alive an' all, which'll please the kid no end."

Jonas ignored him and went on staring at the sky.

"Wassup?"

"Seth Carver is Ava Vispilio. He wants to be Nin because he wants her luck."

Skerridge drew in a sharp breath.

"I know how it will go," went on Jonas. "He'll try to win her confidence. He's already got a head start because of the whole glass lions thing. He probably caught up with her, maybe at Hilfian, maybe before. Maybe even saving her life or something on the way."

Skerridge cleared his throat noisily.

"Then he'll tell her that I'm dead, being gentle about it, of course, but inside he'll be relishing Nin's pain." Jonas clenched his fists, and deep in his eyes lightning flickered.

"Then he'll try and get her alone. He'll spin her some story. Something about the ring being a protection charm or whatever. And she'll believe him because he's Seth. And then she'll put it on."

Skerridge gulped.

"And then Nin will be trapped forever in some tiny corner of her own mind, watching helplessly while Vispilio kills and tortures his way through life, relying on her luck to save him from Strood." Jonas clenched his fists tighter. His gray eyes grew darker, storm cloud dark, and the lightning in their depths grew brighter.

"Look, yer upsettin' yerself. I'll . . ."

"I want to be angry," snarled Jonas, "because I need to be angry to do this." And then he tipped back his head and howled.

Skerridge backed off.

Far on the horizon the storm clouds wheeled in the sky, changing direction. They moved swiftly. They were so high up, they didn't have to avoid the Raw. And soon they were close enough for Jonas and Skerridge to hear them.

What they heard was a clamor of baying and howling mingled with the distant thunder. This was the sound of the Hounds as they tore across the sky, hunting for any Quick souls foolish enough not to run for cover.

But underneath the terrible baying there were voices that called and sobbed. These were the voices of the Quick souls that the Storm had swallowed. It had turned them into Hounds, but in each one a tiny shred of humanity was left, grieving over the life it had lost and would never have again.

And underneath the cries of pain there was another sound. The sound of one voice. The voice of the Storm.

Skerridge shivered, shrinking back into a huddle on the ground. The Land had many voices, and this was only one. But the Land was the greatest Fabulous of all, and it made him feel afraid and awed all in one big uncomfortable bundle.

Jonas blocked out the cold wind, the darkening sky, the hillside with the trees tossing their branches before the gale. He focused on that one voice, trying to hear what the Storm was saying. And what it was saying was this:

"DON'T. WANT. YOU."

"It won' work!" yelled Skerridge, over the thunder and the howling wind. "Ya was up there an' then yer escaped. An' once a Quick's escaped the Storm, it'll never 'ave 'im back."

"I don't want to go back," howled Jonas, "I want HELP!"

By now the sky was filled with boiling clouds. Lightning lanced toward the hillside and a tree exploded into crackling flames. Skerridge tried to scrunch up even smaller, just in case. This had nothing to do with him; it was between a Quick soul and the Land. Skerridge was just an innocent bystander.

"Without Nin, the Drift will die!" Jonas cried over another roll of thunder.

179

The wind whipped about him, nearly knocking him off his feet as he drew in a deep breath. He tried to hold in his head everything he needed to say. He filled himself with the need to get to Nin, to save her, so that she could stop Strood. And then he flung his arms wide, threw back his head, and let out the breath in a howl that matched the Storm. The answering blast of icy gale nearly flattened him.

"WHY? CARE?"

Jonas held in his head a picture of Strood's army, streaming over the Land like a golden tide. Then of the last trace of the Seven wiped from existence. The Raw exploding outward, ever outward, each swath joining with others until there was nothing left. And then of the Storm, blowing over the empty mist that sent tendrils up into the sky, growing higher, devouring even the clouds, even the dawn fires. Even the Storm.

And then, last, he brought Nin to life in his head. The girl who got away from Strood twice. The girl who got away from the Storm.

Thunder rolled across the sky, shaking the ground beneath Jonas's feet. Rain came down like knives, slashing the air. Lightning broke the sky, striking the earth right where he stood.

And when it went, he went with it.

Within moments the hillside was calm. The grass, flattened by the gale, stood up again. The trees ceased their thrashing and the sun came out. A squirrel bounced down the trunk of an elm and across the grass. It didn't get far because Skerridge had come over all peckish and felt he needed some fuel before he got going again.

As he munched, taking care not to eat the tail (which had a fur-to-meat ratio that made it not worth the effort), Skerridge watched the Storm race into the distance, heading for Hilfian. It was moving at high speed and, unlike Skerridge, could take a direct route. More than likely, it would beat him to Hilfian, even if he got lucky with the Raw.

He just hoped that would be fast enough.

23

FALLING

W ha's that?" Jibbit pointed to something in the sky, something that looked like a puff of smoke, only bird shaped.

"Land Magic," muttered Stanley. "Smoke 'awks sent ter keep watch. It means they know we're comin'." He was peering back through the tide of yellow-eyed faces loping along behind him, crammed shoulder to shoulder. Some of them had a singed look and there were less than there had been an hour earlier.

"Blimmin' Skerridge," he muttered.

The bogeyman had been raiding them, using his fire-breath to polish off those tiger-men unlucky enough to be traveling on the outer edges of the army. But Strood had allowed for heavy losses from their journey through the Heart and from attacks by Skerridge; it was why he had made such a vast army. So even after all that, the horde was still big enough to crush Hilfian several times over.

Jibbit had abandoned his perch on Hathor's helmet and was riding on the tiger-men. The troop was so tightly packed that he could move from spot to spot on the raft of furry bodies and keep an eye on Dunvice, who was commanding the first platoon while Stanley was off inspecting the others. Jibbit had a plan about hiding when they got to the fighting bit and so he wanted plenty of notice before they arrived. He didn't want to be too close to the werewolf-Grimm though, because Dunvice was in a bad mood and that made her unpredictable. Jibbit didn't like unpredictable. Especially not when he was so close to the gr . . . gr . . . flat thing the horde was walking on.

Dunvice had been in a fierce temper ever since the waterfall. Jibbit didn't blame her. She had lost the skinkin, and if the creature got to Ninevah Redstone before the army had a chance to take her alive, then Mr. Strood would not be pleased and Dunvice's chance of a pleasant death wasn't worth a faerie's pledge. She had been Strood's favorite, but right now she could feel herself falling from grace with every minute the skinkin got closer to its prey.

Jibbit wondered what the skinkin was up to right now. The thing was taking the same route as the army and some of the tiger-men claimed to have seen it. One of them even claimed to have eaten it, but had died before Dunvice could question it to find out if it was telling the truth. The fact that the tiger-man had died unmentionably in a torn-up-from-the-inside-out kind of way, as if something had got bored and taken a shortcut out of its innards, hinted that perhaps it had indeed been telling the truth. Either way, the incident had not improved Dunvice's temper one bit.

Ahead, trees rose in deep green and shadowy gray against the afternoon sunlight. The tiger-men covered the ground fast, racing on toward the woodland with Dunvice in the front row and Jibbit riding the tide like a natural-born surfer.

Light flicked into shadowy gloom as they entered the wood, but it didn't slow the tiger-men down as they jumped easily over dips and hollows and fallen branches. They were silent save for the steady hiss of their breath, and the shadows were filled with the yellow glint of their eyes. As Jibbit's section drew close, he got ready, and when the time was right, just as they were entering the wood, he jumped. For a moment he was in the air, and then he felt bark scrape under his stony paws and grabbed.

Dangling from the branch while the platoon raced on below him, Jibbit was just getting a better grip when something said "Boo" ever so gently in his ear.

Jibbit hooted.

"No need ter carry on," said Skerridge indignantly. "I was only bein' friendly. Now shut it or I'll chew yer up and spit yer out."

Jibbit glared at him. "I'm a stone," he snapped. "Yoo don't chew stones."

Skerridge bared a row of six-inch-long jagged yellow teeth that looked like they could make gravel out of a mountain, and winked. "Wanna try?"

The whole of the first troop was under the trees by now. Jibbit could hear Dunvice shouting orders to the army, telling them to gather inside the wood, so that the trees shielded them from any watching eyes.

Skerridge drew in a deep breath and a chill crept up Jibbit's spine. He knew about bogeymen.

"Erm," he asked apologetically, "doo yoo mind if I shouts a warning?"

For answer, Skerridge breathed out.

The woods ignited. Trees transformed into burning pillars and bushes spat fire. The tiger-men inside the wood didn't have time to scream, they were instant ash.

On the town-side edge of the wood, where she had been taking a careful look at the way ahead, Dunvice sprang for safety. She barely made it and had to roll on the ground to put her armor out.

Jibbit's tree went up like a bomb. Fortunately for him, he was pretty much fireproof. Unfortunately for him, with the tree gone there was nothing to stop him from falling all the way down to the gr . . .

By the time Stanley got there it was all over. Skerridge was long gone, leaving the spreading fire to do his work for him. The beautiful wood was just so much ash. So was most of the platoon.

"Why did ya stop?" he roared at Dunvice. "Why 'ang about in a wood wiv a bogeyman on the warparf? Tha's anovver platoon gone! What wiv everyfin', we've ended up wiv less than 'alf the troops left!"

Dunvice didn't have an answer. It had been a mistake, was all. Her leather armor was blackened with smoke and ash, and she had lost a lot of her hair. There were burns on her face and hands, too, and in the midst of all the raw flesh and dirt, her eyes glowed like yellow suns. She snarled at him and it was so ANIMAL that Stanley backed off.

"No wonder yer farver died o' fright," he snapped irritably, "when yer was little more'n a blood-curdlin' glow in yer muvver's eyes." Then he stomped away to get the remaining platoons in order.

Jibbit was hooting with panic. He had been hooting for so long he had run out of voice and his beak just made soundless gropings at the air. He was lying on his back, wings spread, staring desperately at the sky and shaking.

The reason he was staring at the sky was so as not

to see what he was lying on. It was lumpy, covered in ash, and stretched away from him in all directions with absolutely no hint of below. A tear leaked from Jibbit's eyes and his paws clawed at the air helplessly.

There was a sound to the left of him and he turned his head, sensing danger. Terror crept over him like a gray shadow, but it wasn't his personal terror, it was something external. He could feel its chill wash over his stony surface, like icy water that had never known the sun. He stopped hooting, because even hooting was not enough for a feeling this alone, this hopeless.

And then, out of the cinders of the wood, came the skinkin. It loped on, through the shadows that seemed to get darker where it passed, its eyeholes searching for its prey. Jibbit tensed as every bound brought it closer. Its paws touched him for a fleeting moment as it landed on his middle and leapt on again. And then it was gone, taking the fear and the shadows with it.

Jibbit lay still until someone said, "Oy, get yer knobbly bum over 'ere an' get in line wiv the rest of 'em."

Jibbit squinted up at Stanley, the goblin-Grimm's bulk outlined against the sky like a minimountain, then flip-flopped onto his front and considered his position. The gr . . . gr . . . ground was still there and it was bad. But other things, things with eyeholes full of death, for example, were worse. As it turned out, ground was manageable. Besides, he needn't stay on it for long.

He spotted something and began to climb.

"Galig's teef," muttered Stanley. "Now I'm a blimmin' jungle gym!"

Strood's army charged on. Rather than cross the charred bones of their companions, they were going to double-back along the foot of the hills to the lower

slopes where they could climb without too much diffi-
culty, and come at the town from over the ridge. Riding
on Stanley's helmet, Jibbit was still looking out for a
place to hide, but nothing useful appeared. As he gazed
desperately around him, a shadow swept across the
scene. Almost as one, the army looked up.

Storm clouds were racing high above their heads
in a torrent of purple-gray, and deep inside the boiling
mass, lightning flickered. A thunderclap broke right over
them and its bone-shaking rumble made the tiger-men
flinch and whine. "Gabriel Hounds!" yelled Stanley to
Dunvice. Only the Quick needed to fear the Storm, but
although the tiger-men had been fashioned from crowsmorte, they were Quick in their blood and knew instinctively that the Storm meant danger. The horde faltered,
but hung together, eerie eyes gleaming in the half-light.
The Storm was bothering them, but it wasn't something
they could attack and that made them angry.

"Don't worry," yelled Dunvice, her voice almost
swallowed up in another crack of thunder, "it won't be a
problem. The way I see it, tiger-men are like us Grimm.
They may be part Quick, but they don't have souls and
that's what the Storm is after. I'm more worried about
the rain."

Stanley had to agree. The tiger-men almost certainly wouldn't like rain. He looked up anxiously, but
he needn't have worried. The Storm was already moving on, racing over the hill toward the town as if it had
a purpose.

24

A QUICK HEART

Taggit had told Nin to keep out of the battle by hiding in the cellar under the long bank of mud huts that served as a general store, where the other children and their mothers had already taken shelter. She argued vigorously, but in the end had to give in. Even so, instead of going straight there, she went to look for Seth first.

She knew she should tell Hen or Hilary, but they would have said no, so she just called out, "Going to find Seth, won't be long," as she hurried past a distracted-looking Doctor Mel.

Nin wanted to talk to Seth because she felt embarrassed about not believing him even when he obviously thought he was right. It must have been pretty nasty, finding a body like that and thinking it was Jonas, so she wanted to make sure he was okay. She was also kind of curious about the present.

She found him in an upstairs room above the main hall. The stairs she had climbed to the narrow landing were really just a ladder of bound branches, and the room, one of two, was small and low-roofed with a door of closely woven twigs. In it was a rough table pushed against the wall, and a bench.

Seth was sitting on a seat built into the small window, studying the faerie spindle closely. Something glimmered on the sill next to him, casting a fiery light. He looked up.

"Hello, Nin," he said. "I've been waiting for you."

"What's that?" Nin stared at the square of flickering color.

Seth chuckled. "It's cloth of fire." He looked cheerful, if a little grubby, and Nin noticed that he wasn't wearing his traveling boots. Maybe he thought they'd get ruined while he dug in the pits.

She came over to sit next to him on the window seat, picking up the cloth of fire from the sill. It was so bright she expected it to be hot, but it wasn't. Just warm and with a texture like liquid silk that made her fingers tingle.

"It's yours," said Seth. "Enjoy it while you have the chance."

Nin looked up at him.

"It's the day of reckoning, girl. You know that." He smiled at her, his green eyes looking straight into hers. "Strood could still win the battle. Don't kid yourself that it's a done deal in your favor."

With a sigh, Nin glanced away from him, her eyes turning to the window. It was filled with greenish glass, the first real window she had seen in the Drift. Sunlight fell into the room through its bubbly and uneven surface, but on the horizon she could see a line of dark cloud.

"I know," she said. "But I have to think we have a chance or what would be the point? Look, I've still got this." She pushed back her sleeve to show Seth the shadow spell.

Seth put out a finger and touched it. "You know, for it to have lasted so many decades it must have its own center of energy, or be connected to something living. Like how the sorcerer's spells are fed by the Quick. Or like that memory pearl of yours. That's not a spell as such, but it's the same sort of thing. Its magic stays alive as long as you do, because the memories are a tiny part of you, even though they belonged to other people."

Nin frowned, turning over his words. And then, suddenly, something vital fell into place.

"It's not a spell to *find* Simeon Dark," she said, excitement making her breathless. "It IS Simeon Dark! Well, sort of . . ." She paused, fitting it together in her head. "Strood told Skerridge that for Dark to be safe from the plague he had to be so well hidden that even Dark doesn't know where he is. Like he's already dead and gone, just a memory in people's heads. So his spell disguised him and then took away his true identity." She gazed at the ribbon in astonishment. "I think the ribbon is like his memory of himself all locked up, waiting to be released."

"Hmm, clever," said Seth. He looked thoughtful. "The spell would have to make sure he still had a memory of some sort, though. It couldn't wipe out everything, or Dark's new persona would really stand out. Dark would have gone into hiding in the last few days of the Seven, sometime *after* the Final Gathering had failed."

Nin nodded. "So a new person popping up who could *only* remember back as far as those last few days would be a bit obvious?"

"Uh-huh. So maybe the spell let his new shape remember some key things, but made him see them from a different angle. Even in his new shape Simeon would remember the Final Gathering, because he was there, but he'd remember it from outside, as if he were someone else watching and not taking part."

Seth's eyes glinted as he looked at the shadow spell, shifting nervously under his gaze as if it sensed what he was thinking. It tightened its grip on Nin's arm. She thought she heard it hiss, but was too intent on following the idea to wonder why. Or to notice that Seth used Dark's first name. Almost like he had known the sorcerer personally. Seth shot her a glance, aware of his slip, but she didn't see that either.

"Sure, if he was hidden as a Fabulous or Grimm that would work," she said. "It would be weird if he didn't remember the Final Gathering 'cos, according to Skerridge, practically every Fabulous left alive was there, watching. He and Taggit were. But if Dark was disguised as a Quick, it would be the other way around and *remembering* the Gathering would be the strange thing. Most Quick wouldn't be that old. Hen's pretty ancient and even she can only just remember it." She frowned. "Do you think Dark could be pretending to be a woman?"

"Wouldn't put it past him." Seth laughed. "But he's a sorcerer, so I don't buy all those stories about him hiding as a Quick . . . unless it's a very powerful Quick, of course. He'd want to be somewhere he can control people." A fleeting expression crossed his face. Realization.

Nin nodded. "You mean, like, if he can't use magic because he doesn't know he's a sorcerer, then he'll want some other form of power?"

"Something like that." Seth waved a hand, dismissing the subject. "Anyway, now that you're here, do you want your present?"

"I thought the cloth of fire was it?"

Outside, the line of cloud was eating up the sky,

covering the Land with shadow as it raced on toward the hills on the edge of the town. Lightning glimmered in its depths.

Seth laughed. "Oh no. The cloth is just a pretty nothing. This is serious." The laughter faded out of his eyes and he leaned close, then glanced away, as if embarrassed by what he was going to say. Nin felt a flush touch her cheeks.

"Thing is," he went on after a moment. "I'm not a brave type, not really." Nin opened her mouth to disagree hotly. After all, he had jumped off the tower with her.

He shushed her with a touch of his hand. "I'm not, believe me. So when I find devices to sell, I keep some of them back. Some of them useful, like the boots, and some other stuff."

"You mean like weapons?"

He nodded. "It's a dangerous world out there! But also things to protect, to keep me safe or to warn me about danger. Only, right now I know that it's not just me in danger. It's not just you either. It's the Land. Everything. And the key to solving it all is you."

"I know people think that." She sighed. "But . . ."

"It's not guaranteed. Like I said before, Strood could win. But if anyone in the world can undo him somehow, it's you. So, what I want to give you is this . . . a protective charm, see?" He pulled one of the rings from his finger. It was a thin strip of gold, swirled about with symbols that made Nin's eyes smart to look at them.

The darkness was really gathering now as the boiling clouds stole the light, racing over the hill. Seth's face was cast in shadow, but his eyes were still bright, still fixed on Nin. Outside she heard a shout of alarm as people dropped what they were doing and ran for cover. She jumped as lightning flickered, closer now. Trees began to dip and sway.

Seth held out the ring. "Here, take it and wear it. You'll hardly even notice it's there."

Nin's head was swimming slightly and the rumble of thunder seemed like something she could feel in her bones. The stinging had gone from her eyes and the gold band gleamed in Seth's hands, calling to her. Before she knew it she had reached out a hand to touch it, then drew back. She pulled her eyes away to look at Seth. "You need it more than me, so you should keep it. I'm supposed to be lucky."

"Please, Nin." Seth put his head close to hers. "I want to do something to help. Maybe getting this ring is part of your luck, did you think of that?" He smiled into her eyes. "Besides, I want you to be safe."

Nin felt her face redden and glanced away, her gaze instantly caught by the ring, which shone now like fire. Burning in her head. Persuading.

"Come on." Seth took her hand and turned it over. "This finger I think."

He slipped it on.

Now the thunder was close enough to shake the town hall, but Nin didn't hear it. Her world was focused on the ring. As Seth pushed it over her knuckle it seemed to CHANGE, its intricate design thinning to a simple twist of silver and one blue stone. And in that moment . . .

In that moment, she knew what she had done. "It changes each time," Nemus Sturdy had told her once, "changes to match the soul it's captured."

HELP ME! she screamed, but no sound came out. She would have pulled her hand away, but he was holding it too tightly. Not Seth. Ava Vispilio.

And then it wasn't her hand anymore.

When lightning hit the ground just outside the town hall, those Quick who hadn't already fled indoors, dove for cover. Even the Grimm took shelter, though the Storm couldn't hurt them. Everything stopped, but only for a while. They all knew it would pass soon. And it had better. The enemy was on its way and there was work to do.

In the dazzle of the lightning bolt a figure appeared, a shape that staggered and fell to its knees in the grass while the heavens opened and rain lashed down in a torrent. Thunder boomed and there was more dazzle, but farther away. For a few seconds the rain was like a wall of water, then a curtain that swayed and lifted around the dark shape, now struggling to its feet and lurching across the grass. Then, as suddenly as it had come, the rain lifted and the dark shape was Jonas, running toward the town hall, his face white and his eyes full of weird light.

As he burst in through the door, Doctor Mel looked up, startled, her arms full of blankets. "Where's Nin?" gasped Jonas. "Please!"

"Erm . . . upstairs, I think," said Mel. "Are you Jonas? Don't worry, she's fine. She's with Seth."

Jonas ran for the ladder. At the top, he burst into the nearest room.

Seth was there all right, but he was no danger anymore. The boy was lying on the floor in a spreading pool of blood. Vispilio's first act in his new body had been to cut the throat of his old one. If the real Seth had been left alive to regain control of himself, he might have told them things about Vispilio that Vispilio didn't want them to know.

There was no sign of Nin.

As Jonas turned to go his eye caught movement through the greenish glass of the window. It looked as if the top of the hills outside the town had come alive and was stirring like a restless beast. For a moment it didn't make sense but then he realized what it was—the heave and surge of many jostling bodies cresting the rise and gathering there. Metal glinted in the afternoon sun. Lots of metal.

Leaving the room, Jonas stood at the top of the ladder and thought for a moment. He knew he was on his own. No use looking to the others for help finding Nin, they had a battle to fight.

Leaving Seth's body where it lay, Jonas went back to the ground floor. Here the main room was quiet, laid out with beds and bandages and potions, waiting for its first casualty to arrive. Those few selected to act as nurses were outside, standing in the sun with their hands shading their eyes, watching the hills. A sense of breathless tension hung over everything.

Tilting his head, Jonas sniffed the air, searching for any trace of Nin.

25

BEYOND TERROR

Nin was in the cellar, retrieving the pack that Seth had left there and checking through the leftover magical artifacts, looking for anything useful to steal. Or rather, her body was. Her mind was cowering somewhere inside, still screaming with shock.

She was beyond terror. There were no words for what it felt like to watch helplessly as your own hands cut someone else's throat, to hear your brain think someone else's thoughts. To understand that your body was going on with someone else's life as if you weren't there. As if you were nothing, not even a blip on the radar.

She couldn't scream or fight or even cry because none of those things were in her control now. Her view of the world was slightly distorted, like looking through thick glass, but still there. She could hear, too, though the sounds were tinny and distant. But that was all. Her sense of touch had gone completely, and if she tried to move, she could feel the instruction leave her mind, but it went nowhere. Her body carried on doing something different, operating to HIS commands. She was absolutely powerless.

And raging at herself. How could she have been so deceived by lies and charm? How could she not have *seen* what Seth really was?

Trying to calm herself, Nin took the mental equivalent of deep breaths. She pushed the image of Seth from her mind, the real Seth, bleeding and dying. It was too horrible to deal with right now, and if she remembered it again she would start screaming and never stop.

You can't feel panic, she told herself firmly, *because panic is just chemicals and things in your body and you don't have one of those right now.*

It didn't work. She might not have the right chemicals for real panic, but her mind was doing a pretty good impersonation. To do something, anything rather than just howl silently, she watched what Vispilio was doing.

The cellar was lit only by the thing in the corner, the device wrapped in thick cloth that couldn't hide the glow coming from inside. By its golden light, Vispilio had found some amulets and rings to take and was stuffing them into a small bag, already half full of the magical jewelry he had removed from Seth's body. Although the glowing thing in the corner was obviously powerful, he was ignoring it, and Nin wondered briefly what the thing did, how much power it really held.

It was clear the device unnerved him and Nin realized that she could feel his fear of it. Focusing hard, she found she could sense Vispilio's ideas and emotions. They were sharp, full of edges and harsh, cruel colors. She tried to pick up what he was going to do next. It wasn't hard. She was no threat and he didn't care what she found out from him because she could do nothing with the knowledge.

When he had finished here he was going to leave before the fighting got started. She guessed the traveling boots must be in his pack, so he would use those to get away quickly. As to where he was going . . .

In his head Nin could sense his burning desire to find Simeon Dark. The feeling connected to the desire was one of safety, and suddenly she knew that when he found the sorcerer he was going to steal him. She remembered from stories of the Final Gathering that Vispilio was said to be more powerful than Dark, though only by a little, so he must be counting on the magic in his spell being strong enough to let him take over Dark's body in the same way that he took over Quick.

It won't work, snapped Nin, unheard. She deliberately whipped up her anger. It felt better than despair.

If Strood's right and it's all about knowing who Dark is, she went on, *then as soon as you find him you'll know it's him, and his spell will break and he'll be back. And a REAL sorcerer has got to be better than your stupid old spell. Besides, you need Quick because you need their life to live on, and even if Dark is disguised as a Quick, that's all it is. A disguise. What are you going to do about that, huh?*

She got no answer, but there was something in the jumble of his mind about if he was in Dark, who was a sorcerer, then he'd BE a sorcerer again and could use Dark's magic to make everything all right. And then she understood.

Vispilio wanted his power back. And he wanted it so badly he was prepared to overlook holes in his plan you could drive a train through just so that he could fool himself into thinking it was possible. Even if a part of him knew it wouldn't work, he had to try. He would do anything, kill anyone, risk everything just to be a sorcerer again.

He even had an idea about where to find Dark. He'd already told Nin half of it.

Dark was a sorcerer, and if he was going to live in disguise, then he wouldn't settle for just any old disguise. Vispilio was convinced that Dark would be hidden in some form that meant he could wield power.

Real power.

Power over life and death. The power to kill, to turn the world on its head if he felt like it.

Strood.

The surges of feeling and image that she was picking up from Vispilio told her the story. Vispilio thought that Dark had already used his sorcerer power long ago to undo the real Strood, or to hold him captive somehow. Then Dark had disguised himself as Strood and taken his place. After all, in the modern-day Drift, Strood was even more powerful than the Fabulous.

Nin gasped, struggling with the idea. It would mean that far from coming back and helping her save the Seven and the Drift, it was Dark who was killing them in the first place.

Suddenly Vispilio raised his head and stared into a corner of the cellar, the opposite one to that occupied by the shining thing. On that side of the room it was still dark and Nin got the feeling that something had just arrived and was crouched there. Whatever it was, it sent a chill into Nin's captive mind. Vispilio's eyes, her eyes, couldn't see it in the shadows but they could both feel it, watching. And *it* could feel *her*.

It's looking for me, thought Nin, horrified.

Vispilio frowned. "Skinkin," he whispered out loud, and Nin felt his thoughts narrow, focusing, ready to run if he needed to. She also picked up something else. According to Vispilio, the thing, the skinkin or whatever he had called it, seemed puzzled.

It's looking for me, Nin thought, *and it thinks it's*

found me, but I'm not ME right now so it's not sure. It can't see me properly because my mind is hidden behind Vispilio's.

The shadows shifted and the thing moved, flicking toward the bright hole in the ceiling that was the open trapdoor. Nin caught a glimpse of something leaping up into the room above, something that looked like a long-legged hare but . . . too thin. Too much bone.

Vispilio relaxed, ran a wary eye over the cellar, then turned back to stashing the bag of jewelry safely in his pack.

Nin reeled with shock yet again. As he scanned the scene, Vispilio's eyes had passed over something lying on the floor. A small, lumpy man-shape. Jik. Dead.

WHAT HAVE YOU DONE TO HIM! screamed Nin, fury burning through her. And this time Vispilio paused. She felt him smile.

"I'm killing him," said Vispilio, speaking out loud. To Nin, his voice sounded distorted and small, as if she was on the end of a bad telephone line.

"Remember that cloth of fire?" he went on. "That cloth is the essence of the mudman. I spun it out of his body, like the bogeyman spun your mother's memory of you right out of her head. Technically the mud-rat's not dead yet, but his body can't exist without his essence, nor his essence without his body. So in a few hours that lump of mud will crumble and the cloth of fire will fade and go out, unless they are joined back together. I could save him. If I felt like it. But I won't."

I HATE YOU, screamed Nin again, *HATE YOU!*

Vispilio laughed, and as he did, through the trapdoor the skinkin had just left by, someone else dropped into the cellar.

* * *

Startled, Nin spun around. Seeing Jonas land crouched and ready at the foot of the ladder, she left the pack and pulled a knife from her belt.

Jonas leapt at her and she sprang to the left, dodging him and heading for the ladder. She made it up several rungs before he recovered and came after her. Grabbing at her jeans he pulled her down again, almost ripping her back pocket off.

A bright square of color slithered from under his fingers. Unnoticed, Jik's essence fluttered to the floor, drifting beneath the table. It lay there, its glow lost in the golden light of the unknown device.

Nin kicked and struggled, but Jonas held on, twisting her to pin her knife arm against the ladder so that he could focus on the other hand, the one with the ring. He wrenched Nin's fist open, raising welts on her palm as he dug under her fingers to pull them out. On the third finger was a silver band with one blue stone in it. He seized it and pulled.

Nin screamed with rage as she tried to yank her hand free, and the ring flew off, hit the edge of the ladder, and skittered away. Half expecting Nin to collapse, Jonas loosened his grip and smiled with relief.

He was celebrating too soon. There was always a moment, a couple of seconds, before Vispilio lost control of the body he was in.

Nin twisted sharply, jabbed Jonas hard and ran, heading for the ring. A look of shock on his face, Jonas staggered and fell to one knee. He forced himself up and got Nin in a tackle that brought her crashing to the floor.

She thrashed for a moment, biting and clawing, then suddenly the tension went out of her and she stopped.

"Nin?" Jonas tried to move, but pain shot through

his back and chest, and his head spun. There was something sticky on his hands.

Nin looked up.

"I stabbed you!" she gasped, her face white with
fear.

Jonas struggled to sit. The stickiness was all over
him, coming from a wound in his side. Nin crawled over
to him, getting blood on her hands and knees. "Help!"
she shouted, trying to dam the flow with her hands.
"SOMEONE HELP!"

"They're outside." Jonas was growing pale as more
and more blood leaked from between their combined
fingers.

"I'll get Doctor Mel." Nin scrambled up, her head
spinning. "Don't die, Jonas, please don't die!"

She ran for the ladder and scrambled up it, leaving
Jonas alone in the cellar.

Upstairs, Nin headed for the door, her heart hammering frantically as she yelled for Doctor Mel. Part of
her registered how silent the town seemed with everyone gone to the battlefield, how her voice rang on the
waiting air.

Hen and Hilary were further away, keeping watch
on the edge of town, but Doctor Mel had stayed near
their makeshift hospital. Hearing Nin's call, she turned
and hurried inside.

"No time to explain," Nin gasped. "In the cellar.
Jonas. Stabbed."

Mel nodded and snatched up bandages. "Hot water,"
she said, "and bring a bowl."

Nin darted toward the small kitchen room, off to the
side of the main one, where a fire kept two cauldrons of
water bubbling.

Halfway down the ladder, a gleam caught Mel's eye,

a single shaft of light more focused and silver than the glow of the unknown device and coming from a spot over by the wall. Jonas was lying on the floor, silent and unmoving, so she stepped off the ladder and toward him. But the gleam shone out again like a lighthouse beacon and something about it went straight into Mel's head, bypassing thought. Calling to her.

She changed direction and went to look. The gleam was coming from a ring that lay abandoned on the floor. Mel leaned down to pick it up.

She put it on.

Grabbing a bowl from the stack on the table, Nin was about to fill it with boiling water when something shifted in the darkness between the door and the cupboard next to it. The skinkin. She felt it see her, recognize her. This time there was no confusion. It had found its prey.

Nin had picked up enough from Vispilio's mind to know that the skinkin was unstoppable, that was its magic. It was made to kill its victim, so kill its victim was what would do. And that meant Ninevah Redstone.

Dropping the bowl, she darted back out of the kitchen into the main hall, where she paused. Her instinct was to head for Jonas and Mel, but they couldn't help her, and Mel needed to be free to tend to Jonas. So she turned to the door outside, intending to run to Hen. Hen would know what to do. Her hesitation was a mistake.

Out of the corner of her eye she saw the shadows shift. It was amazing how many shadows there were in a day-lit room. Under the beds, in corners, behind shelves or cupboards. She froze, her heart thudding and her skin chilled and clammy. Was that a movement, over to the left of the door? She snapped her head around and saw . . . what? The pattern of dark and light resolved itself into the dips and hollows of a catlike face, with just sockets for eyes, watching her.

Another shift of light and it was gone.

Outside, Nin thought, *it went outside and it's waiting for me to come out so it can get me before I can find Hen.*

As silently as she could, Nin turned and ran to the ladder. She climbed, trying not to fumble the rungs with her trembling hands. At the top, she hurried toward the second ladder at the end of the corridor, the one that led to the roof. From there she could get across the rope bridge to the bell tower and then down the tower into the street, bypassing the skinkin while it watched the main entrance.

Icy with terror and shaking so badly she could barely hold the rungs, Nin made it to the top of the second ladder. Here was a small square room with a door out to the roof. Stumbling through, she felt air on her face and dragged in a breath.

In the last hour she had been a helpless prisoner in her own body and an unwilling accomplice in murder; she had seen one friend lying dead and had stabbed another; and now she was being hunted by a relentless assassin. It was more than a Quick mind could cope with and the world was spinning about her as her body began to shut down from shock and exhaustion.

And then, rolling in from the hillside that overlooked the town, Nin heard a distant roar. It sounded like thunder, but she knew it wasn't. It was the shout of many voices raised in a cry that shook the air. There was no help coming any time soon. The battle had begun and Nin was on her own. Blackness swarmed in from the edges of her vision.

I'm passing out, she thought from somewhere far

away in her head. She crashed to the roof floor and lay there, senseless.

It was the best thing she could have done.

Two floors below, crouching in the shadows of a barrel just outside the town hall door, the skinkin hissed as Nin's consciousness winked out. It had been about to give up waiting and go after her, but it needed her consciousness to track her down. Asleep, it was as if she had vanished.

It settled where it was for now. Sooner or later its prey would wake up. Then it would find her easily enough.

26

ANGEL

Even in the cellar, Jonas heard an echo of the battle cry that shook both air and ground. He sat up. The pain had subsided a little and the bleeding had slowed, thanks to the bandages that Doctor Mel had dropped. Once she had gone, Jonas had managed to reach the fallen dressings and had packed some of them over the wound, binding them tight with the others. "It's begun," he murmured.

Although Jonas hadn't been in Hilfian to hear the reports from Skerridge's spying trips, the Storm had carried him over Strood's army and he had looked down and seen them. So he knew that the townsfolk were outnumbered. It would be little short of a miracle if they made it to nightfall, let alone tomorrow.

His eyes fell upon the thing in the corner. The device wrapped in roll after roll of material, but still glowing. He watched it for a moment. Even Vispilio had left it alone. It radiated power so fiercely that Jonas was ready to bet no one wanted to touch it. But power on that scale was exactly what they needed. He swallowed hard, then moved toward it, grabbed one end of the wrapping, and pulled. Light beamed fiercely and the material disintegrated into ash under his touch, revealing at last what lay beneath.

It was a sword, its blade burning silver white, with rubies at the hilt. The symbol etched on its shining surface was the outline of a bear on its hind legs, its great arms outspread as if to embrace or attack.

"The sign of King Galig of Old Celidon!" murmured Jonas, his face full of wonder. "This is Galig's Sword?" He leaned forward to grasp the hilt.

As soon as his hand touched it he felt the world shake and twist and heard a sound like tearing metal. Light burned his eyes as he doubled up trying to hide his face from the glare. A crack ran across the dry earth of the floor and up the walls, but he held on to the sword as tightly as he could. If there was any chance that whatever was coming might tip the balance in their favor, then he had to risk being burned up in the process.

Forcing himself to look up, Jonas saw a man striding toward him. He was silver-haired and clad in a blue surcoat over bright chain mail. At once, the shaking stopped and there was only the man, standing, surrounded by brilliance, studying him. His arms were crossed and Jonas got the feeling that he was waiting.

Still clasping the sword, Jonas got painfully to his feet. As he rose, he staggered slightly and winced.

"Are you . . . King Galig?"

"I am the shade of Galig, King of Celidon," said the man. He looked sternly at Jonas. "I am the last part of his magic, which dwells in the sword that you are holding now. Something in your heart has called to me, Quick boy. Tell me what it is. But be warned, if it is not enough to have summoned me in good cause, I will kill you."

"There's a battle." Spots of color showed on Jonas's

pale cheeks. "The end of it may mean the difference between life and death for the Land."

Golden eyes watched him, measuring his words. Galig didn't look that impressed. Jonas had no doubt that, shade or not, this magic could wreak death in a moment if it chose.

"All right," said Jonas, reassessing the situation, "the truth? If we fail it will mean the difference between life and death for . . . for one I care about. Nin might save the Land, true, but that's not what counts to me. What counts to me is simple. The world is a better place with her in it."

Galig leaned toward him. He smiled a slow smile that bared white teeth shaped to points. His look was so fierce it made Jonas's skin prickle.

"Now I hear you! And my answer is this. I see that you are injured and weak, but if you want to fight, let me in and I will give you and your army all the strength I have until the sun goes down. Trust me, the magic I give will endure for one glorious battle only. Just one. Then even this last rag of a great king will be done."

Jonas opened his mouth to answer, but Galig raised a hand. "First, be warned. While I am in control, you will be a helpless passenger, unable to act until I leave you again." He saw the look on Jonas's face and smiled. "Don't worry, in spirit you will still be there with your friends. You will see the sights and suffer the hurts of battle with me as I fight. It will be hard on you, though, I can take a lot of pain and you must bear it all."

Jonas smiled back. "I survived the Storm Hounds, I'll survive you. I'll let you in. I'm strong."

Galig laughed and the sound rang around the room. "So I see! Are you sure you're just a Quick? Now, be ready."

The shade moved forward, stepping into Jonas so that the form of the dead Sorcerer-King merged with that of the fourteen-year-old boy with a stab wound in his side. Jonas cried out as his shape twisted and stretched, growing taller and broader. He felt the power coursing through him, mending, improving, making him STRONG.

Galig bent Jonas's arms and flexed his fingers. And then he went to join the fight.

In the main hall Hen and Hilary stared in open-mouthed astonishment as Jonas strode past. He didn't acknowledge them, or even glance their way. He looked like some kind of avenging angel, walking in a halo of light and clasping a sword rimmed with fire nearly as bright as the fire in his eyes.

"Well," said Hilary, "somebody's done a deal with Old Celidon!" She ran over to the cellar and looked in. Sure enough it was dark. The wrapped-up thing in the corner that nobody wanted to look at was gone.

Hen peered over her shoulder and smiled. "He had the guts to do what no one else dared to, eh. He always was a brave boy."

"What's that?" Hilary pointed into the cellar.

The darkness wasn't complete. Now the main source of light was gone, a glow, the color of dying embers, shone faintly. It reminded Hilary of Jik's eyes. "Jik?"

She climbed down carefully, picking her way by the light that came in from above. Groping under a table for the glow, she pulled out a square of cloth. It lay on her palm, its reds and golds melting together, flickering like the flames they came from.

"Faeries used to make cloth of fancy from the essence of a Quick," whispered Senta's Spell thoughtfully in her

head. *"They spun out the Quick's soul and left a shell that lived on for a short while till it died of emptiness. That is not Quick, but it's more than just fire too. Brighter, more alive..."*

Hilary glanced at Hen, who had followed her down. The old woman's face was creased with concern. She understood magic as well as any Fabulous.

With Hilary holding up the cloth like a flag of light, they could just make out a lumpy, man-shaped patch of darkness. It looked like what it was. Dried old mud. They could see the empty holes of Jik's eyes and the thin crack running at an angle across his chest, deeper and wider in the middle. "How do I make this right?" Hilary whispered, kneeling beside him.

"You have to get the fire back inside," said Hen firmly. "Magic will do the rest; it has its own way."

Hilary thought for a moment. Then she folded the shimmering square over and over until it was a tight wedge and poked it into the crack in Jik's chest where it was widest. The cloth went in like a dream, slipping from her fingers and soaking into the earthy body. There was a fiery glow that faded, disappearing inside.

It seemed like forever while they waited.

At last, a spark glimmered in Jik's eyes. It brightened steadily. And then it wasn't a spark anymore, but a flame.

It wasn't long before he was strong enough to follow Jonas into battle.

27

BATTLE

As they crested the rise, Strood's army saw the enemy for the first time. Stanley shouted the order to stop. He wanted to make sure they were all together and ready for the charge. The horde came on, rank after rank gathering on the hill at his back, roaring and hissing with pent-up bloodlust.

Thoughtfully, Stanley studied the opposition.

The townsfolk of Hilfian were assembled in the fields in front of and below Strood's army. More than half of them were Quick, Stanley noted, but not much more. A lot of Grimm had made their way to Hilfian too. Goblin-Grimm, mainly, and goblin-Grimm were known for their toughness. They were doing a good job of looking menacing, shaking their weapons, some of them even roaring back, their deep growls rumbling over the tiger-men's shrieking. And the two great, shaggy Grimm at the back of the townsfolk army, both of them the color of old chestnuts, were probably half werebear. They'd be slow but horribly strong. And relentless too. Werebear-Grimm would fight to their last breath.

All the town's Grimm clutched spiked balls on

chains, short swords, and axes, but the Quick were armed with the most unlikely bunch of weapons Stanley had ever seen. Pickaxes and kitchen knives bristled from every angle, scythes and long-tined forks stuck out at random.

From the top of Stanley's helmet, Jibbit leaned down and pointed a stubby claw. "Ooo look, they got m-m-magic," he said, hooting nervously.

"Get a grip," muttered Stanley, sighing at the scraping of claws on his helmet as the gargoyle took him seriously. The creature was right though. Some of the Quick were clutching magical devices, mainly wands or staffs. "Not many though," he said. "Too few to make a real difference."

His eye was caught by Taggit standing alongside a couple of other true goblins, all glaring hideously up at Stanley and his hordes, their yellow eyes narrowing as they picked out a target worthy of their attention. Next, Stanley spotted a slim fellow with skin like black velvet and yellow-green eyes who just had to be a werecat. The mudman was nowhere to be seen and neither was Bogeyman Skerridge. Stanley gazed along the stretch of the hill to the east, where the slopes were steeper and higher. There in the distance, beyond the farthest reaches of his milling army, he could make out a flaming tree and a long burnt scar in the green of the hilltop. It looked like Lord Grayghast was already at work keeping the bogeyman busy. A werewolf was easily a match for a bogeyman in strength and speed. Skerridge's main advantage would be his firebreath, if he could stand still long enough to use it. Grayghast's would be his endurance, his talons, and his sheer savagery. It would be a fair fight and Stanley just had to hope the werewolf would come out on top.

Turning back to 'the horde, Stanley inspected the banked-up flood of fangs and needle claws, of eerie purple eyes glowing scarlet with hunger for the kill. They covered this stretch of hill, surging restlessly against the minimountain that was Hathor, the giant-Grimm. Their lithe, steel-strong bodies flexed and flowed everywhere around the fixed rocks of the armor-clad Grimm guards and the two huge granite-faced Fabulous goblins.

Next, Stanley looked up at the sky. It was late afternoon, and even if by some miracle the townsfolk army lived to see sundown, they wouldn't see it rise again the next day. Come nightfall, Strood's bogeymen would be along to burn whatever was left to the ground.

The CO allowed his insides to unknot a little. The battle wasn't going to be quite the pushover he had hoped for, but in the end victory was sure to be theirs on numbers alone.

"Now!" Dunvice hissed in his ear, making him jump.

Clearing his throat, Stanley raised an arm. Seeing the move, the tiger-men stopped surging and tensed, ready to run. Eyes gleamed. Muscles coiled like gathered springs.

Watching them from the bottom of the hill, Taggit muttered, "All right everyone, 'ere it comes. You know the plan."

With a shout, Stanley gave the signal to charge and a cry went up from both sides, rumbling into the air like thunder. The ground shook as the horde took off, pouring down the hillside in a torrent of shadow and gold, with hungry eyes and unsheathed claws.

And then, too late, alarm bells went off in Stanley's head. Something wasn't right. Why were the bigger, heavier townsfolk at the back and not in the front line?

His brain clicked into action. The smaller ones were at the front because they were faster, which meant they were all going to . . .

The townsfolk turned and ran like the blazes.

Stanley screamed, "PULL BACK NOW!" at the top of his lungs, but the tiger-men's charge was speeding up and their roars drowned his voice.

Dunvice heard him, though, and dropped to all fours, leaping just as she reached a suspiciously neat spread of heather and grass. Seeing her spring, many of the tiger-men copied. Not so the Grimm guards.

Three of them, either too stupid to realize or going too fast to pull back, plunged into the pit that opened up under their thundering feet. The first wave of tiger-men went with them.

Stanley seethed with fury. He had lost most of his first line, though it could have been far worse.

Jibbit clung on to Stanley's helmet as the CO charged to the left, spotting a narrow wall between two pits where he could cross. As he went by, he looked down. Most of the victims were dead, thanks to the spikes at the bottom. Those that weren't soon would be. Hopefully for them.

Dunvice howled a war cry, rallying the tiger-men to her. She led the way, charging over the last stretch of ground toward the clover fields on the edge of Hilfian where the townsfolk had stopped running and regrouped. The same spot where they stood now, their weapons ready, watching a tide of death pour toward them.

Watching the approaching troops, Taggit, leading the townsfolk, tried not to let fear take hold. He knew about Strood's army of tigerlike warriors from Skerridge, and had even passed it at a distance on his way to Hilfian.

But knowing about it in his head and seeing it hurtling toward him in all its golden-coated, deadly-eyed glory were two very different things.

Worse, he could feel the townsfolk around him beginning to doubt their ability to stand against a force this great. He didn't want them to lose courage; they would need every ounce if they had any hope of surviving.

"Hold yer ground," yelled Taggit, determined to ignore the growing panic pressing in around him as the townsfolk stared into the savage teeth of the approaching enemy. "Let them come to us. . . ."

As if anybody was likely to charge!

There was movement at the rear and the wedge of townsfolk opened, heads turning as someone strode through them toward the front line. "Jonas?"

The boy just kept on walking. It had to be Jonas, it looked like Jonas, and yet . . . he seemed taller, older, and stronger; even his old black coat had taken on the look of dark iron. You could almost hear it clank like armor. And no Quick ever burned with power like that. It came off him in a wave of light that swept over the band of Quick.

"Galig's teeth!" muttered Taggit, standing aside. "What's come over 'im?"

Jonas raised his arms, both hands folded around a great sword rimmed with white fire. Behind him the townsfolk raised their own weapons. The light broke into glimmers that settled over the villagers, sinking into them. Changing them. Suddenly, the Quick looked less like Quick and more like Grimm. The Grimm looked . . . terrifying. Galig had brought the spirit of his army with him and that spirit was giving them strength.

Taggit felt exhilaration sweep through him. This was real magic. Sorcerer magic, forged in the old world of Celidon where Fabulous walked the Land and the sorcerers were the greatest of the Fabulous. And it was on their side.

Jonas didn't stop; he just kept on going, holding the sword aloft as his pace increased until he was running, charging to meet Strood's army as it hurtled toward them across the grass.

A massive roar rose from the throats of the townsfolk as they fell in behind the shade of Galig, stampeding toward the enemy.

Although Jonas had no control over anything his body did, he could see the misty shades of the past warriors as they settled over the townsfolk, giving them strength and skill beyond anything they had prayed for. And more. As his vision adjusted and he saw more clearly through Galig's eyes, it was soon the townsfolk who were shadows.

He could see now how Galig's army must have looked in the past, when his warriors were alive and at their peak, and stared in astonishment at row upon row of long-dead Fabulous he would never see in real life.

There were ranked hordes of roaring, chain mail–clad goblins and werewolves that streamed over the ground in a flood of shadow. There were steel-clad sorcerers, and elves, too, tall and willowy with shining skins. There were things that Jonas could not name but that made him shudder, things with beaks and talons and eyes like night, and things that ran in a spiderish way that made him want to look elsewhere fast.

Jonas thought that, if Galig was using him as a bridge to channel all this Fabulous strength into the present, it was going to be a very short battle.

Until he saw the opposition.

Strood's goblins loomed from the charging horde like solid, spiked-ball-on-a-chain waving, metal mountains. His armored Grimm bristled with gleaming weapons. But it was the tiger-men that made Jonas's heart clench with fear. There were so many, their gold-and-dark mass covered every inch of ground. The flood was so vast that even though the front of the army was almost at the foot of the hill, there were others still cresting the rise, pouring over it with no end in sight.

The horde was close enough now for him to see the bared needle teeth and unsheathed claws. In that last second before the two armies met and clashed together, the heat of breath and burning energy from the tiger-men hit Jonas like a wave. All he could see was their purple eyes, on fire with excitement at the thought of killing.

As strong as Galig's Fabulous army had been in the past, it was still only a ghost army in the present, fighting through the bodies of living Quick and Grimm. Jonas could only hope that it brought enough of its old glory with it to help them survive.

The tiger-men sprang with easy grace, their muscles like steel under the silken coats, their fangs bared in a roaring scream of eagerness for the fight. Then, as the armies finally came together, everything became a blur of action around him, full of savage tiger faces and glinting metal, the sound of shouts and snarls and clashing steel. He saw Taggit whirling a great ax, his skin shining with sweat as he faced a goblin as massive as himself; and Jik battling with another, a female. Jik was doing a good job of keeping his enemy confused, jumping over her and diving into the earth, then springing up like a leaping fish right under her nose. She had already wounded herself badly by getting tangled up in her own spiked ball and chain.

In the background was a medley of battle-stained Quick and Grimm, their faces strained, but their eyes alight with the power that Galig had given them. And everywhere was the rippled flood of the tiger-men, drenched in blood and pouring against Jonas in waves, all claws and fangs and savage eyes. In Jonas, Galig sliced through them as if they were made of mist, the white-hot sword in his hands weaving a pattern of light against the darkness of pressing bodies and shedding drops of fire that cut like knives. The noise of screaming, of metal on metal, and metal on flesh, and the heat, and the stink of burning and of blood like hot iron was overpowering.

And then Galig stumbled on a rock and fell to one knee. The rock uncurled and looked at him.

"Is magic," it mumbled nervously, glancing at the sword, then rolled aside, tucking its head back under its paws.

Galig bent, caught it up, and threw it to a battered-looking Floyd, who had just lost his weapon.

"Here, friend, use that!" cried Galig above the screaming and howling. "It might as well be good for something."

And then, suddenly, a huge shape loomed, so close it seemed to fall on him, its bulbous face seamed on one side by a network of burns from the fire shed by Galig's sword, its mouth open in a snarl of yellow teeth, and its eyes hot with rage. Jonas heard the whistle as Hathor, Strood's giant-Grimm, whirled a spiked ball at his head about to take him down. In that moment Jonas saw the weapon, dark iron slick with blood and traces of hair, hurtling through the air toward him, but it was coming too fast for him to leap aside or parry the blow. A split-second before it cracked his skull, something shot out of the ground, something that looked like the Land come alive, made of earth and glinting with crystal. "Jik!" he shouted as the mudman smashed into the giant-Grimm's face, sending it reeling as it dragged the spiked ball with it. Taggit leapt in, with Floyd at his side, and all their shapes were lost in the struggling crowd, leaving Jonas shocked at how near his body had come to death. Galig might be the shade of a Sorcerer-King with a magic sword, but he was fighting in a Quick's body.

They fought on, and soon Jonas began to lose track of everything but the sword he was holding and the relentless onslaught of the enemy. As Galig's Fabulous spirit and magic sword cut through the tiger-men in droves, Jonas felt every blow and injury, until it was all one long blur of shape and sound and color and pain.

At last, on the horizon behind the town of Hilfian, the sky turned to liquid gold as the sun began to drown in a sea of its own light, and Jonas felt the wrench as Galig stepped away.

The sword became too heavy to hold up anymore and he staggered, going down on one knee. Looking up he saw the shade of the Sorcerer-King standing over him. The white-hot light was fading and the shape of Galig was just a silver outline in the air.

Jonas glanced around. The battle was still going strong and he felt cold fear as he realized it was far from done. Half the townsfolk Quick were dead, and many of the Grimm, too. The Fabulous werecat was gone and only one of the goblins remained besides Taggit. Strood had lost many of his Grimm guards, and both Fabulous goblins. As he scanned the field, Jonas could see the half-werewolf Dunvice taking on a group of townsfolk, and the two goblin-Grimm, Stanley and Floyd, silently fighting each other. But the worst thing was the tiger-men. With Galig's help they had killed so many, the creatures were piled high. But every townsfolk left alive was matched by at least two tiger-men. And they were tireless, still seething with the desire to kill, whereas the townsfolk were exhausted.

And now they were losing Galig's power too. Jonas could see it, sparking out over the battlefield in flashes of dying light.

"I wish I could stay," whispered Galig, his eyes dark holes in the silver shape, "but my part is over and I thank you for it. It felt good to be alive again for one last hour."

"And I thank you," gasped Jonas. "Without you we would have died for sure. There were so many!"

Galig's last trace was fading now, with nothing left but the eyes and the voice.

"Great Merlin be with you," he said, and then the light went out, the shade of Galig was gone, and the sword was just a useless lump of metal.

28

GATHERING DARK

As the sun disappeared into a pool of molten gold and the sky overhead became a translucent turquoise that would quickly deepen into nighttime blues, a bogeyman lay on his back on the hillside, still and silent in the gathering dark. He was battered and bloody and wearing the ruin of a fancy waistcoat. Next to him a pile of burned bones glowed red-hot on the scorched and seared earth. The smell of smoke and cooked werewolf was dreadful.

Skerridge coughed. He opened one eye. The other was a bit of a problem as his face seemed to have swollen up, what with all the bruises from the time Grayghast had battered him against a tree until it splintered down to a stump. Skerridge peered blearily at the broken and smoking remains of the stump and then at the broken and smoking remains of the werewolf.

"'Ow d'ya like *that*, stinky breff," he muttered.

It had taken a long afternoon of playing chase-and-fight round and round the hill, but finally Skerridge had gotten a lucky break and had managed to deep-fry the werewolf. Now the question was, what was happening in the valley below? Had the townsfolk been overrun by mad tiger-men or was Ninevah Redstone's luck holding out?

Skerridge lay where he was, in a heap in the middle of the hillside, staring at the sun as it sank beneath the edge of the world. He should go and find out the answers, but he was exhausted and every bone in his body hurt. Superspeed was beyond him right now—he didn't have the energy—but he thought if he lay still and had a rest for five minutes he might be up to at least a fairly quick shuffle.

The first minute had just begun when he saw the tombfolk.

They came striding over the hill looking like death incarnate, white as bone and dressed in rags of skin and hair. Fortunately for Skerridge they were too far away to see him and walked on past. Moments later his sensitive bogeyman ears heard Taggit shouting the retreat. Someone must have spotted the tombfolk heading toward Hilfian.

Skerridge had barely heaved a sigh of relief when the last of the sun disappeared. Three minutes later the BMs joined the party.

Arriving in a hiss of speed, they stopped on the hillside close to where Skerridge lay. There were two of them and Skerridge noticed at once that they were the same two that had escaped the tombfolk with him after frying Azork's Hive: Polpp and Rainbow. He also noticed that something was up.

"We're s'posed t' be after the Redstone kid," Rainbow was mumbling, "Strood's orders. Get the kid, burn the town."

"Oo cares?" snarled Polpp. "I couldn' give a faerie's

pledge fer the blimmin' Redstone kid. What I'm worried about is us BMs."

Flattening himself against the ground and trying to be invisible, Skerridge gave an inner groan. He could see that Polpp was angry and thought that Rainbow had the edgy look of someone who was gearing up to do something bad, but was a bit nervous about it. Things didn't bode well.

"I been finkin'," went on Polpp. "An' what I'm finkin' is this. We're turnin' into wusses an' it's all 'is fault. Strood!" He spat out the name, his red eyes glowing feverishly. "'Come an' work fer me,' 'e said . . ."—Polpp put on a mincing voice that was actually nothing like Strood at all—"'an' I'll make yer the most Dread Fabulous ever so's ya won' die.' So now we all do what that blimmin' Strood tells us, 'cos we're scared 'e'll give us the sack. But 'e lied, don' yer see? We ain't Dread Fabulous no more, we're jus' Strood's Scary Servants!"

The twin fires of Rainbow's eyes rose and fell in the darkness as he nodded. "Le's do it," he said suddenly, his nervousness falling away as he spoke. "Le's go rogue, like Skerridge 'ere wha's lying on the ground 'opin' we ain't seen 'im. No more workin' fer Strood? We could be REAL bogeyman again, yeah?"

The two bogeymen swapped grins, baring teeth like knives of bone, and just at that moment the night seemed to gather more closely around them, cloaking them in darkness. Skerridge stayed still and quiet. Whatever was coming, he didn't want to be part of it. They were going rogue all right, but in a way that had never occurred to Skerridge.

"Right, no more workin' fer Strood," Polpp said firmly, his eyes smoldering like red-hot beacons. "We ain't gonna burn the town an' we ain't gonna bovver wiv the kid. But there's all them Quick an' Grimm down there jus' beggin' fer a bitta mayhem an' murder, so le's go an' 'ave some REAL bogeyman fun, eh? Le's go make 'em scream!"

The air fizzed and the newly REAL bogeymen were gone, leaving Skerridge alone on the dark hillside. He heaved a sigh. On the one hand, with Strood's BM's gone rogue, at least Hilfian wouldn't be razed to the ground with no hope of any survivors. But on the other hand . . .

Skerridge shuddered, remembering how the REAL bogeymen had looked somehow bigger, more THERE than before. More part of the night. He supposed he must have been like that once, back in the days of Celidon. Vague memories of a crazy bogeyman raid on Beorht Eardgeard and a lot of extremely annoyed sorcerers tripped through his head, but it all seemed very hazy.

"Watch out 'Ilfian," he mumbled, "the bogeymen are comin' t' play!"

He sighed again, got to his feet, and shook himself. His five minutes' rest had come and gone and it was time to go and give the townsfolk a helping hand. It would be a shame if they survived Strood's army just to die horribly at the hands of a pair of BMs.

Reluctantly, he followed the sound of screams rising from the town below.

"It's all right," said Hilary soothingly to Senta's Spell, "we're barricading the doors. No tiger-men will get through that!"

Around her was a hive of activity as people piled beds and furniture against the door, even the injured doing their best to help. Someone was nailing boards over the windows. Others stood ready with weapons, on guard against anything that might break through.

"And the tombfolk?" snapped the Spell.

"We'll hide in the cellar and hope they don't find us."

Jik appeared at her elbow, his flame eyes worried. He had arrived, with Floyd in tow, to warn them that tombfolk had been seen heading down the hill toward town. Now he was sensing something else and it wasn't good. A shadow had crept over his inner fires and it had to do with Nin.

"I might have guessed the girl hadn't gone off meekly to hide with the others!" said Hilary, after one look at his face. "Where is she?"

They set off, hurrying up the ladders toward the roof. But they were too late. The skinkin got there first.

Up on the roof, Nin was awake at last, revived by the cool air of oncoming night. Unconsciousness had given her brain and body time to deal with the shock, and although she was still shaky, she was feeling better than before. She knew she had been asleep for some time because it was dark, the last trace of daylight already fading from the sky.

A scream rose into the air, making her flinch. It was followed by shouts and then more screams. Glancing around, she saw a low wall enclosing the roof, so she got up and went to look over it.

Below her, lit by the silver globe of the moon, she could see the grassy tops of the buildings that surrounded the town hall. Beyond them was the battlefield, backed by the rise of the hill. It all looked like something from a nightmare. The field was dotted with running shapes, the Quick townsfolk, the Grimm, and the remaining Fabulous from both sides, all hurtling toward the town, their legs pounding as they headed for any hiding place they could find. Some were being carried by others and some were lolloping along, trying to ignore their injuries as best they could. Weapons lay discarded on the ground, glints of silver amid the over-coat of dead.

The tiger-men were running too. Some of them were going after those fleeing to the town, but most had turned their attention the other way, toward the seven tall shapes moving at a steady pace down the last stretch of hill. A pace that was not going to stop for anyone or anything. Tombfolk.

For a wild moment Nin thought they had come to help, but then she understood. Although Azork might attack Strood's army as revenge for the loss of his Hive, the people of the town would be in danger too. The vampire tombfolk would make no distinction between sides.

In the lead, Azork spread his arms and the others followed. The tiger-men swarmed on, roaring and howling. They didn't know what the tombfolk were, they just saw another enemy to fight.

The tombfolk's pace didn't falter for a moment, but the tiger-men began to stagger and fall, their charge interrupted. The air around them filled with a red mist that rose from the struggling shapes on the ground, shapes that were breaking apart where they lay. The tiger-men were made from crowsmorte and blood, and the tombfolk were drawing out every last drop of blood. Which left the crowsmorte. Blooms sprang up everywhere and began to spread across the battlefield, feeding on the bodies of the fallen.

As the tombfolk strode on, the last of Strood's

tiger-man army crumbled before them. Even those that got close to the Hive had no chance to do any damage. They were snatched up as if they were nothing, then torn apart, their blood drunk and the remains tossed aside. And as they fed, the tombfolk took back the beauty stolen from them by the day. Their skins began to shine and their eyes to fill with stars again. Even so, they went on, seeking out every last drop of blood. The battle was over, but Nin could see a long and terrifying night ahead.

And then a line of dull red light flared on the edge of town, leaving a streak on the night air like the trail that might be left by something moving very fast. Screams broke out and fire glowed briefly, followed by more cries and a long shriek.

Bogeymen! After all the townsfolk had gone through, all that fighting, now what? Tombfolk and bogeymen.

Nin put her head in her hands and hot tears spread on her cheeks as despair swept through her, so intense that she felt her heart stutter in its beat. Ice ran down her spine and her scalp prickled. Suddenly the world seemed far away because she knew, she just knew, what was BEHIND HER.

Slowly she turned. The skinkin was there all right, crouching next to the door. It was a shape in the darkness, a patch of deeper night with bone-white highlights around the paws and eye sockets, and it was so still she could almost have fooled herself that it was just a trick of the moonlight.

Then it bared its teeth and hissed.

With a cry, Nin ran, looking for the rope ladder over to the bell tower. It had gone. Before the battle began, someone had cut it down to make sure no enemy used it to get into the town hall. She could see it, hanging loose against the side of the tower, out of reach and useless. The blood drained from her face as she realized that she was trapped.

She glanced back. Just one hope. If the skinkin came after her then she might be able to get back down the way she had come. Trembling, she stumbled to the wall that surrounded the stairwell and then paused, waiting, listening. Nothing. She was numb with fear but forced herself to move, creeping around the square of the wall until she was back where she had started.

It was still sitting by the door. It had her helpless and knew it.

Nin felt her heart contract with fear as the skinkin turned its bone-socket eyes to look at her. She clenched her fists and stepped toward it. Another step; three more and she would be past it into the stairwell and down the ladder. Trembling so badly she thought her body would shake apart, she inched closer. With one, loping hop the skinkin moved. Now it was between her and the doorway.

Nin's breath came in gasps. "It's just skin and bone," she told herself, "you can rip it apart with your bare hands."

She forced her legs to move, and for a second she really believed that she had taken another step, only she hadn't. She was standing in the same place, rooted to the spot while the skinkin looked at her, filling her with terror and loss and awful, heart-wrenching loneliness, like darkness gathering inside her. Lights sparked at the corner of her vision and the shadows began to close in. Her heart fluttered. Through it all she thought she heard someone call her name, but Nin knew she must have imagined it. "Move!" she shouted at herself, but instead of leaping at the thing and smashing it to nothing, she sank to the floor, trembling as hopelessness took over.

At the sound of movement from behind the skinkin she looked up, but she didn't see what came through the door. As far as Nin was concerned, she was cornered by something relentless and terrible, and she was utterly, completely alone.

"Nin!" Hilary paused as she saw the skinkin crouched in the doorway between her and the girl. *"Step over it,"* said Senta's Spell. *"It won't hurt you unless you get in its way."*

Without stopping to worry about what she was doing, Hilary jumped over the skinkin, landing next to Nin. She grabbed the girl under the arms and began to drag her away toward the outer wall.

In the stairwell, Jik inched nearer, planning to grab the skinkin from behind and pull it apart. But as he stepped close a wave of despair flowed over him, making the flames of his eyes dim to almost nothing. Still, he reached out a hand. The moment he touched the skinkin, feeling its fragile bones against his mud palm, one of his fingers broke and crumbled. A crack ran up his arm.

"Stop!" yelled Hilary. "Senta's Spell told me. No living thing can survive contact with it. The skinkin kills with fear and hopelessness . . . like . . ."—she listened again—"like the Dead of Night, whatever that is."

Jik stepped back, knowing she was right. He couldn't touch it. "Nik likik thik?"

"That's right," said Hilary, "no living thing . . . Oh . . . you're thinking about Azork?" She looked doubtful. "You could try, Jik, but why would he want to help?"

Jik shrugged, then leapt right over the skinkin and

ran. In two strides he was at the wall and diving over it. Hilary looked just in time to see him hit the land below, only he didn't *hit* it, he went *into* it, like a diver entering the water. And then he was gone.

Hilary turned back to Nin. The girl's face was deathly pale and wet with tears, and around her arm the spell had gone dark, almost black. Her eyes, full of shadows, were fixed on the skinkin. "Don't look at it," Hilary said softly, taking Nin in her arms. "Don't listen to it. You are lucky, remember, you can't die!"

Nin knew it was a lie. Everything was clear to her now. The Dark Thing was right and she alone was responsible for all the pain and the death. Ninevah Redstone, who skipped through danger while those about her bled and burned. The townsfolk of Hilfian were being devoured by vampires and ripped apart by bogeymen. The Seven would soon be gone and so would the Land. Jik was facing death. Jonas was dead. Strood had won and she would die alone and terrified in this horrible world and never see her mother or her brother again. And when she was gone, her mother wouldn't even mourn her. All the past they shared, all the good times and the bad, would be gone forever when the memory pearl died with her. There would be nothing.

And it was best that way.

"Come on, dear," said Hilary, hugging Nin to her. She kissed the girl's forehead. "You must fight."

Nin turned her eyes to Hilary's face. They were sunk so deep in their sockets that only a gleam showed. Hilary could feel Nin's heart beating, but each heavy pound was too far apart, and the gaps were getting wider. Panic gripped her.

"Nin!"

In front of them, the crouching skinkin seemed bigger than before. Its hunched back looked more menacing, the claws on its bone-paws were longer and sharper.

Nin drew in a breath, then let it out. And there was one last thump that shook her like a leaf before her heart stopped beating and Ninevah Redstone died.

29

SKINKIN

Swimming through the earth in his search for Azork, Jik burrowed out of the ground on the outskirts of Hilfian. He paused, taking in the scene.

Everywhere he looked he could see chunks of mud huts. The chunks were scattered untidily about as if the huts had been hit by a bomb—or maybe torn apart by something very strong and enthusiastic. Further on, past the remains of the mud huts and beyond the edge of town, he could make out the battlefields where the tombfolk had finished off the tiger-men and were moving on, looking for the townsfolk.

He was about to head toward them when a screaming Quick hurtled past, pursued by Polpp in Hook-Handed Horror form, waving the hook screwed into the stump of one arm and screeching with crazy laughter. Darkness came off the bogeyman in waves, leaving a streak of extra-dense night in his wake. Also in his wake went Skerridge, an expression of desperate determination on his face.

Jik stared after them. He guessed Skerridge was trying to help the Quick, but it looked like he was having a hard time of it. With a shrug Jik turned his attention to the tombfolk. By now, they had made it to the edge of town where they had run into trouble with one of the bogeymen. The Queen was glaring angrily at Rainbow, who was standing in her path, grinning at her. Spirals of golden light surrounded her, she was so full of life. "Stand aside, bogeyman," she hissed. "On the ground, we are indestructible. Do you know what that means?"

Rainbow snickered, gathering the dark around him like a mantle.

"Means yer'll still be alive after I pulls yer 'ead off!" he said, flexing his fingers.

With a shake of his head Jik left them to it and moved on again. Azork was not with the Hive and it was Azork he wanted. He found the once-sorcerer on the edge of the battlefield, surrounded by spreading crowsmorte. By now the bobbing purple heads with their bloodred centers were so thick that he could see no ground between them.

Jik ikked as he stumbled on a gargoyle-shaped stone, buried in the crowsmorte. It was mumbling to itself, so he dug it free.

"Thank yoo," it said, shaking the dirt out of its ears.

It wandered off over the field, stopping every so often to shudder before it moved on. Jik watched it for a moment, then turned to Azork, who was studying him thoughtfully.

"I'm still dying," the once-sorcerer told him. "I remember a time when I loved and even the memory is enough to tear my Armor of Dread apart. My spell is broken, and without it to help me endure, I will soon be . . . nothing."

Although all the life he had consumed hung around

Azork in a bright halo, Jik could see in his eyes that it was true. "They know it too." Azork glanced in the direction of the other tombfolk.

Following his look, Jik saw a silver column spiraling up, higher and higher against the night and the smoke. The Queen was leaving, taking her Hive back into the skies. Rainbow had won that little showdown.

"Hikik nik yik," he said simply, turning back to Azork.

Azork shuddered at Hilary's name. "Why should I care if she needs me or not," he hissed.

He turned his back on the town, but Jik somersaulted over his head, landing to stand in his way. Tombfolk and mudman exchanged a long look.

Jik's meant: You are going to die, so why not die well? Why not spend the last of your life helping Hilary Jones save Nin and save the Drift?

And Azork's meant: I care nothing for the Drift. If I can't enjoy its beauty, why should anyone else? I was the Daemon of the Night, King of the tombfolk, and now I'm nothing, a once-sorcerer with no power and no future. And all because of one wretched Quick. So why, in Galig's name, should I help *HER*?

Jik shrugged, then turned and walked away. He went slowly to give Azork time to think about it. He just hoped they wouldn't be too late.

Behind him, Azork hissed angrily. But he followed Jik to the town hall anyway. Only, he wasn't going to help.

Hilary had reminded him of his past love for Senta and that was destroying the spell that kept him alive. So if he was going to die, then he would have one last act of revenge before the end. He would kill Hilary Jones. And maybe killing the Quick who had broken his spell would reverse the damage she had done and save him.

It was his one last chance to survive and he was going to take it.

On the town hall roof, Hilary had given herself up to tears. The skinkin was still there too, watching them, waiting. Hilary guessed that it hadn't quite done its job yet. It had been created to kill the *legendary* Ninevah Redstone and that legend would only die when Hilary Jones stumbled out into the world to tell it what had happened. Then the news of Nin's death would spread like wildfire, burning up everyone's hopes of saving the Drift, making her just another kid who would be forgotten in days. And when that happened the skinkin would finally be free.

"Is it too late, then?" asked a familiar voice.

Startled, Hilary looked up to see Azork hovering in the air before her.

"Everything's over," she said. "All these amazing people, this beautiful Land. Just as I've found them all everything's going to die." She half-smiled, rubbing her arm across her face to blot some of the tears. "That's a little selfish, isn't it?"

Azork drifted down, his feet touching the roof, making him solid again. Outlined against the fire-lit sky he looked cut from night, all stars and darkness.

"But then, sorcerers are a selfish breed." Hilary sighed. She looked down at Nin's body and stroked her hair sadly, then touched the spell with her fingertip. It glowed softly in reply, but stayed dark, as if in mourning too.

Azork's star-filled eyes glittered as he stepped forward, preparing to kill. He would tear the woman apart, he thought, and drink her blood straight from her body. He reached out.

"I'm glad you came," Hilary was saying, "even if it is too late."

She looked up at him again, her clothes stained with the blood of many injured, messy and exhausted with her hair dull and matted and her white face smeared. Her eyes were still brimming with tears. "I'm sorry I hurt you." She sighed. "Even if you are Dread."

There was a sound like tearing silk. Azork shuddered as threads of light appeared, running over his skin like spider webs. The stars in his eyes went out.

Hilary's eyes met his. The night went on around them, but something had changed. "I was going to kill you, but I can't," he said. "Because of you I remember what it is to love, and although I swore I would never feel that again, seeing you now . . ." Azork smiled ruefully out of eyes that were now only silver. "My stupid heart just let me down. I've fallen in love all over again."

Underneath all the tears, Hilary blushed. She didn't know what to say.

Azork struggled for a moment, a tangle of emotions running across his face. Some of them were old, bitter ones and some of them were new. He had loved Senta and she had hurt him. But now he had fallen in love with Hilary, and he would never know if she could have loved him back. There was not enough time. But maybe there was one thing he could do. He reached a decision and stepped forward. Then he leaned toward Nin, stooping low over her. "My spell is gone," he said. "I'm dying anyway. But I'll give my last strength to help the girl if it will make you happy. I'll give her my life."

He breathed out and life poured from him in a flood, bathing Nin in light. Hilary gasped. She could see it, soaking into the girl's skin, running into her mouth and up her nose and even squeezing under her eyelids. She felt Nin's heart stutter into a beat. And then another.

She was only half aware that around them the night grew colder for a moment and a tremor ran through the Land.

Azork felt it and smiled grimly. Every act had its backlash, and the bigger the act the bigger the repercussions. He had brought someone back from the dead and the price would be enormous. And he didn't just mean the cost to him, the loss of his last precious hours of life. It was more than that. For an act this huge there would be terrible consequences. He turned his head to search the shadows. Something was there, watching.

Nin stirred and moaned, then settled again, her eyelids flickering. She didn't wake up, but now it was sleep, not death.

"Her body is still damaged," Azork said, "her heart has been weakened and her brain clouded with the strain of fear and despair. But she's alive. The rest is up to you and your friends."

He stepped back. With all his life shed, he looked thin, insubstantial. The cracks of light on his skin had gone and now he was as he once had been. Slender, dark-skinned, and silver-eyed. Hilary could see right through him; as she watched, he was becoming a ghost. "You're fading," she said.

Azork smiled at her. "Just remember, I didn't do this for Ninevah Redstone, or for the Land. I did it for you."

"Thank you," breathed Hilary, her eyes fixed on his, two points of soft light in the darkness. A breath of wind stirred her hair and rustled the few leaves growing from the wall. Then it tore the last traces of Azork apart like mist and he was gone.

"Thank you," said Hilary again, to the empty sky.

Hilary had forgotten the skinkin. Even as Jik appeared in the doorway, his flame eyes peering anxiously at Nin, a movement to their left got their attention.

The creature leapt out of the darkness. It was bigger, the size of a large cat or a small fox, and skin over bone, with long ears, yellowed claws, and legs built to run and leap. Its eyes were holes overflowing with shadows that hung around it, and it carried a smell of mold and decay.

Hilary held Nin tight against her, paralyzed with fear. Jik sprang to their side.

Skinkin watched the three living beings with cold anger. It had been cheated. Ninevah Redstone had survived even Death and now her legend was safe for as long as there were Quick to tell the story.

"Wik hikik!"

Hilary tipped her head, listening to Senta's Spell.

"Strood made it to end Nin, but it's failed," she said slowly, "and now it's . . . Well, it can't die as it should, because now it has a task it can't complete. So this is the price we've paid to have Nin alive again. The skinkin has become a new Fabulous."

Skinkin bared its stained teeth at them, then raised its head and sniffed the air, breathing in the night. It sprang and its great leap took it over their heads, flying through the air to land on the bell tower. Trying again was not an option. Now the one person in the Land that Skinkin could never attack was Nin. Every Fabulous had its rules.

On the bell tower, outlined black against the

moonlight, it threw back its head and let out a cry like many people screaming their last. The sound echoed through the night and everyone who heard it—Quick, Grimm, or Fabulous—stopped what they were doing to listen. Then it sprang again and was gone.

30

CROWSMORTE

Along the rim of the world, a seam of red fire exploded into life, burning away the long night and casting a doom-filled light across fields that were dark with crowsmorte, each purple flower splashed with scarlet that matched the dawn. Their scent made the air both heavy and sweet at the same time and they covered everything so thickly that it was hard to tell where the fields ended and Hilfian began.

Slowly people appeared from their hiding places. A couple from a hut here, more from another, and a whole gaggle from the cellar underneath the ruined mud building that had once served as a general store. Taggit was among them, as was Jonas, white-faced with exhaustion. More townsfolk, Quick and Grimm, peered out through doors or collapsed walls, then grew bold and stepped into the cool air where a gentle breeze made the crowsmorte nod and blew away the smoke from the still-smoldering barns.

It was a lovely day, if only because none of them had expected to see it.

Over the other side of the Heart, watching the

dawn through the crystal walls of the Sunatorium, Mr. Strood steepled his fingers and studied the row of three . . . beings . . . in front of him. "I was surrounded," said Chief Bogeyman Pigwit. He was huddled up under a very large, very thick blanket with his back turned firmly against the early morning light. He didn't look at all well after a horrible night, rounded off by the huge effort of superspeeding back to the House and finding a way around all the patches of Raw with a bad-tempered stone in his pocket. It had grumbled all the way to the House and Pigwit wished he had left the stupid thing where he had found it, staggering across the battlefield in a daze. "I thought you said there were only two?"

Pigwit blinked. "More'n that. Four at least. There was no escapin'."

"But you're here," pointed out Strood reasonably.

"Barely. Only 'cos I managed t' make a break fer it when they was busy wiv the townsfolk. Six or seven there were, all big bogeymen wiv teef an' everyfin'."

"You're a bogeyman. With teeth. And everything."

"Yeah, but . . ."

"They were REAL bogeymen," snapped Jibbit.

Strood sighed and shook his head at Pigwit. "I sent you to oversee a mere two of your fellows in sorting out the town. A small task, I would have thought. A few mud huts, easily burned. A few Quick, easily fried. A little girl, easily picked up. Instead, what do you bring me?" His quartz eye glittered. "A stone. An insignificant little stone."

Jibbit thought about huffing indignantly, but decided against it. He was on the table opposite Strood, mainly so that Strood didn't have to look down at him all the time, but at least it was off the ground. Jibbit shuddered at the memory of the last few hours, used as a battering weapon in battle, dropped and trampled on, stamped into the mud like . . . like . . . a stone. He had survived though. His worst nightmare had come true and he had survived and now the thought of ground wasn't nearly as terrifying as it had been. But that didn't mean that his yearning for HIGH had gone. If anything it was growing.

Sitting back in his chair, Strood eyed them thoughtfully. Pigwit's eyes were watering in the light, and where he was holding on to the blanket, he had left one of his fingers out accidentally. It had begun to smoke.

"So, Giblet, you are telling me that in spite of everything I have thrown against her—my terrible army, the deadly skinkin—she is still alive?"

Jibbit nodded. His stony paws clicked nervously against the table. There was a strangled squawk from Pigwit as his finger burst alight and he had to stamp on it to put the flames out.

There was a long silence. Strood's eyes, the quartz one by now glowing horribly, fixed on the third person in the group in front of him. The one standing with its arms folded as it leaned nonchalantly against the table. The figure yawned. It was a woman with dark hair and eyes the color of winter. She was wearing a pair of interesting boots.

"I told you she would," Doctor Mel said. "Even I couldn't get to her."

A look of hatred twisted across Strood's face. "It was a stupid idea," he said scathingly. "The luck belongs to her, not to her physical form. Trust a once-sorcerer to overlook something like that. You think that all the Quick are is a body, a lump of flesh to be . . ." He stopped.

Jibbit glanced curiously from one to the other. There was something between these two, something big.

Pigwit was almost doubled up under his blanket, only his red eyes glowing in its shadow.

"Go," said Strood, switching his gaze to the bogeyman. A smile curled his thin lips. "And don't bother me again. Ever." He leaned forward, his voice a soft hiss on the air. "You're. Fired."

Pigwit squeaked and trembled and it seemed to Jibbit that he shrank, growing smaller and thinner until instead of bony he looked spindly. A spindly thing with red eyes and bandy legs. "It's all a state of mind," said Strood calmly as the once-bogeyman ran for the door. "He's no longer Dread, he doesn't have it in him anymore. These Fabulous, they think they're so invincible." He chuckled. "But then, you should know all about that."

Mel glared. "Well, Ava . . ." went on Strood.

The once-sorcerer in the woman's body winced at the familiar tone and bit back a sharp comment.

". . . things haven't gone quite as I would have liked, I'll admit, but it can be still be saved. It seems to me that this is one job I shall just have to do myself."

"You've got a plan?"

"Of course." Strood chuckled. "When do I not have a plan?"

"And it is . . . ?" Vispilio sounded bored, though he wasn't. For possibly the first time in his horrible life he was very far from bored. It was a long time since he had seen Strood and the man had changed. He was no longer Gan Mafig's servant. He was pure insanity wrapped in a skin.

Outside the red fires of dawn were burning out on a clear day.

"Simple," answered Strood, "like all the best plans. Kill. Everything."

* * *

"Are you sure this is the only way?" asked Jonas.

They were back in Hen's hut and he was sitting on the edge of the bed, looking worried. Jik and Hilary were there too, watching anxiously as Hen tipped a potion down the sleeping Nin's throat.

"It's the only way I know," said Hen. "Dissolved, crowsmorte is a potent healer, if used right. And she needs a lot of healing. Azork may have brought her back to life, but he couldn't repair the damage. Her heart is very weak."

"The sisters gave her a crowsmorte potion too. I've never heard of anyone taking it twice before."

Hen smiled. "Nothing venture, nothing have," she said, patting Nin's hand. "Just let her sleep and we'll see. Only thing is, I had to make it strong, so she might have a few funny dreams."

31

CELIDON

Nin was dreaming about music, a kind of soft singing. There was something familiar about it. She didn't know where it was coming from, because the rest of the dream was taking place in a city on a rainy day. She was standing in the middle of a broad street surrounded by buildings that soared above her, sweeping to a white sky, their spires and domes wreathed in mist. Everything was light gray or white stone, but even in such pale hues, lost against the blank clouds, the walls and towers looked magnificent. Fine drizzle veiled her hair with tiny drops and a chilly breeze made her shiver.

Nin knew this had to be a dream; it had that unreal quality, though it was getting more vivid every moment. Before this, the last thing she remembered clearly was going to find Seth. She had a feeling there was more, but that it was best if she didn't think about it for the moment.

The singing faded away, leaving only the soft patter of rain. Now that it was gone, she remembered where she had heard it before. In the sanctuary, when Elinor had given her a crowsmorte potion.

I'm hurt, she thought, *and Hen is trying to heal me. But for now I'm dreaming, so I might as well enjoy it while I can.*

A figure draped in a dark cloak and with a bloodred scarf twined about his neck paused at her side. Beneath the cloak, he was wearing a black silk suit and a bright, embroidered waistcoat.

"There you are," he said, "come along then. Morgan wants to see you."

In that moment Nin saw that she was not alone in the city. There were others, hurrying along the pavement, heads bowed against the weather. Not many, but enough to make her wonder why she had not seen them before. But it was the one at her side that commanded her attention most and she turned to look up at him.

He was tall and slender and the lines and planes of his face were as beautiful as the buildings around them. Nin recognized him at once from the Mansion, but there was more than that. A sense of familiarity about his teasing smile.

"Simeon Dark!"

"Of course." He laughed and she saw that his eyes were gold. Not plain gold, but dappled with flecks of silver. "Come along, follow me and no dawdling."

He set off and Nin started after him, hurrying to keep up. She didn't know what was going on, but then who did in dreams?

Dark turned down a street of stone walls, their gray broken by the shining squares of windows lit against the dismal day. A woman passed them going the other way, and Nin saw that her face was sad and her silver eyes held a fear that made them dark. Looking back as the woman walked on, Nin lagged behind her guide, then had to run to catch up. For the first time she noticed that the pavement was covered in a fine layer of dust. Mixed with the rain it made a paste that coated her boots and splashed her jeans. Its pale color was striking against the dark material of the sorcerer's cloak.

Ahead, the street gave out into a vast square and as they came into the open space Nin gasped. The building at its center made the others look ordinary. It did more than merely soar, its spires and pinnacles reached up in layers of intricate stone until they pierced the sky.

"What's that?" asked Nin.

"That," said Dark reverently, "is the Hall of Galig, built by the King in celebration of his victory over the faerie. It sits here on the banks of the river, at the heart of our great city of Beorht Eardgeard, as a symbol of Fabulous power."

A cart rattled by and Nin saw something that made her tear her gaze away from the Hall. This time she stared in horror.

The cart was laden with goblins and other creatures she couldn't name. All of them dead. They were piled up, their shapes not given the dignity of a covering, their heads lolling against one another, arms embracing the stranger beside them.

Nin looked away, feeling cold in her stomach. Dark watched her with interest. "Plague victims," he said.

"It's happening now? I'm dreaming the past?"

"It began slowly, but now death is coming faster and Fabulous numbers grow less every day."

Nin felt her eyes fog with something other than rain. "I'm sorry," she said.

"Why should the Quick be sorry? We gave you nothing and took everything."

"You gave us magic," said Nin. "We miss it. Honestly."

Dark laughed and moved on. Nin fell into step behind him again.

"All Fabulous die in different ways," he told her. "And not all leave a body like the goblins. Tombfolk dissolve into air, bogeymen become their own funeral pyre. Sorcerers, like many others, turn to dust."

"Dust?"

"What do you think you are walking in?" said Simeon Dark quietly.

Silent now, Nin followed him across the square and toward the river that ran past Galig's Hall. Crossing the bridge, Nin looked down at the swirling waters, stained with red and wearing a skin of broken wood and silver froth.

"Sprites," said Dark, even though she hadn't asked. "Wood sprites and water sprites." He said no more; he didn't have to.

They left the river and the Hall behind them, turning down a broad street of tall, elegant houses, all of gray or white stone. At last Dark stopped before one of the front doors and spoke to it. It swung open onto a long hall, the arched ceiling cut by a twisting ribbon of flame that hung in the air above them. Dark led the way down it toward another door at the end. Behind it, Nin could hear singing, real singing this time, rich and warm. Dark walked on without changing his pace, and the door opened before him, leading into a room that made Nin gasp with amazement.

Light and heat came from a small sun, about the size of Nin's fist. It hung in the center of the room near the high ceiling, burning like the real thing. On all sides were arched windows between stone pillars, and the earth floor was covered with rugs of petals and leaves. There were no cabinets or other furniture, no shelves, and definitely no books.

But the windows amazed her most. Outside, where there should be rain and gloom, was a summer garden of flowers.

Bewildered, Nin turned her attention to the room's occupants. Besides Dark there were three other Fabulous sorcerers. The singing had stopped as they walked in and all heads had turned to look at her. One face she knew at once, for although he didn't look the same as she remembered him, his white beard and gnarled skin told her his name.

"Nemus!" she said happily.

The sorcerer looked at her. "Who is this?"

"More like, *what* is it?" said a languid voice and Nin turned her head to see Azork.

He was clad in magenta silk and stood leaning against one of the pillars, his golden eyes looking Nin over with distaste.

Simeon Dark smiled and drifted over to a space away from the others.

Azork laughed. "Come now, is this another of your jokes, Simeon?"

"No joke. Morgan wanted to see her."

"I did indeed," said Morgan Crow.

The fourth sorcerer in the room was sitting cross-legged in a chair that was really a large flower, and he was watching Nin. A mop of glossy black hair hung thick and loose down his back, and he was dressed in silver and holding an instrument like a mandolin. His face was not intelligent exactly, but interested, curious. He had long, slender fingers heavy with rings, a boyish smile, and white eyes with no pupils.

He was, in fact, wonderful.

"You're real," said Nin, suddenly understanding. "They aren't, but you are!"

"Quite right," said Morgan Crow cheerfully. "This," he waved a hand, "is my world, or at least my memory of it." The mandolin vanished from his hands and he leaned back on the air.

"So you did survive!"

"Of course. I thought that the best way to live on was to make myself one with the Land."

"But your body was eaten by crowsmorte."

"All part of the plan. It absorbed me, so in a way I *am* crowsmorte. I exist here, living in my memory and kept alive by my physical being, which grows all over the Drift."

Nin thought for a moment. "So you feed on the Quick by . . . eating their bodies?"

"Oh yes, and Grimm. I can even break down Fabulous flesh, though it's not a lot of use."

"I suppose at least they're dead when you do it," she said doubtfully.

"Mostly," said Crow cheerfully. "The odd live one, you know. But it's all part of the spell, see. Eating flesh and blood, whether it's alive or dead, is what makes crowsmorte understand bodies so that it can heal them. It may not be as dramatic as Enid or Nemus, but you'd be amazed how people yell for me when it comes to healing their wounds!"

Nin glanced around at the other sorcerers. She could feel them taking her apart with their gazes like something on a dissection table. She understood that while they could see her skin, blood, hair, and eyes more clearly than any Quick, what they couldn't see was HER. To them, she was just a different kind of animal.

"Are they bothering you? They are only my memory of the originals. I can make them go away."

"Please," said Nin. Azork in particular was glaring

at her irritably. Dark was humming to himself thoughtfully and inspecting his waistcoat, and Sturdy was
watching with a faint smile.

There was an almost imperceptible shift in the air
and they were gone.

"Do you want to sit down?"

He pointed to the floor and a shoot appeared,
growing and unfurling into another flower chair. Nin
thanked him and sat in it. On the whole, it was pretty
comfortable.

"Simeon Dark said you wanted to see me?"

"Ah, yes." Crow laughed. "I've heard a lot about
you; rumors spread through the Land, you know, as
well as through the people that live on it. I wanted to
meet you, and this second brew of potion that you've
taken has given me the chance. I might be able to help
you stop Strood." He sighed and shook his head. "We
should really have done something about him, but we
were all too intent on surviving the plague, so we just . . .
didn't. And the world has been suffering Strood's evil
ever since."

Nin shivered.

"Cold? Would you like me to turn the sun up?"

She shook her head. "No thank you, I'm fine. Was it
really like this?" She waved a hand at the window opening onto the garden.

"Oh yes. This is my exact memory. I like to have a
garden through my windows, especially on dismal days.
I love flowers, so soothing and yet so potent, don't you
think?"

Nin wasn't sure how to reply, so she just smiled and
nodded.

"Would you like to see how it was?"

"How what was? Oh, Celidon you mean." She

shook her head. "I saw on the way here. It was . . ." She stopped. Finding a word for the gray mud and the death carts defeated her.

"I know, I know. But that's only because I'm remembering this time right now. Come with me."

He got to his feet and moved out of the door, into the hallway. Crow walked more slowly than Dark, so Nin didn't have to run to keep up. In fact, while he walked he talked, and he often paused or slowed right down. Nin found herself slowing to keep beside him. She danced around him, wanting to get where they were going.

"After the Final Gathering we all went our separate ways. You know what paths we chose to endure beyond the plague?"

Nin nodded. "Except for what happened to Simeon Dark. Or at least, I know that his spell disguised him and then took away his memory. But I don't know who he is, what he's disguised as. I found this in his Mansion." Nin held up the shadow spell for Crow to see. It looked brighter than it had ever been. "It's his memories, I think. Or at least his *real* memories. Seth . . . Vispilio thinks Dark still has a distorted version, so as not to stand out, you see. This will just make them right again. So if I can find out who he is, then the spell will break and he'll remember everything properly."

"Interesting! And he could be anyone?"

"Yes." Nin sighed. "Anyone. Good or bad."

"Are you sure about that? I mean, couldn't he have done away with the physical altogether? It's just a body after all, he could—"

"Grow another one? Like people said about you?"

"I made a prediction once, you know. Well, lots of predictions actually. I'm famous for them. But this was something about 'in the dying days of the Land a Fabulous shall rise from the earth and signify new life.'"

"That could mean Jik," said Nin thoughtfully, turning the idea over in her mind. She sighed. "There are just so many possibilities."

"Simeon was always a tricky one," Crow said cheerfully. "You didn't know what was going on in his head half the time." He chuckled. "In fact, Vispilio once said that even Dark didn't know what was going on in Dark's head! Of course, he didn't mean anything nice by it, but I thought it was kind of cool."

Nin was frowning. "This corridor got very long?" She looked back over her shoulder and the door seemed right where it should be, but they had been walking away from it for ages.

"It's a long way to the past," said Crow, "but we're nearly there now."

Nin felt excitement bubbling inside her. She danced ahead of him, wishing he'd hurry up. And then, at last, they were there and she burst out of the door into another world.

The sun was shining on houses and buildings that could have been made of light, they were so dazzling. Where the spires had risen to clouds before, now they touched a sky of clear, intense blue. A breeze, bearing the scent of lilac, stirred Nin's hair and underfoot the pavement was white marble. "Can we go to the square?" begged Nin. "I want to see Galig's Hall, I want to see the people!"

Crow laughed indulgently and put a calming hand on the top of her head. "All right, the square it is."

They walked back the way she had come with Dark, down the broad street and toward a river that glinted in the sunlight. Golden fish flicked in its depths, and swans, both white and black, sailed its rippling surface. Gardens lined its banks.

"Can we walk by the river?"

"River or square, which first?"

"Oh!" Torn by indecision, Nin hopped back and forth. But she remembered Galig's Hall in the rain and wanted to see the square as it would have been. "The square!"

"Come, then."

They moved on over the wide bridge, Nin still dancing ahead of Crow. People were crossing the river in both directions, and when they reached the square on the other side it was swarming. Beorht Eardgeard had been built by sorcerers, but that didn't mean they were the only ones to live there. The city was full of sorcerers, goblins, werewolves, sprites, and elves. There were many things she didn't know, and some she didn't like the look of at all. And then, towering over the bright river, she saw Galig's Hall as it should be.

With the sun shining on its stone, it looked like some wonderful cathedral soaring into the blue sky, dwarfing every building around it.

Nin gasped. In that moment she forgot all about Simeon Dark. She was eleven years old and seeing things that no living Quick had ever seen, or would see again. The real world was very far away.

"Of course, it's all dying," sighed Crow. "Well, dead really."

Nin shook her head. "It's alive here," she said.

Crow looked pleased. "I do my best!"

"Can we go into the Hall?"

"We could, but I don't think you have time. You're fading."

"What?" Nin looked up at him. His thin, bright face

was growing hazy. She felt fear lurch in her stomach as the real world stirred around her. "But I need more time! I wanted to ask . . ." Around her the people slipped away into nothing.

"About Dark? Of course you do. I think you should look for someone who is like he is. His character won't have changed, not really, not deep down. But most important, though I don't know where he is now, I might have a prediction about where he *will be*. The Dancing Circle."

"I can't HEAR you!" cried Nin, and now only the Hall of Galig loomed in her mind like towers of mist.

"Tomorrow," Crow's voice was fading fast. "Before the sky turns black. IF I'm right . . ."

"Hold on to me," cried Nin, reaching out. "I don't want to go . . ."

And she woke up.

32

KILL EVERYTHING

So now, if you'll just give me those boots." Strood smiled at Vispilio, rose from his chair, and took a step forward.

Suddenly, the once-sorcerer felt very Quick and very fragile.

"They're mine!" Vispilio backed away, eyes flashing angrily. They were Doctor Mel's eyes and flashing suited them. "I came here to offer my help. Together we can . . ."

"No you didn't," snapped Strood. "You came because you are a once-sorcerer—an old used-up has-been—and I am the immortal who owns the Drift." His voice dropped to a snarl. "Do you think I can't see right through you? You think I am Simeon Dark and you've come here because you want to make me put on that stupid ring, to take me over. You're wrong, of course. I know I am not Dark, because I know who Dark is. The signposts are a mile high for anyone who's looking."

"You can't know," muttered Vispilio resentfully, "because if you did, his spell would be undone."

"You got that from the girl," Strood replied. "Who got it from Skerridge, who got it from me. But I didn't tell the bogeyman everything. It's not just about one person knowing, it's about DARK knowing. And the only way he will ever know is if someone tells him."

Vispilio glared. His confidence in his own plan was already draining away, though he hadn't given it up quite yet.

The door to the Sunatorium opened and one of the servants struggled through, panting and almost blue with cold. He was holding a chain and on the end of the chain was the Maug. It bounded into the room, nearly knocking the servant over. Around it, crowsmorte began to die, the vivid flowers falling before Jibbit's eyes, leaving a circle of dead, faded crimson petals and twisted brown stems. The temperature in the Sunatorium dropped sharply.

Jibbit eyed the Maug nervously. It fed on Quick and he was well aware that his stone body was suffused with essence of Quick. Images flicked through his mind of the Maug sucking out his Quick bits and leaving the rest in a gravelly mess on the floor. He decided to be as quiet and as still as possible.

"Aha," said Strood cheerfully. "Well done . . . ?"

"M-Milo, sir," stuttered the servant.

"Good, good. Still alive I see, excellent. Keep it up!"

The servant wrestled with the Maug's chain, finally getting it looped around the bole of a tree. That done, he scampered out of the room. "Now," said Strood, beaming at Vispilio, "let me introduce you to my Death. I call it the Maug—not for any reason, it just seemed polite to give it a name. The Maug was separated from me years ago by the last Seven Sorcerers in a cruel, selfish, and, may I say, badly bungled experiment to see if they could postpone death." He chuckled. "Oh, but I forgot. You were there."

Vispilio glared irritably at Strood. "We did you a

favor," he said in icy tones. "You should have died years ago; you should be so much dust by now."

"True, true, but living a long time isn't the same as being immortal. Immortality has its drawbacks. I have an analytical mind, you know. I can work out what the future holds for someone who will live forever. Do you understand forever? It means time without end."

Right next to Strood's glittering eye a muscle began to twitch. "No matter how weary of life I become," he went on quietly, "I will never reach the end of it. Never. And when the Drift has gone and even magic itself is dead, I will still be here. And then—if I can ask such a dull mind as yours to take a leap of imagination—think beyond that. When the Widdern has grown old and died, when the planet is a lump of boiling rock about to be swallowed by the sun, I will still be here. I will be here when the sun goes nova. I will burn for countless years until the sun goes cold again and dies in its turn. I will hang in the icy void of space and watch the stars go out . . ."

As Strood talked, Vispilio grew steadily paler. He licked his lips nervously.

"So that's forever," said Strood calmly. "Now, shall we discuss the word 'alone'? Alone, as in nothing else in the universe but me?"

Vispilio edged closer to the door. Or, at least, a little farther away from Strood.

"So, you see, far from doing me a favor, you Seven Sorcerers committed a crime so horrible it doesn't bear thinking about. All things considered, it's amazing I've managed to stay sane!"

Strood gave his darkness-dripping Death a friendly pat. "But we'll come back to your crimes in a moment. First I want to try a little experiment of my own."

The Maug licked him in a companionable way, its dark within dark eyes watching him attentively. After all, Strood was its master. More than that. The Maug was part of Strood. His Death, by now long overdue and yet unable to claim him because of a spell woven decades before that, had driven a wedge between them.

Vispilio watched, a frown creasing Doctor Mel's creamy forehead. "You see," Strood went on, "it occurred to me the other day, that maybe I could do more with the Maug. It is, after all, MY death. It's a pretty unique relationship and I don't feel that I have properly explored all the options."

"For example?" Vispilio sounded thoughtful, as if he too were thinking things through. A look came into his eyes, one of amazed realization (quickly covered up) followed by one of cold calculation. "How much command do you have over it?" he asked softly. "Does it come when you call?"

"Hmm?" Strood was barely paying attention. He waved a hand dismissively. "Oh, possibly. It's always here, so I've never had the need to try. No, I'm thinking of something more dramatic. Like . . . why a dog, do you think? Why not . . . something less . . . limited?"

Vispilio gasped as the Maug's great body shuddered and heaved. The creature opened its mouth in a silent howl, then leapt into the air. Its great shape hung for a moment, then twisted and tore apart, exploding soundlessly into a thousand smaller fragments that filled the air in a swirling mass. Each one began to reshape itself, pushing out beaks, spindly claw legs. Wings.

The Death birds rose, circling upward to mill about just below the crystal roof of the Sunatorium. They hung there in a black cloud, dribbling shadows like rain that dissolved into the air as it fell. "Much more convenient,"

259

said Strood, "for sweeping through the Drift, devouring every living thing they see. Don't you think?"

As if given a signal, the Death flock veered and dipped, heading for the door. It burst open under the pressure of many small bodies and they streamed through into the hall and then out of the nearest smashed-in window. Through the crystal walls of the Sunatorium, Jibbit watched as they poured into the sky, a funnel of inky shadow that gathered above the Terrible House in a spreading and eerily quiet cloud. There were none of the normal bird sounds, no twittering or singing, just the whir of thousands of small, darkness-dripping wings.

The Death flock wheeled in the sky. Then it headed inland.

Strood went to the door and locked it, pocketing the key.

Vispilio cleared Doctor Mel's throat, feeling suddenly nervous. His plan had undergone a rapid rethink. Far from taking Strood over and ruling the Drift, it had become more like just getting out alive. "So, what? They'll finish off anyone still living?" he said, trying to buy time. "And what about the girl? Isn't that just a little dull? Giving her the same fate as everyone else!"

"Oh, the Death flock will head straight for Hilfian, it is intended only for those Quick and Grimm who survived my army. I have other plans for the girl, as I'm about to demonstrate. I'm going to deal with her personally." Strood beamed. "Now here we need to backtrack a little. Remember that bungled experiment I referred to? The one that made me immortal? I'm sure you do remember, because I believe it was you, Ava, who established my immortality by throwing me to the wolves."

Strood held out a hand. It was smooth with new skin and the only odd thing about it was a bluish-black tinge to the fingertips. "Hmm." He held out the other one, also tipped with bluish-black, but this time seamed with so many scars it looked like miniature crazy paving.

"As you can see, torn apart as I was, I healed up again."

"I remember," said Vispilio, coldly.

Strood looked at the woman in front of him. He looked right through her skin to her heart where the once-sorcerer was crouching like a spider at the heart of a web. "So do I," he said. He smiled warmly. "And so, to make amends, you can help me test the fate I have in mind for young Ninevah." He took a step forward.

Vispilio took a step back.

"You may have noticed," Strood went on, "the strange discoloration to my fingers?"

Vispilio nodded, his eyes darting anxiously this way and that. Jibbit could see that he wasn't used to being nervous and didn't know how to handle it.

"Does it remind you of anything?"

In fact, it was Doctor Mel who knew the answer, but Vispilio had already ransacked the contents of her captive mind. "Faerie pox?" he said. "A nasty disease visited on the Quick by the faerie race when they wanted to clear a village. It died out with the faeries."

"Funnily enough, not all of it. Mafig . . . remember him? He was the Quick apothecary who helped the Seven create the Deathweave . . . Well, he saved a man's life once by distilling the pox right out of him. Kept it as a memento. I discovered it in my laboratory, though I didn't think I'd find such an interesting use for it."

Strood advanced on Vispilio, evil glittering in his quartz eye. It was doing pretty well in the other one too. Vispilio had backed right up against Jibbit's table, eyes widening with horror. "I drank it," went on Strood. "Of course, it can't kill me, because I'm immortal. Which means I'm just . . . a carrier . . ."

Vispilio went white, then drew Doctor Mel's body up to its full height. "Do your worst," he hissed. "In my own way, I'm immortal too. It can only hurt for a while."

"True," said Strood as his fingers touched the middle of Mel's forehead. "But it can hurt A LOT."

Strood's finger left a pink mark. The pink deepened to red. A pimple appeared and became a spot, which became a pustule surrounded by angry-looking skin. Another pimple, and another, both already swelling. Vispilio stopped glaring at Strood and reached up to scratch. The pustules burst, smearing sticky white goo over Doctor Mel's once-smooth forehead. More pimples, spreading down around the eyes, nose, and mouth. Vispilio scratched again. The itch was irresistible.

"Ugh!" He looked with disgust at his fingers, which had already begun to swell. "Well, Strood, I don't think much of your fearful disease."

His voice sounded thick, slurry, as if his tongue was too big. Which it was. The ends of his fingers were turning black and puffy. He coughed as his tongue, now too black and swollen to fit in his mouth, popped out and lolled. His eyes bulged and Strood smiled as he saw panic arrive in them.

"Changed your mind?" he said. "I'm guessing the pain has begun, something like every inch of your skin splitting open. Which it's going to do in just a few minutes. Oh, and the struggling to breathe can't be fun."

Vispilio gave a strangled gasping sound, his eyes now so swollen they bulged out of their sockets. His arms flailed as he sank to the ground.

Watching, Jibbit made a disgusted face as the smell, something like rotten fruit, reached him. Vispilio screamed as great rips began to appear in his skin. Pus oozed out of them. "Just think, once you could have saved yourself. Once, when you were more than just a passenger in a Quick body. Only a sorcerer's touch can stop the faerie pox. No wonder the faeries hated them, they always had to be better at everything."

There were more screams and rips, then a wet popping sound followed by a horrible slithering one as Vispilio descended into a pool of mush, some clothes, and a nice, clean, leftover skeleton. The ring dropped off Doctor Mel's finger bone and Strood reached down to pick it up and clean it off on a handkerchief. He looked up to see Jibbit watching anxiously.

"Not immortal," he explained warmly, "an immortal cannot die. According to the story, Vispilio will only live again if his spell finds a Quick to wear the ring. I'm going to make sure it doesn't."

Jibbit nodded, trying to make the gesture as humble as possible.

Strood beamed as he examined his blackened fingertips. "Well, that worked, then. I shall enjoy using the faerie pox on the girl even more now that I know exactly what's coming to her." He fished Vispilio's boots out of the pile of clothing and mush.

"Hmm, a little ickier than I would have liked, but they'll do."

Cautiously, Jibbit raised a claw. "Erm, but how will yoo know where she is?"

Strood's smile widened. "Oh, I've got that covered too." Out of his pocket he took a circle of metal, its rim etched with twisting symbols that made Jibbit's eyes water to look at them. Balanced on the outer edge of the rim was a ruby. "Interesting thing about faeries, you know. Hopeless sense of direction. Made a lot of compasses. There are tons of them scattered about the Drift."

He held it up.

"Find me Ninevah Redstone," he said, and the ruby rolled to point south.

33

FOR THE WOLVES, AVA

Arafin Strood stepped out of the Terrible House for the first time in decades and sniffed the air. It felt cold in his throat and lungs, probably something to do with the stretches of Raw towering against the sky in all directions.

He was wearing Vispilio's boots strapped on over his usual black silk suit. He held the compass in one hand and had a rope strung around his neck. It was a strange rope, woven from freshly plucked stalks of crowsmorte twisted together in a complicated plait. Jibbit, tucked under Strood's arm, wondered what the rope did and was ready to bet it wasn't nice. He also wondered why Strood was taking him along on the trip and in particular why Strood had strapped Vispilio's ring to his back with twine, wound uncomfortably around his useless wings. Again, he was ready to bet that he wouldn't like the answer. So he didn't ask. Just to be on the safe side.

"Hang on," said Strood cheerfully.

Jibbit had never seen him in such a good mood, not even when he was throwing people to the tigers or sending them to die horribly in the Engine.

Strood took a step forward and Jibbit hooted as the ground spun beneath them, whirling along in a blur. Coming to a stop, Strood turned to look back. Far behind them the House reared against the horizon. The boots had carried them so far in one single step that they had caught up with the Death flock as it sailed through the morning sky, on its way to bring doom to Hilfian. "Well, well," said Strood. "Though bear in mind that we will have to go the long way round."

"Because of all the Raw?" said Jibbit timidly.

"Naturally."

Strood set off again. Each step was like flying very low over the ground, but jerky because every time Strood's feet touched the earth there was a horrible jolt. The pace was dizzying and Jibbit closed his eyes, praying that the journey would soon be over.

Although Strood was carefully avoiding most of the patches of Raw he came across, even though it often took him well out of his way, there was one patch he was planning to visit. "You see," he explained to Jibbit, "if I land right on the edge of the nothingness that you described to me, the nothingness at the heart of the Heart, then we should be able to stop for a while without our mode of transport being eaten away entirely."

"But if we miss the edge and end up in the middle of the Raw . . . ?"

"Then I'll get out again quickly."

"And if we miss the other way and end up . . ."

"Then we will fall forever into nothingness," said Strood comfortably. "It's a gamble, but what is life without a little risk, eh?"

Jibbit was silent. He thought it best. Instead he fixed

his eyes on the mist walls of the Heart, looming against the sky.

"Here we go," said Strood, and took a step.

His calculations had been meticulous and so the step was only a small one to make sure he didn't overshoot. There was a moment of freezing fogginess and then a jolt as they stopped.

"Just as I thought," said Strood.

They were standing on a single ridge of rock, like a raised pathway stretching across the nothingness. A way behind them, the Raw hung like a luminous curtain, its surface shifting restlessly, as if it didn't like being on the edge of death. Their ridge ran out of it, its rocky surface topped with a faint layer of mist that Jibbit could barely see.

"There you are," said Strood cheerfully. "It would take that days to dissolve these boots away. Or the compass for that matter."

"Where does it go?"

"Ah. Good question. Right across the Heart, I believe. You see, the mud creature, the so-called New Fabulous"—he chuckled to himself—"had to have cut across the Heart somehow to reach the Redstone girl in time to be part of our little story, and being made of mud he couldn't use the river. So, even though you told me that there was nothing here in the heart of the Heart, I knew there had to be a way across."

They were both quiet for a moment, stone and madman, standing together on the single thread of rock that ran across the heart of the Heart. Around them the emptiness was so complete that Jibbit thought it would crush him with the weight of its dark, silent nothing. Though it had to be somewhere nearby, he couldn't even hear the river; its great rushing was swallowed up in the emptiness. To distract himself he looked down at their path of rock and wondered where it went before it reached the other side of the Heart.

"Well," said Strood briskly. "It's been interesting. I'm glad I stopped off, and not just because I have a task to perform here."

"A task?"

"Vengeance to wreak, that kind of thing. You see, there is always a gap between legend and the truth. According to the story, Vispilio will die if no Quick puts the ring on within . . . say . . . a few days. Frankly, I think that any evil genius worth his salt would not take such a risk quite that stupid. I suspect that in reality he could last for years sealed in that ring. Centuries even. Until someone found him. So, I will make sure that no one ever does."

Jibbit gulped.

Strood held him out over the edge of the path, dangling him over the void. The ring, tied to the gargoyle's wings, clinked against his stony back.

"I would say it's been nice knowing you, but, frankly, I couldn't give a damn. You are, to me, just a handy weight."

And then Strood let go.

He watched for a moment as the gargoyle fell, plummeting down into the darkness. It made no noise and Strood's last glimpse was of its stony eyes and beak opened wide with shock and its paws spread out and waving wildly. The tied-on ring glinted once, shining out with a red light that soon dwindled to a tiny spark in the darkness before it vanished altogether.

Arafin Strood smiled. "For the wolves, Ava," he said, "for the wolves. May you fall forever."

And then he took a step, the traveling boots whirled him away, and he was gone.

✳ ✳ ✳

Jibbit had no time to cry out. His last glimpse was of Strood's face watching him as he fell, a red light flaring in his quartz eye and a smile playing across his thin lips.

The feeling of shock wore off quickly enough, and after a few minutes Jibbit got used to falling. He wasn't afraid of hitting the bottom, because there wasn't one. Even so, he didn't fancy the idea that the falling could last forever. He felt it might get boring after a few years. It was already quite dull.

He took stock of his surrounding. Up—nothing. Down—nothing. To the left—nothing. To the right— the side of the ridge rushing past him revealed only by the faint haze of Raw clinging to its irregular surface. He had a nasty feeling that it would only rush past him for a few miles before it ran out altogether and then there would be nothing on that side too.

The thought terrified him into action. He flailed with his paws, trying to catch on to the bumps and folds of the rock. Instead he managed to turn his body over so that he was facing down instead of up. Now he could sense the nothing rushing up to meet him, could FEEL the point at which the rock ran out. Then there would be only him and the ring in the middle of all that eternity.

Now he hooted at the top of his voice.

He flailed again and managed to spin over, end to end. Something caught him hard in the back and red-hot pain flared through him. He spun giddily, and then whacked into the wall, front side against the rock and face down toward the void. Even through the agony, the knowledge of what was ahead if he failed made him stick out his paws and shove his beak in, using them as a kind of break to slow himself down. He slithered and clung on, his front paws plowing into the cliff face and sending chips of rock flying into the void. He slowed. A bump came up, like a minileroge, and at last he ground to a halt, his front paws and beak jammed against the jutting edge, his eyes staring wildly over it into the emptiness spinning away below him.

And something else too. Still falling, turning over and over in the air as it plunged on into the darkness, was a lump of rock. His wings! Broken off, he realized, when he had smashed into the cliff the first time. Tied to them, glinting with a red light that held something of rage and something of sheer terror, was the ring. It glimmered, a spark that dwindled fast and then was gone, swallowed up in forever.

Tears leaked from Jibbit's eyes as he hugged the wall of rock, working his fingers and toes deeper in even as he wept. He stayed like that for a while, facedown toward the darkness, until the shock and panic wore off. Then he took stock. The damage to his back was not too bad. Although he couldn't see the ragged, lumpy mess left by his broken wings, he knew that he hadn't been cracked through because he was clearly holding together. His top half was still joined to his bottom half and that, when you got right down to it, was the thing that mattered. He had lost a finger, and possibly a couple of toes, and his beak felt chipped, but he was basically whole.

Next he looked at the Raw nibbling at the face of the rock wall he was clinging to. The Raw was taking a long time to eat the rock away, probably because of all the nothing that was in turn eating away the Raw. The Raw didn't seem to be doing any damage to Jibbit at all, and he wondered if the dose of Quick soaked into his stony being was offering some protection. It was cold, he knew that. Any creature of flesh would be facing frostbite, but Jibbit wasn't a creature of flesh.

Satisfied that he was in no immediate danger, Jibbit inched the fingers of his right front paw over a little. He followed with the toes of his left back paw. Then he shifted his left fingers over, followed by his right toes and so on until he had turned right round and was facing up. Then, quickly regaining his confidence, Jibbit began to climb.

He climbed for a long time up the pitted, ice-cold face of the rock until finally he made it to the ridge that led through the heart of the Heart. From there he went on, hurrying across the terrible nothing, trying not to notice the way the silence was so utterly silent.

At last he reached the other side, where the Raw thickened again and other ridges reared on either side, spiraling away across the scarred and pitted Land. On this side of the nothing, he could hear the eerie voice of the river and suddenly he remembered. When they had been traveling through the Raw on their rafts, they had passed something that loomed over the banks of the river.

Something amazing.

Something that reached the sky.

Looking up, Jibbit saw it, rearing through the mist in a tower of towers, light gray against the white and most definitely there. Although he had conquered his fear of the ground, it didn't mean he wasn't longing to be high again. And what was ahead was most certainly high.

Jibbit's heart leapt with joy and he hurried on toward it.

34

BEFORE THE SKY TURNS BLACK

Nin had woken up feeling well, but as fragile as glass. Her memory of the last day was back too, and although it was painful and frightening to think about Seth, Vispilio, and the skinkin, sleep had put some distance between her and the events and that helped to keep the horrors at bay.

As soon as she had told about seeing Morgan Crow and about his prediction, Taggit had bundled them all into a cart belonging to one of the townsfolk. The cart was harnessed to an ancient horse that seemed to Nin to be all bone structure and nostrils topped off with a worn-down ridge of mane. It set off at a brisk pace, taking them to find Simeon Dark.

The Dancing Circle was high on a range of hills that lay between Hilfian and the remains of the Savage Forest. They had long ago rattled through a narrow pass in the lower hills to the north of the town, curved around the wall of Raw, and headed east. For some time the land had been rising steadily, although the slope was gentle enough not to slow the cart down by more than a little. It was getting steeper, though.

"Accordin' to Crow, the last sorcerer will arrive at the Circle before the sky turns black," said Taggit. "But that don't mean Dark will be himself. He'll still be in disguise."

"But we'll know him *because he's there,* right? And once we know him, the spell will break and it will all work out." Nin frowned. "I suppose the sky turning black means by night falling?" she went on doubtfully, adding a sharp "ow" as the cart rattled over an extra-bumpy bit.

She sent a glance up at the sky, currently a soft-looking blue, spotted here and there with patches of cloud like becalmed ships. Then Nin touched the shadow spell around her arm, feeling its cool and silky spiral shift restlessly. Ever since she had woken up, it had been edgy, as if it knew the search might be coming to an end.

Taggit gave her a questioning look. "What else could it be?"

"I don't know, but it's a prediction isn't it? And predictions shouldn't be that tidy."

"She's got a point," said Jonas. He looked pale and Nin guessed that the wound in his side—mostly healed by Galig's magic, but still tender—was not responding well to being thrown about in a wooden wheeled cart. "After all," he went on, "look at '*a tide of golden darkness.*' Hardly clear, and yet it was perfect for Strood's tiger-man army."

"Dik fikik tik skikik."

"Eh? Oh yeah. The skinkin. I guess '*carrying death to one*' about covers that, right?" Nin looked thoughtful. "And wasn't there something about '*when there is life again in the Heart, so shall the lost be found and the ruined made whole*'? No, wait! That was Azork just trying it out."

"Erm, guys," said Jonas suddenly. His voice had an edge to it. "Call me crazy, but I think the sky is due to turn black sooner than tonight. Look, on the horizon and headed this way!"

Jonas was right. Along the eastern skyline, in the direction they were traveling, stretched a thin band of inky darkness. "It doesn't look like normal rain clouds," said Nin, "but I can't put my finger on why."

"It's not the Storm," Jonas spoke firmly.

"Whatever it is, it's comin' this way fast," said Taggit softly, "and when it gets here the sky is gonna turn black, all right." He pulled the horse to a standstill. "Thank Galig, we're nearly at the Dancing Circle, but we can't take the cart up this last slope, it's too rough. We'll have to hurry if we want to make it before *that* does!"

"What I wanna know," muttered Stanley, "is what Strood's gonna do next? Somefin' nasty, o' course, but what?"

He was studying the wheel ruts cut into the grass in front of them. He and Dunvice had survived the long night after the battle by hiding out in a hut on the edge of town. Now they were following the tracks of the cart carrying the Redstone girl and her friends.

Dunvice snorted irritably, as if she didn't care.

"Yore just as scared of 'im as the rest of us," grumbled Stanley—recklessly, in view of her current mood.

"You're an idiot, Stanley," Dunvice snarled. "I'm not scared of HIM. He's back at the House. What I'm scared of is the thing right behind us."

Stanley blinked as chunks of thought began to shift about in his brain. The feeling of despair that had dogged him all morning, the way Dunvice kept glancing nervously over her shoulder, the rustles in the undergrowth that he had thought was the breeze.

"Great Galig help us," he muttered. His blood froze in his veins. The chill didn't so much run down his spine as settle in and start a family. "The . . . the . . ."

"Skinkin," hissed Dunvice. "It's after us. Or me more like. I'm the fool who kept it in a cage."

"But it's meant to kill the girl?"

"It failed. Didn't you hear that hideous scream last night? Somehow it failed and now it's grown a will of its own. Strood's made a new Dread Fabulous to terrorize what's left of the Drift." She snarled again, froth dribbling at the corner of her mouth. Her eyes were the eyes of a wolf at bay. "I'll bet the evil-hearted son of a gutter dog knew what he was doing too. The skinkin was a sick, hellish experiment. And now the thing KNOWS WHO I AM. We're following the girl for *me*, not for Strood. Finding her may be my only hope. Maybe if it sees her again it will forget about me." She glanced over her shoulder and her eyes were like wildfires, hot and yellow with fear and rage all mixed up.

Behind them the long grass waved and rustled. Stanley stood for a moment, taking in the world. He was taking it in because with the skinkin on their trail it had dawned on him that this might be the last chance he got to look at it.

Around them, the grass was spotted with buttercups that shone like drops of melted gold. There was another, shaggy-headed bloom too, as bright a blue as a summer sky, and suddenly Stanley wanted more than anything to know what that bloom was called. The grass and the flowers bent in the breeze and he could hear the soft rustle of their movement. The meadow was hemmed on one side by a wood of dark trees, and from its center rose a wall of Raw that sent misty snakes reaching into the sky. Stanley could smell its cold iron scent on the air. Along the skyline he could see other stretches too, white smudges as if someone had erased part of the landscape. Even so, the Land was beautiful. So beautiful that he thought his heart would break with the loss of it. With the knowledge of all the time he had wasted not noticing.

I joined the wrong side, he thought, and regret filled him up to overflowing.

"What's that," muttered Dunvice suddenly, "that horrible cloud coming this way?"

Looking east, Stanley saw a strip of blackness racing across the sky, casting a shadow over the Land as it sped toward them. He had seen the Maug close-up many times, and as soon as he saw the way the inky mass coiled and moved, he knew exactly what it was. Not clouds. Death. Strood's Death, to be precise.

At the same time he was aware of stealthy movement behind them. Or rather, behind *him* because Dunvice had taken off and was running. He felt a chill flow over him, like misery made liquid. He dropped to his knees.

Something leapt past him. It moved in great springs, seeming to fly when it was off the ground, and barely touching the earth where it landed before it was off again. It was shrouded in shadows, but he got a sense of its thin, skeletal body and of eyes . . .

Dunvice was screaming as she ran, directionless, just heading for anywhere that wasn't there. The wolf was all gone from her now and she was a blubbering wreck, stumbling, falling, picking herself up to run a little farther. She kept turning to run backward, as if facing it would help, as if she couldn't bear to have it BEHIND HER. And then she fell and didn't get up, and the thing . . . skinkin . . . landed on top of her and sat on her chest, its eyes that weren't eyes pinned to hers, crushing her heart with loneliness and fear.

Stanley staggered to his feet and ran, half backward because he couldn't bear the thought that the thing might be BEHIND HIM and he had to keep looking to see. Something caught at his foot and he tripped. His vast Grimm bulk crashed to the ground, face first, arms spread-eagled. Shuddering, he lay there, waiting for death at the merciless stare of the skinkin. It was all over for him, he was sure of it.

"Oy! Stanley," yelled a voice.

A hand grabbed him roughly by the shoulder and hauled him up. Hauled him so up that his feet dangled for a moment before whoever it was planted him back on the ground.

Half sobbing, Stanley looked up into the Halloween face of the ex-gravedigger.

"Taggit? Taggit Sepplekrum?"

Behind Taggit were other shapes. He could see the pony and trap now. It had been hidden by an outcrop of shrubs. A whole gaggle of people were running away from the trap, heading off up the steeper slope of the hill and over its top. He could see the girl and the boy and the mudman and a great knobbly shape that had to be Floyd. At the sight of his old friend, Stanley felt something bubble up in his chest.

Without thinking, he joined in, following Taggit and

the others as they thundered toward the Dancing Circle, determined to get there before the flood of darkness overtook the sky.

Nin was running hard to keep up with the others. The shadow spell was a ribbon of purple fire on her arm, constantly moving, twisting with energy. *Dark will be there,* she told herself, *he* has *to be there.*

Over the crest of the hill the land dipped sharply and then leveled out to a wide stretch of green grass. Ahead of them, on the plateau, she could see a ring of trees. All dead, that much was obvious from their bone white trunks and naked branches. Against a background of faded blue, the pale forms reached up to the sky. Their shapes were so strange, she had a horrible moment where she didn't recognize them as trees, but saw them as if they were the skeletons of people, struck suddenly dead in the middle of a complicated dance. Each one had a twisted look—some bending, some reaching—and their branches were like arms flung out and up. As she drew closer she thought she could see the shapes of faces in their trunks.

They were Fabulous, once, she thought. *Alive and Fabulous.*

"Tree Lords," panted Floyd in her ear. "Kings of the forest. 'Ullo, Stanley."

"'Ullo, mate," said Stanley, falling in beside him. He looked bloody and battered and his eyes had sunk so far into his face, they were barely visible. But he was grinning away as if something heavy had been taken off him. "Wha's up, then?"

"We're gonna find Simeon Dark, see. Stop Strood."

"Righto," said Stanley, humbly but happily. "Count me in."

He glanced nervously at Taggit and Jonas, but they were too busy running to worry about the past. It was gone now, wiped away by this last mad dash to save the Drift, if not forever, then at least for another day.

Coming to a breathless halt inside the circle of trees, they watched the mass of inky cloud racing toward them. The table of land on which the Dancing Circle stood was halfway down the steep plunge of the hill, and Nin could see the Drift laid out before her, rolling away to the east. The Savage Forest was a brown scar cutting across the landscape, but before and beyond it were meadows and woods and a sparkling strip of the river to the south. A white smudge on the horizon was probably the Heart.

Over it all, the strange cloud flowed across the sky in a tidal wave of liquid black, casting shadows as it came. Far on the skyline, a thin band of blue showed where the mass of cloud ended. "There's something familiar about the way it moves," she said.

Stanley cleared his throat. "Strood's Deff," he offered. "Dunno 'ow, but it's the Maug. See 'ow the shadows seem t' drip off it? 'Ow it swirls in the air like a great flood o' spilled ink?"

"Of course," said Jonas softly, stepping toward Nin.

Floyd and Taggit did the same. They didn't know that Strood had sent the flock to Hilfian with no stops on the way, and they thought it was looking for Nin. They gathered around her protectively, overshadowing her with their bulk as if they could hide her. There was no point in running because the Maug would be faster, and besides, they were here to find Simeon Dark, their last and only hope.

"It won't see 'er," muttered Taggit suddenly. "It's flyin' too 'igh."

Outside the Dancing Circle something rustled in the long grass. Stanley heard it and flinched. *It's watching,* he thought. *Skinkin is here and it's watching.* He realized that this was the creature's last chance to die. If Nin failed, then the Drift would be dead in a day or so and, as everything died with it, skinkin would get the death it longed for. But if she succeeded . . . if she found Simeon Dark and he put a stop to Strood, and the Drift lived on for a little longer, then there really would be a new Dread Fabulous to roam the dying landscape, chilling the hearts of all who heard it scream.

Skerridge sent a glance around the Circle at Nin, Jonas, Jik, Floyd, Taggit, and Stanley as they stood anxiously waiting for Simeon Dark to arrive before Strood's flying Death did. It dawned on him that, including himself, there were seven of them, an echo of the Seven Sorcerers and the Final Gathering that had changed the world and given it Arafin Strood. The thought made his bones tingle. It seemed right somehow, that this group of seven players in the great game of Ending Strood should be here. Even Stanley, though he had been so long on the other side.

As the chill shadow swept relentlessly toward them, Skerridge shivered. But it wasn't only because of the Death flock. The sorcerer would be in the Dancing Circle, Crow had said, before the sky turned black. The seven people currently in the circle had all arrived before the Death flock filled the heavens with its inky darkness and there wasn't a lot of time left for anyone else to show up. The conclusion was inescapable.

"Dark's one of us, ain't 'e?" he said. "'E's 'already

'ere an' we just 'ave t' work out which of us it is!"

He sent a penetrating look at Jonas. He'd been wondering about the boy ever since the Galig's sword incident. So did Taggit and Nin. Stanley took a surreptitious glance at Floyd, who was watching Nin. Jonas shot a look at Jik who was staring thoughtfully at the sky.

"There's still a moment yet," said Taggit calmly.

Now the flock was almost overhead, its great mass eating up the sky and its shadow tearing over the last stretch of land toward them. Watching it, Jonas frowned. "Taggit's right. It's too high up! The Maug can't be after Nin. If it was coming to the Circle it would be flying lower by now."

"I'm bettin' it'll fly right over our 'eads," said Skerridge suddenly. "I'm bettin' the evil git 'as sent it to 'Ilfian to finish off the survivors!"

Jonas paled. "Hen, Hilary!"

"Right," said Nin firmly. She touched the spell on her wrist, trying to will the last sorcerer into view. Hilfian wasn't far away, the Death flock would be there in no time.

"We need Simeon Dark, NOW. At least it can't be Strood, because he's not . . ."

Through the pillars of the dancing trees, something blurred in the distance, heading toward the hill. It made Nin's eyes hurt as if she were trying to focus on two different places at once. She winced and blinked.

". . . here," she finished.

And suddenly Strood *was* there, neatly dressed in a black silk suit that didn't go at all with the leather boots strapped around his legs. He was standing an arm's reach away from Nin, smiling at the circle of shocked faces. Everyone froze.

Overhead, the Death cloud swarmed on, spilling its chill shadow over the Circle and its occupants.

Turning the sky black.

35

ANY ONE OF US

Strood glanced up at the inky flood as it swept over their heads. From it, shadows fell like rain.

"I see my Maug flock is making good time," he said. "Excellent. Should be at Hilfian in minutes, I believe. That's one thing sorted, anyway. I have other plans for all of you." He beamed at the stunned group. Nin backed away, her mind churning. Skerridge was right, one of the people in the circle was really Dark in disguise.

It could be any one of us, she thought, *even Strood.*

And the awful thing was, Crow had said that Dark's character wouldn't have changed, not deep down. So if Dark was a sorcerer, and sorcerers loved power, then Strood had to be top of the list of possibilities.

Her heart turned to stone at the thought.

"Well, now," Strood was saying. "I didn't expect such an excellent turnout for my grand finale. Seven, I see. How . . . meaningful."

Even as he spoke, he swung the crowsmorte rope from his neck in one easy movement, twirled it around his head and threw. It spun through the air, its stalks

already alive and twisting, and hit Skerridge before anyone had a chance to register what was going on. The
stalks twined, swiftly pinning the bogeyman's arms to
his sides as it began to put out shoots.

"Oy!" yelled Skerridge indignantly, more with fury
than anything else. Yet.

Chaos descended as everything happened at once.

Strood sprang toward Nin, his blue-black fingers
reaching to touch her face, but she was already on the
move. She scrambled backward out of his way, then
ducked under his outstretched arms and ran.

As she moved, she saw Jonas and Jik rushing to
help her. Taggit, Floyd, and Stanley had leapt in to free
Skerridge from the crowsmorte, and all four of them collapsed in a tussle of bodies and roots and rapidly bloom-
ing flowers.

Strood spun to catch her, but Nin darted left and
kept going, hurtling around the inside rim of the Dancing Circle. Strood followed, inches behind her and laughing excitedly. Jonas sprang at Strood, who dodged out
of his way then dove around Jik, leaving the mudman
spinning.

Nin tore past the heaving mass of Fabulous, Grimm,
and madly growing crowsmorte. She heard Skerridge
yell something that might have been "Stop it! Stop growing in my 'ead, ya blasted, blimmin' POPPY!" followed
by a lot of strangled gasping from Stanley and bellows of
fury from Taggit. A boot flew past followed by a shower
of crowsmorte petals and a dented helmet. The helmet
hit Jonas, who staggered and fell. Jik, diving to tackle
Strood, ikked wildly as a tentacle of crowsmorte lashed
around him, dragging him to the ground and bump-
ing him over the grass before—not finding any flesh or
blood to eat—it let go.

Nin ran on. She didn't go outside the ring of trees, partly because she didn't want to leave the others, and partly because she hadn't yet given up on Simeon Dark. She was easily keeping ahead of Strood and knew that as soon as they could, Jonas and Jik would grab him. So she kept going, starting her second lap of the Dancing Circle.

The sky was still inky and the chill cast over the land by the Maug flock, flying high above over their heads, was getting into her bones. She heard Jonas shout and saw him spring back onto his feet. Jik was already up and running toward Strood.

Good, she thought with a surge of relief, *they'll get him any second.*

And then her foot hit a stone and her ankle wrenched, throwing her backward against a tree. For a moment she faced Strood, eyeball to glittering eyeball.

Arafin Strood smiled indulgently. "That was fun," he said. "Haven't played chase in years. Quite a day *this* is turning out to be."

He reached out with his blackened fingers and gently touched her forehead.

"Ow," said Nin, clapping a hand to her head. She glared at Strood.

Triumphant howls and shouts along with some major ripping sounds came from the other side of the clearing. Breathless, Jonas arrived at her side. There was a cut on his head and blood smeared on his cheekbone. He was about to take Nin's arm when Jik leapt in and shoved him away.

"IK!"

"Don' touch 'er!" yelled Skerridge, appearing next to Jik.

There was a crowsmorte bloom growing out of

the bogeyman's ear, but otherwise the stuff had been stamped into oblivion. The others staggered up, clothes torn and eyes wild. They all stood there, staring at Nin and Strood and slowly registering that it was too late.

Nin stepped away from Jonas, her face pale and her breath coming in short gasps. Her blue eyes fixed his gray ones with a steady gaze.

"They're right, Jonas. He's done something, don't you see?" she could feel it already, spreading over her forehead. The skin was tight, swollen, and itchy, hot with something bad. She put a hand up and it came away with yellow pus spilling over her palm. Even as she looked, her fingers began to swell and darken.

Strood stood, quietly watching Nin's face as the lumpy boils spread. "I've killed you," he said softly, "that's what I've done. Given you faerie pox. And if you touch your friend here, even for a final good-bye, then he'll die too. Painfully. Like you."

"Take it back," snarled Jonas, his eyes lighting with fury.

"Or what? You'll kill me?" Strood chuckled. "Come now, boy, we both know there is nothing you can do."

Jik stepped forward and pushed a mud-made hand into Nin's. The disease was spreading backward across her scalp and forward down her cheekbones. And up her wrists to her arms, too, making the spell shift about uncomfortably, its colors turning to a dark gray touched with crimson. She coughed and something spattered onto her raised hand. The disease was inside her now, clogging her lungs and pushing up under her skin. Her whole body felt stretched. It was uncomfortable, but she knew that uncomfortable was just the beginning. Strood was about to win, unless she did something fast.

"We know that Dark's already here." Nin swallowed

as pain began to blossom somewhere in her middle. "We just have to work out who."

All eyes were on her now, hanging on her words. She wished they wouldn't. She wished one of them would help her, but it was *Nin* who had to help *them*. One of them at least. Dark. Suddenly, while her body fell apart, somewhere in her head the pieces began to fit together.

"I think . . . I think Dark's spell *wants* him to be free," she said through swollen lips. "The spell was made to keep him from death and it disguised him so well that even he doesn't know who he is. But it's not working anymore, is it? The Land is dying and so will everything in it, however carefully it's hidden."

Her tongue was swelling now too; her voice sounded thick and the pain was a hot knife in her insides. Jonas stepped toward her and she could see how much he wanted to put his arms round her, try to make it better somehow. She pulled back, shaking her head, hanging on to Jik.

"What I'm saying is," Nin mumbled past her tongue, "now, the best way the spell can keep Simeon Dark from death is to break. That way he can come back and save us, save the Drift. But the spell can't break itself." She stopped, struggling for breath. She knew the answer was in reach, but she just couldn't get it.

"It can only break when someone tells Dark who he is," said Strood cheerfully, "so you had better hurry up, girl, hadn't you! Let's see, you have around five minutes before you are incapable of speech. Screaming maybe, but not speech. And . . . say . . . seven before you are a puddle on the ground. And just remember, Dark's spell is designed so that nobody can guess it."

"Unless," said Taggit, suddenly. He looked at Strood, a slow smile crossing his ugly face. "Unless they're someone very lucky who 'appens t' be dyin' of somethin' only a sorcerer can cure."

Jonas glanced at Strood and saw that what Taggit said was true. It was written on Strood's face. Even he wasn't perfect. Every plan has its flaw and Arafin Strood had just spotted the catch in his. "Not quite as I intended things to work out," he said. His smile had become brittle and his quartz eye glittered horribly in his pale face. "But never mind. What is life without an element of risk?" He looked at Nin. "Come on now, time is running out."

Watching Nin struggle, Skerridge felt something expand in his middle. Panic. A complicated thought came into his head about this being IT. THE END. Because if this girl died then it was all over and everything would die, torn apart by the Raw and doomed to become nothing but eternal darkness. Because this girl was the last chance. HIS last chance. He shook the feeling off and stepped forward to lean over her, his red eyes inches from Nin's, the crowsmorte bloom bobbing.

Overhead the cloud of Death was nearly gone, darkening the horizon beyond the hill as it swarmed on toward Hilfian. It left a shadowy haze in its wake, but following that was clear sky.

Nin looked up. Behind Skerridge she could see the dark slash that was Strood as he waited for the disease to get her before her luck could tell her what she had to say. She could sense the tension, crackling like fire in the hearts of those watching. It felt as if the focus of the whole world was here, on *this* stretch of grass, in the center of *this* ring of trees. Because what was about to happen here was going to change everything.

"Come on, kid," said Skerridge gently, "ya know, doncha?"

Overhead, the shadows left by the Death flock began to break up and a shaft of sunlight fell through the trees, bathing Skerridge in light. And suddenly Nin understood what Crow had been trying to say about Dark's character being the same. Crow hadn't been talking about Dark as a sorcerer, but Dark as a *person*. And Dark as a person was a joker who loved disguises and liked to stretch the rules.

It was obvious really.

"BMs don't go out in the sun," she gasped, "but you do. You're not a proper bogeyman, and that's because you're not a bogeyman at all. You never were! You're a sorcerer in disguise."

Leaving her arm, the shadow spell broke apart, sending its colors flying through the air, swirling around the startled group of watchers.

"It's you, Skerridge," said Nin. "You're really Simeon Dark!"

36

THE LAST SORCERER

Skerridge bounced backward as the shadow colors gathered into a cloud and surged toward him. They surrounded him, their light filling his eyes with a kaleidoscope of blues and purples, and then were gone. Inside his head, memories began to rearrange themselves, shifting their perspective, details clicking suddenly into place. As they did he realized just how dreamlike the old ones, the memories that he had thought were real, actually were. Now he was seeing his past from the right angle and it made everything different.

He gulped. He had been at the Final Gathering all right, but he hadn't just been *watching*. He had been part of it. Alongside the other sorcerers he had helped to cast the Deathweave, had persuaded Strood to drink it, had failed to stop Vispilio throwing Strood to the wolves. And then had walked away from the results.

Horror swept through him at the memory and he groaned, shuddering and putting his bony hands over his face. He was part of the creation of Strood and so he was also part of the destruction of everything he had come to care about.

"It's all right," mumbled Nin gently through her swollen lips.

Skerridge opened his eyes again and grinned a slow, relieved grin as a happier thought arrived. Of course it was all right! It was absolutely, fantastically all right! He could sort it all out NOW! A bit late, true, but that was better than never. He was a sorcerer and he could save the world. Not to mention Ninevah Redstone.

He stepped toward her, shaking off the bogeyman shape as he moved, his bony limbs thickening to a sorcerer's slender figure, the hairiness disappearing, except for that on his head, which turned fair. Lastly, in a single blink, his eyes glowed gold, strangely flecked with silver. Simeon Dark was back.

Dark leaned toward Nin, smiling. In spite of the row of neat, perfectly formed teeth, the look was pure Skerridge. The crowsmorte bloom had gone from his ear, but he was still wearing his tattered trousers and the worse-for-wear fancy waistcoat. He reached out with one slender hand to touch her forehead. To take back what Strood had given her.

Strood dove, grabbing Dark around the waist and hurling him to the ground a split second before his fingers touched Nin. "You won't win it all, Simeon Dark," he hissed. "At least I'll make sure the girl dies."

The sorcerer vanished from Strood's grip, then flicked back into view a few feet away. For a moment Dark wondered how he had done it, but then remembered. With magic he could rearrange himself to be pretty much anywhere.

Springing back to his feet, Strood got between the sorcerer and Nin. With a flourish he pulled a sword from a sheath at his belt. Its thin blade shone with a light that made the air around it glitter.

"Elven silver," whispered Taggit. "Impervious to magic."

Those watching edged away, leaving the sorcerer and the immortal facing each other, tensing for the first move. As she staggered against a tree for support, Nin was shocked at how useless her legs felt, like lumps of soaking cotton wool. She sank slowly to the ground, feeling something inside her burst. Jonas crouched beside her, white-faced with fear.

In the middle of the Circle, Dark sighed. As his memory unearthed one inventive spell after another, it left part of him still reeling from shock at this new discovery of himself. On top of that, not one of the spells he was coming up with would put an end to Strood. Only Strood's Death could do that, and to work out a spell to undo the Deathweave would take time—the one thing they didn't have.

He shot a glance at Nin. All he needed was a moment to rearrange himself over there and heal her. Perhaps if he got Strood out of the way . . .

"Hah!" he shouted triumphantly, flicking his fingers. Strood vanished. Dark turned toward Nin, flicked out of sight and then materialized again, standing right next to her. At the same time, the air blurred and Strood reappeared in exactly the same spot as Dark. The two of them collided, bouncing back, away from Nin.

"Forgot the blimmin' boots," muttered Dark.

Strood grinned savagely and whirled the sword, taking a firm stride toward Dark.

Backing away, Dark breathed in deeply. He didn't need Natural Bogeyman anymore to produce a little thing like firebreath. A blast of white-hot flame poured from his mouth, forcing the watchers to scrabble further away. As Nin moved, another split ran down her back and she knew that the end was near. Her insides felt like hot liquid and each breath was a struggle.

Strood burst alight, but stalked on toward Dark anyway, a pillar of fire with an elven sword and the air of something that was never going to stop. A lump of glittery stone dropped out of the flaming mass and rolled away as sorcerer and immortal circled one another.

The flames finished burning anything burnable and went out, leaving soot-stained bones. They were still upright and waving the sword menacingly, though Strood had stopped moving forward. Nin wondered why until she realized that he was waiting for his eyes to heal so that he could see properly.

Dark stepped lightly across the clearing. Sensing the movement, Strood turned his head. Already, blood vessels were forming on the bone, flesh was growing. He got a better grip on the sword and began to lurch across the space after Dark, eyeless and earless, it didn't matter. He was coming to kill them anyway.

Nin's world was growing dark, and the pain settled into one great ball of fire in her chest as her heart got ready to explode. She sagged, and Jik shoved his arms around her chest, holding her up. Jonas turned, wild-eyed with fear, looking for the sorcerer.

Dark reached them, leaned forward, and pressed a cool hand to Nin's forehead. "There you go," he said, "all better now."

Nin gasped as the pain began to recede at once. Behind them, Strood whirled the sword, bringing it down in a blow that should have cut both the sorcerer and Nin in half. Only there was a sizzle of hot air and suddenly Nin's world became a blur of movement so fast she could feel her molecules spin. Then everything was normal again, except she was on the other side of the clearing, slung over the sorcerer's shoulder. "Was that real superspeed?" she mumbled, steaming. "As opposed to nearly superspeed?"

On the plus side, it had dried out some of the pus and she didn't appear to be cooked. She saw that her split skin was already healing.

"With knobs on," said Dark proudly, setting her on the ground. "Note that you are not currently a cinder! We sorcerers can do almost anything, you know."

There was a howl of rage from across the clearing. Strood swung the sword wildly, forcing the others to leap back out of the way. He had eyes now. Two new ones with no trace of quartz. And a few bits of skin.

"Ahh," said Dark, raising an eyebrow. Light flashed from his fingers and suddenly Strood was wearing a smart white suit. Nin was glad. He was healing up pretty fast and things could have turned embarrassing. This time there were no scars, and if he hadn't been an immortal, insane, death-dealing psychopath, he might have looked quite nice.

Angry though, definitely angry.

Vision restored, he spun toward Nin, whirled the sword up over his head, and threw it. The blade sailed through the air, a shining silver-white streak hurtling straight for Nin's heart. She stepped neatly to one side. The sword flew past her and stuck in one of the Dancing Trees, where it quivered, singing quietly.

For only the second time in his long and cruel life, Arafin Strood completely and utterly lost it. He went nova.

"You," he snarled having just discovered that he now had lips to snarl with, "you sniveling, scrawny, insufferable little BRAT." His voice rose to a scream. "How dare you challenge me!"

Nin edged toward Dark, feeling hurt by the sniveling

comment. She was sure she had only cried when it was really bad. She wasn't too keen on scrawny, either.

Stood pulled himself up to his full height. He was quivering all over with fury, his face twisted up with it, his eyes like chips of black ice. "That's it," he said, "it ends NOW!" He flung back his head and screamed. It wasn't a word, but it still sounded like a command that echoed through the air in spreading ripples until it reached its target.

Back in Hilfian, the Death flock's approach to the town had been hidden by the wall of Raw, which blocked people's view of the horizon. It took them completely by surprise, appearing over the top of the Raw and crashing down on them in a tidal wave of inky black.

Shouts of alarm rose as the air grew cold. Ice ran over puddles and ponds, leaves began to wither on the tallest trees, and flowers pulled in their petals sensing night in the middle of the day. The shouts turned to screams as the Death flock swept over Hilfian, a hundred thousand wings whirring and a hundred thousand beaks open, letting out a trilling that was made of raw fear. Everywhere, everyone ran.

"Get to the cellars!" yelled Hilary above the clamor of frightened voices. "We'll be safe there!"

She darted into the town hall, calling to the patients to move as Maug birds poured into every hut, broken or whole, through every gap and crevice. Their chill put out fires and froze barrels of water, and where they found life they swept around it hungrily and then moved on, leaving only husks of flesh and bone.

Ahead of the flood, people snatched up their children and ran, screaming. Goats and chickens were devoured in a heartbeat, their tiny lives extinguished as the flock ate everything Quick in its path. Even the Grimm weren't safe. The birds just ate around the Fabulous parts and left the remains. Only the Fabulous would survive this attack and there was nothing they could do to help the others.

In the town hall, Hilary leaned to pull open the trap door.

"Great Galig help us," whispered Senta's Spell in her head as she looked up to see Death birds pour in through the door. Around her, people screamed, trying to bat away the swarm of tiny, icy bodies and sharp beaks. "Galig can't do anything now," said Hilary as the flock poured toward her. She shut her eyes, feeling cold surround her. She held out her arms to let the birds feed. If she was going to die, it might as well be quick. The chill cut into her like knives as a hundred tiny beaks dipped into her skin. She felt their darkness surging through her veins, exchanging life for death.

Suddenly, a ripple ran through the flock. Not a sound so much as a vibration echoed from every beak. For a moment, the birds swirled in confusion, and Hilary could feel their icy bodies buffeting against her. And then the pain and the cold lifted. Opening her eyes, Hilary saw the flock rising again, pouring upward into the sky and gathering into a dark mass over the town. Around her, people began to stir and groan. Most people. One or two lay still.

Overhead the Death flock circled and began to move, heading back in the direction it had come from as if in answer to a summons. As they went, the birds began to pick up speed. Bewildered, Hilary watched them go.

In the Dancing Circle, the air shimmered and something in the light changed and then was gone. Nin glanced up at Dark. He was frowning.

"That felt like magic," she said.

"No magic," snapped Strood. "I summoned the Maug. Change of plan, Hilfian can wait. My Death flock can feed on you first, all of you, Quick and Grimm!" He glared at Dark and Taggit. But especially Dark. "The Fabulous I'll deal with later."

Jonas ran across the clearing to Nin. Already a streak had appeared on the skyline, a slash of inky darkness that grew, racing back from Hilfian. As it tore across the sky, the Maug flock had changed, the thousands of bodies losing their form and running together, merging into a single mass. Now it was no longer a flock, it was just one great Death, answering its master's call with horrifying speed. "You won't escape this time," sneered Strood, "even your Fabulous friends can't help you now."

A look flickered across Dark's face. It was the same look that had crossed Ava Vispilio's earlier that day— sudden realization as the penny dropped and after all these terrible years he finally understood how the Deathweave worked.

"They won't have to," he said sadly. "What just happened, it wasn't magic, it was the breaking of magic."

Nin shivered as the cloud of darkness flowed swiftly across the sky. The Death swirled, dipping toward the Dancing Circle. Trees dropped leaves suddenly heavy with ice, and frost ran over the fields, spreading in a crisp coat. Skinkin felt it coming and howled a howl of longing to be part of that death. "You see, the terrible thing is," Dark went on softly, "the Deathweave did precisely what we said; we were just too scared to trust it. The potion would have let us live for *exactly as long as we wanted to*. When we had had enough of life, all we needed to do was . . ."

". . . call it back!" whispered Nin.

Strood went white as he understood. The summons he had just sent to the Maug had ended the spell that kept them apart. He had called his Death home and it was coming. Fast.

"Help me!" he said. His eyes had gone wide and dark and for a second Nin saw the face of the man he used to be, a long time ago before it had all gone so horribly wrong.

Inky shadow poured from the sky in a whirlpool of darkness, funneling down toward its master. It streamed right into Strood and for a moment there was silence.

In all the years that had passed, Arafin Strood had been through many deaths. They all scrambled to kill him at once.

He screamed as the faerie pox, which had been raging uselessly in his body for the last day or so, worked out that it could finally get him and moved in, determined to be the first. Boils erupted all over his skin, appearing, swelling, and bursting in one very fluid moment. They had to travel fast because his flesh began to fall off almost at once, the old scars where the wolves had pulled him apart opening up like fault lines all over his body. And then there was the faerie venom, racing to turn him into mush before his skin was eaten away by the pox. It all happened in the space of one terrible scream.

And there was Dark's blast of firebreath, too. Just as Strood's soft bits were dissolving to reveal a shocked-looking skeleton, he burst into flames.

Everyone leapt back as the skeleton burned fiercely before it exploded, showering red-hot bones and steaming dribble everywhere.

The echo of Strood's last scream died away and silence settled, broken only by the soft crackle and spit of flames. Then the smell of barbecue and acid caught up with the watching group's noses and everyone began to cough and splutter.

"Well," croaked Dark through streaming eyes and a sore throat, "I guess that's the end of Arafin Strood."

But they watched the remains sizzle for a little while longer, just to make absolutely sure.

37

WEDNESDAY

D'you think," Nin said thoughtfully, "that I might've got it wrong about Wednesday? I mean, even if bad things did happen on a Wednesday—Toby ceasing to exist, being stolen by Skerridge, and all that—the fact is that I survived them all against the odds. Like, it's Wednesday today and we've finally managed to beat Strood. He won't be killing off the Seven and weakening the Land, which means the Raw will stop spreading so fast and the Drift will go on for a few more years at least."

"So, you mean that really Wednesday is your lucky day," said Jonas. "The day you succeed against the odds?"

"Yeah!" She nodded firmly. She, Jonas, and Jik were back in Hilfian, sitting on the grass outside the ruins of the town hall, waiting for Simeon Dark. He had promised to take them back to the Quickmare at No. 27. From there they would get through to Dunforth Hill and then Nin would go home. She was still hoping to persuade Jonas to take his memory pearl too, though he had always said he wouldn't.

She flopped onto her back and stretched out, amazed

at how nice it felt not to be running away or fighting for her life for a change. Around them, people were busy mending huts, setting things to rights, and generally being happy to be alive. The sun was shining and the sky was a glorious clear blue, and right now Nin felt wonderfully free. "In a lot of ways, I'll be sorry to leave it all," she said softly, "and really sorry to leave Jik, but he's . . . well, he's growing up now and it's time he went off to be his own Fabulous. Besides, we know where the gateways are." She took a sidelong glance at Jonas. "I suppose I should say *I* know, since you think too much time's passed for you to go back to the Widdern. Not that I agree. I mean, you must have a family who would want you back even after four years. And we'd still be friends. . . ."

"It's more than that," said Jonas slowly. "It's all I've seen and done. I don't know if I could fit in again." There was a thoughtful look in his eyes. "I'd be expected to be normal. School and everything."

Nin scrunched up her face, thinking about it. "Yeah, true it would take time. But you've got me. And what would you do here anyway? Hilary is going to stay and help Hen, Taggit, and the others put Hilfian back together. Skerridge . . . sorry *Dark* . . . is going to open up his Mansion again, and wants to free all the people held prisoner in Strood's Terrible House and help all the servants, too. After all, he knows what Strood was like to work for!" She sent an affectionate glance at the mudman standing in the sun, soaking up the heat. "Jik wants to go traveling and see what's left of the Drift. So, would you stay in Hilfian too?"

Jonas shrugged. "Ready then?" Asked a cheerful voice right behind Nin, making her jump. "Do you have to do that? You'll give someone a heart attack!"

Dark chuckled. "No, but it's fun."

He was no longer wearing his old tattered trousers, but had replaced them with a suit of dark silver. He still had his waistcoat though. It looked a lot tidier and all the bloodstains had gone.

"You're getting used to being a sorcerer again then?"

"It's not been easy." Dark blew out his cheeks thoughtfully. "I mean, one minute there I was casting a spell to keep me safe and then all of a sudden it had rearranged my memory, changed my shape, and given me a whole new identity! I spend the next few decades stealing kids for Mr. Strood without a clue who I really am until suddenly I'm back as a sorcerer, battling a complete madman. Not to mention being the only one of my kind left." He looked sad for a moment, then smiled again.

"Sorry," said Nin.

Dark waved a hand airily. "You've got nothing to be sorry about. You only saved my life. Well, are you ready? Said all your good-byes?"

Nin got to her feet, thinking of Hen and Hilary and Taggit and Floyd. And even Stanley. The good-byes had been difficult, but not too difficult. She knew where the gateways were. It wasn't the last time she would see them, she was sure of that.

"Come on then," said Dark. "Can't hang about all day. I'm a very busy sorcerer you know."

And then they weren't standing outside the town hall in Hilfian anymore. They were on a hillside in the warm morning sun looking up at the blank windows of No. 27 Dunforth Hill, Driftside.

"It's that easy, is it?" said Jonas with a laugh.

"It's magic," said Dark cheerfully. "We sorcerers can do that."

Nin laughed. "Don't get too bigheaded now, I

remember you when you were just a bogeyman."

"Yik!"

Dark chuckled. "We had some times, eh! Not all of them good, I'll grant you. But definitely exciting. Oh, and bear in mind, I'll be offended if you didn't drop by now and then for a chat. And you really shouldn't offend sorcerers." He smiled. "Just give me a shout when you come Driftside. I'll hear you."

"You could come and see me?"

"I know I used to go Widdernside for days at a time, but that was when I thought I was a bogeyman." Dark looked up at the towering walls of No. 27 and sighed. "I think my Widdern days might be over."

Nin nodded, and turned to Jik. "When you're back from traveling and all that, well, you know where to find me, don't you?"

"Yik. Alwik." He reached over and took her pink hand in his dusty, crystal-studded one for just a moment.

Jonas put a hand on her shoulder. "Come on, kid. Time to go."

When they reached the gate of No. 27, Nin looked back. Jik and Dark were still there. She followed Jonas down the side of the house, trying not to hear the Quick-mares scratching at them through the walls. And then they were through.

Watching them go, Dark said, "I suppose I could try it. Maybe if I do Skerridge shape, I won't feel it so much?"

"Yik!"

"Let's see, how does it go?" He flexed his fingers. "Red eyes and kind of horrible . . ."

Dunforth Hill looked exactly the way it always had. Jonas led the way up the hill until they were just across the road from Nin's house. She glanced over her shoulder and saw a bogeyman perched on a nearby wall, next to an odd-looking mud statue. The bogeyman was wearing a tattered pair of trousers and a (still clean) fancy waistcoat, so she waved. It waved back and the mud statue raised a hand in farewell. She felt pleased that they had come to see her safely home.

The house sat in the sun, a pine tree casting its cool darkness over the garden, looking peaceful and untroubled. It was going to be troubled pretty soon, but there was nothing Nin could do about that. She wondered what on earth she was going to tell her mother. She wondered if Toby had remembered what she had told him. If he would be waiting.

"She's going to remember me again, which is nice. But she's also going to realize that I'm the second of her kids who's been missing for ages and she hasn't even noticed. What's that going to do to her?"

"You have to tell her the truth," said Jonas firmly. "It's the only way she will ever be able to forgive herself." He took a deep breath. "Thing is, Nin," he went on nervously. "I know I said I wouldn't, but . . ."

"You're gonna take yours too? That's great!" Nin gave him a big smile. "And don't worry about school. It'll be weird for a bit and they'll have to give you extra classes, but you'll catch up really fast. And I'll be right here . . . or at least . . . where does your family live?"

"Both together, right?" said Jonas, ignoring the question.

Nin nodded. They dug into their pockets for their memory pearls. Copying Jonas, Nin threw hers quickly into her mouth and swallowed. For a moment, silvery strands spun in the air above their heads, making a halo around them both.

Nin didn't feel the memory of her that spun out, back to her mother and her grandparents and all those who loved her most or knew her best. But she did feel the memories of Jonas as they glimmered in the air, some of them spiraling straight into her head.

She gasped as it all came rushing back. Jonas teaching her to do handstands in the garden. Jonas stealing her ice cream. Jonas helping her build sandcastles and laughing when she was scared of the sea. Jonas helping her with math when she first started school . . .

When her head was refilled with the memories that should have been there for years, except that some bogeyman had stolen them, she stared at her brother, speechless.

Who grinned and said, "in answer to your question, little sis, I live right here."

He came and put his arms around her and she hugged him back as hard as she could. "I'm sorry I couldn't tell you," he said, his breath tickling her ear. "It wouldn't have made you remember. I would just have been some stranger claiming to be your brother. Better that you think I was just your friend."

There was a crash of broken china and a cry from the house as the memories of two more missing children rushed back into Lena's head. It was a terrible cry and it made Nin feel weak.

She left Jonas and ran. There was no need to ring the doorbell. The door was already open and Lena was there, with Toby pulling her along, hurrying her toward the rest of her family.

Nin got there first, beating Jonas up the path and running straight into Lena's arms.

✳ ✳ ✳

"Well, that's it then," said Dark, who was again disguised as Skerridge, as the door closed on Nin and her family. "Though what their muvver's gonna make of it, Galig knows!"

Jik sent him a look.

"Come on," said Dark with a chuckle, "a disguise ain't complete unless ya do the voice as well. Don't suppose it's quite right, but at least I'll 'ave a go."

Jik shrugged.

The bogeyman heaved a sigh. "Truth is, I feel kind of guilty for puttin' the kid through all that. My spell needed to break, an' as soon as it laid eyes on Nin—not that it's got eyes as such bein' a spell, but ya get the idea—it saw she was lucky. So it knew that out of everyone she 'ad the best chance to work out who I really was, see? My spell is the reason I lost 'er when I'd never lost a kid before. It was workin' inside me, even though I didn't know it!"

Jik nodded. He'd been wondering.

Dark mopped his brow with a corner of waistcoat. "Bit hairy, this Widdern lark, even in disguise. Still, ya never know till ya try and I feel kind of okay. Feet're a bit tingly, mind you."

They started off back to the Drift, Dark still looking like Skerridge. "Y'know I kinda like this shape. I might use it now an' again. Specially if I decide to take the odd trip Widdernside. It was fun scarin' the socks off all them kiddies."

Jik gave him a stern look, then went back to studying the horizon, checking for new patches of Raw. It was a habit he'd got into. There were none. "It's slowed down already," said Dark, seeing his look. "We've gotta few more years yet, an' who knows, maybe that prophecy of Crow's'll come true. Then the Raw might even start to recede and the Land'll come back! Slowly, of course, but wouldn't that be somethin'!"

He glanced at Jik. "Ya remember the one I mean? About somethin' livin' in the Heart an' makin' every-thin' all right again."

"Nik Crik, Akik."

"Oh yeah, right. Azork's prophecy, then. No wonder it was so dumb." Dark sniggered, then sighed. "Shame really."

Jibbit still hadn't reached the top of the high thing. His gargoyle heart was pounding with happiness, because of all the cathedrals that he had ever dreamed about, this cathedral was the greatest and best. It didn't just tower against the sky, it soared, its spires rising in tier after tier of pale stone. And there was only him to enjoy it. It was a relief after all the excitement to have his own space again.

At last he scurried nimbly up to the tallest spire on the highest roof. It was so high that it reached above the Raw, piercing the mist to break into open air. Twining his tail around the stem, just above the words that said, "King Galig of Beorht Eardgeard built this," Jibbit settled on the tip.

Here the sun was warm on his stone head and back, and even if the Raw still swirled below him, Jibbit could sense the giddying drop at his feet. It made him happy.

And he knew that if there was anywhere in the Drift that a gargoyle was born to live, it was right here.

In the Heart.

Nin crept into her mother's bedroom.

They had told Lena everything and it had been enough to send her into serious shock. It had been the right thing to do though, Nin was sure, because learning about other worlds peopled with strange and terrible things was surely better than believing that you had forgotten your own children.

Now Lena slept, worn out with all the things she had learned.

As quietly as she could, Nin placed a candle on her mother's bedside table. It was the crowsmorte candle that had helped to bring a little peace of mind to Jonas, just after they had escaped the Hounds on their journey to the House.

Carefully, she lit it with a match then stood back. In the gathering Widdern dusk the candle glowed with a warm yellow light and gave out a scent of clover and honey. She remembered Crow's voice, singing to her when she had taken the potion, and hoped her mother could hear him too.

Lena didn't move, but after a while, Nin thought she saw some of the shadows leave her face.

She watched for a moment longer, then went downstairs to find her brothers.